PRAISE FOR LISA GRAY

"Lisa Gray explodes onto the literary stage with this taut, edge-of-the-seat thriller, and her headstrong protagonist Jessica Shaw, reminiscent of Lee Child's Jack Reacher, delivers a serious punch."
—Robert Dugoni, *New York Times* bestselling author

"Mazey Los Angeles noir for fans of Sara Gran. I'm liking it a lot."
—Ian Rankin, bestselling author of the Inspector Rebus series

"*Thin Air* is an exciting whodunit that kept me guessing until the end. PI Jessica Shaw is so capable and strong, I couldn't get enough of her!"
—T.R. Ragan, bestselling author of the Lizzy Gardner series

"One of this year's best new thrillers . . ."
—*Evening Standard*

"You'll find this one hard to put down."
—*Daily Record*

"The very best sort of detective fiction: gritty, real and gripping with a brilliantly-realized main character."
—Cass Green, *Sunday Times* bestselling author

"A fast-paced, perfectly plotted killer of a thriller with a fantastic female lead and a cracking premise."
—S.J.I. Holliday, author of *Violet*

DARK
HIGHWAY

ALSO BY LISA GRAY

Thin Air

Bad Memory

DARK
HIGHWAY

A JESSICA SHAW THRILLER

LISA GRAY

THOMAS & MERCER

Text copyright © 2020 by Lisa Gray
All rights reserved.

Published by Thomas & Mercer, Seattle

www.apub.com

Amazon, the Amazon logo, and Thomas & Mercer are trademarks of Amazon.com, Inc., or its affiliates.

ISBN-13: 9781542021135
ISBN-10: 1542021138

Cover design by Dominic Forbes

Printed in the United States of America

For Ben, Sam, and Cody—with much love

PROLOGUE

There were four of them in the car. Five if you counted the dead woman in the trunk.

Nick sat in the back seat, way too close to her for his liking. He pinched his nose and breathed in heavily through his mouth. He was convinced he could smell her even though he knew that was unlikely. He didn't think she'd even be cold yet. But what the hell did he know about this stuff? There hadn't been much blood at least. Something to be thankful for.

The car bounced beneath him as it hit a rough spot on the blacktop and the nausea that had been churning away in his gut leaped right up his throat. Nick tasted vomit in his mouth and swallowed hard. Sucked in a big lungful of air. Next to him, Junior didn't look too good either.

Dusty turned around and glared at Nick from the front passenger seat. The crusty dried blood around his nostrils appeared black in the gloom. His eyes had a wild look about them. Coke and liquor and . . . something else.

Something bad.

Nick could see that now.

"Would you quit with the panting?" Dusty snapped. "You sound like a mangy old dog begging for a treat. Get a fucking grip of yourself."

Nick turned away and looked out of the window. The moon was as perfectly round and white as a dinner plate. It cast an eerie glow over the flat desert landscape, the mountains far off in the distance nothing more than shadowy purple outlines. They passed a bar that had long been shut up for the night and a motel with a single light burning. Along the roadside, a dozen or so mismatched mailboxes were jammed into the dirt like a row of metal flowers. The homes they belonged to were set back off the highway and shrouded in darkness. Nick envied the inhabitants of those houses, no doubt fast asleep in their beds. He wondered if he'd ever sleep soundly again.

He thought about the woman. Christ, he couldn't even remember her name. That would be the booze and the shock, no doubt. But he figured he'd be hearing it plenty soon enough. How long before she'd be missed? How long before they'd start looking for her? He knew she had family. She'd said as much when she'd begged Dusty not to hurt her.

Her pleas had been ignored.

As for Nick and Junior and Zee, they'd stood back and let it happen. Frozen by their fear of Dusty and what he was doing, and what he wanted them to do, and what he did to her in the end.

They were every bit as bad.

Every bit as guilty.

Afterward, they'd wrapped her body in trash bags, like she was a piece of garbage, and carried her out to Zee's car like they were told to by Dusty. Of course, they didn't use *his* wheels to get rid of the body. There was no chance of Dusty messing up his brand-new Miata for a dead girl. In any case, the old Cutlass that Zee had inherited from his daddy had way more space in back and no way was Zee going to argue once the decision had been made.

Cade was the only one who'd had the balls to stand up to Dusty. He was the reason she'd been there tonight, the one who'd persuaded her it'd be a good idea to come along. Nick could tell straight away that Cade was real sweet on the woman. The goofy grin on his face when he'd first introduced her. The way his eyes had followed her all evening. Her smile suggested she was sweet on Cade too.

Then Dusty had shown up and everything had gone to shit.

Later, when Cade had refused to get in the car, Dusty had given him a look that said he'd be next to find himself stuffed in the trunk. But the guilt and grief and anger written all over Cade's face had clearly been stronger than any hold Dusty ever had over him. He'd walked off into the night, shoulders hunched, hands plunged deep into his jeans pockets. Didn't look back.

Nick wished he'd had the balls to stand up to Dusty too.

They drove on. The terrain was sparser now. Only the occasional lonely property or rusted trailer to break up the empty desert chaparral. They passed a road sign warning: "Next Services 100 Miles." The four young men traveled in silence. No conversation, no music on the radio. The only sound was the gentle thrum of the Oldsmobile's engine. The car smelled of windscreen washer and old Camel cigarettes and fresh body odor. The sweat on Nick's back stuck to the velour upholstery through his t-shirt.

"Pull over here," Dusty said after a while.

Zee eased the car onto the shoulder. Cut the engine and headlights. Only that big, fat moon illuminated the otherwise dark highway now. Dusty opened the glove compartment and removed two flashlights. Handed one to Zee and then got out of the car. The others followed him. Dusty turned on the flashlight and popped the lid of the trunk. Nick didn't want to look—already knew what he'd see inside—but he couldn't help himself. A shovel had been tossed carelessly on top of the dead woman. Its blade glinted under the flashlight's pale beam. Nick heard one of the others retch, followed by a wet sound as vomit hit blacktop.

Nick's eyes met Dusty's cold, hard stare. "What?" Nick asked. His voice was raw, barely a whisper.

Dusty nodded toward the open trunk. "Grab the shovel," he said. "Then start digging."

1

JESSICA

Jessica Shaw plucked a photograph at random from the pile scattered across the table and turned it over in her hands.

It was a great shot. Real and unfiltered and natural. Taken with a proper camera, rather than the latest model cell phone. There was a developer's stamp on the back for one of those one-hour photo places she was always surprised to discover still existed.

These days, it was usually all filters and pre-sets and social media apps adding bunny ears and lolling dog tongues to selfies. Why anyone would want to make themselves look like a human sex doll or cartoon character was beyond Jessica. As a private investigator who specialized in missing persons cases, sometimes it was a bigger challenge sourcing a recent image that actually looked like the person who'd disappeared than it was tracking them down.

Thankfully, there would be no such problem this time. The woman was in her early twenties, with beachy blonde hair hanging in messy waves past lightly tanned shoulders, accentuated by a black dress with spaghetti straps. She had pale blue eyes and a generous scattering of freckles across a snub nose that looked like they'd been drawn on with a pencil. The kind of girl who'd be described as "cute" and who didn't need makeup to look good.

The scene had been captured at a restaurant, probably Mexican, and a half empty margarita glass and a chocolate fudge cake sat in front of her. The cake drooped slightly to one side as though drunk and two lit candles—a two and a three—had been planted into the thick frosting on top. Jessica thought the woman's smile, reflected in the candlelight, carried a hint of embarrassment and she guessed the waiter had probably led the rest of the patrons in an enthusiastic rendition of "Happy Birthday" moments before the shot had been taken.

The name of the woman in the photograph was Laurie Simmonds and she had been missing for two months.

"That was taken exactly a year ago. Today is Laurie's twenty-fourth birthday."

Jessica looked up. It was Laurie's mom who had spoken. Renee Simmonds was as dark as her daughter was fair. Yoga-toned and glossy-haired, she would have been a walking advertisement for healthy California living were it not for the faint waft of cigarettes not quite disguised by her expensive perfume. A brunette in her fifties, she was dressed simply in slim-fit blue jeans and a black silk blouse, but the rock on the ring finger of her left hand, which could probably be seen from outer space along with the Grand Canyon, betrayed her wealth.

Jessica noted the woman's careful use of the word "is" rather than "would have been." There were three of them around the table—Renee, Jessica, and another private investigator called Matt Connor—and none of them were willing to address the elephant right there in the room with them, namely the fact that Laurie Simmonds may not still be alive. Even so, Renee's hazel eyes shone with a sort of fierce defiance that said she wasn't giving up hope just yet.

Jessica held up the photo. "May I hold onto this one?"

"Of course." Renee hesitated. "Will you be working the investigation too?"

"Yes, I will. Is that a problem?"

"No, not at all." Renee turned her attention from Jessica to Connor, the owner of the agency and the one whose name was on the front door. "It's just that, when I spoke to you on the phone yesterday, I was under the impression this was a one-man operation."

"Jessica is new," Connor said.

Renee's eyebrows lifted a fraction in an unspoken question.

"She has a ton of experience," he added smoothly. "Especially with missing persons cases."

Talk about an understatement. What he didn't say was that Jessica, herself, had been a missing person, snatched from her home as a toddler. The kid on the side of the milk carton. Completely unaware that people had been looking for her for twenty-five years until she had stumbled upon the truth about her tragic past last year.

It was while working the case in Eagle Rock, a neighborhood in northeast Los Angeles, that Jessica had first crossed paths with Matt Connor. Over the few days they'd spent together, she'd found him to be equal parts infuriating and arousing. He was also one hell of a liar and Jessica still didn't know if she could trust him. But, with no plans to return to her native New York any time soon, she needed to keep clocking up the hours required for a California PI license and Matt Connor was her best hope for a quick and easy solution. Hell, at least she'd get to hang out at the beach all day and call it work. She'd tracked him down to a bar in Venice the night before and asked him for a job.

Today was her first day as an official employee of MAC Investigations. She had a pretty good idea what the "M" and the "C" stood for but, so far, not the "A." She just hoped it wouldn't turn out to be "Asshole." What she did know was that she was pumped about this case. As they'd shared a couple of Scotch on the rocks the night before, Connor had told her what little information he'd had at that point: Laurie Simmonds was an artist who lived and worked in Venice, she was single, in her early twenties, and hadn't been seen or heard of since her VW camper van was found abandoned by a roadside in the desert.

Jessica set the photo aside, turned to a fresh page in her yellow legal pad, and wrote the date at the top. Connor did likewise and she let him take the lead with the questions.

"Let's start off with a little more background on Laurie," he said. "She's an artist, right?"

Renee nodded. "She shares a creative space with another artist, a sculptor by the name of Elizabeth Mann—that's Mann with two 'N's—down near the Boardwalk. It has the triple purpose of being a studio, gallery, and retail space. They're best friends, as well as working together."

"She lives alone?"

"Yes, in a two-bedroom apartment on Speedway, not far from the studio."

"Two bedrooms but no roommate?"

"No, she likes her own space. She paints there too. Often late into the night. Being on her own suits her."

"When we spoke on the phone, you mentioned she was single at the time of her disappearance."

"That's right. No boyfriend."

"She wasn't dating? You know, something more casual?"

"If she was, she never mentioned it. But it's possible, I guess." Renee smiled sadly. "We're close but I suppose daughters don't tell their moms everything, huh?"

The question was directed at Jessica. She smiled back, like she understood. Even though she didn't. Her own mother had been murdered when Jessica was three years old, the night she was abducted. She'd never had those girl talks with her mom or anyone else. Even if she had, she sure as hell wouldn't have told anyone about any guy she was casually sleeping with. She figured Laurie Simmonds would be much the same.

"But she'd tell you if she'd fought with someone?" Connor asked. "Like a girlfriend, maybe?"

"Sure, but she didn't mention any arguments. Didn't seem upset about anything. Elizabeth said the same thing. Honestly, Laurie is just the sweetest person. I can't imagine her pissing someone off enough for them to hurt her."

Jessica looked up from the pad where she'd been furiously scribbling her notes. "What about money troubles?"

"No, none."

"She's a successful artist, then?"

"She's very talented."

"So, she's making a good living from her work?" Jessica pressed.

A pause. Then Renee said, "Well, no, not exactly. Laurie's father and I help out with the rent on both the apartment and retail space. I know it bothers her, relying on handouts from her mom and dad. But, like I said, she's got real talent and she'll get the recognition and money she deserves one day. I'm sure of it."

Jessica smiled. "I'm sure she will."

Connor said, "Speaking of Laurie's father, I was under the impression he'd be here with you today?"

Renee's mouth pursed into a tight line of disapproval. "Trey had to work. Trey always has to work." She sighed, her features softening. "That's not fair. This whole business has hit us both really hard. I guess throwing himself into work is his way of dealing with things. If you need to speak to Trey, you can arrange a time to stop by the house."

"Sure, we'll do that." Connor paused a beat. "Okay, Renee, this might be tough but now we need to ask you about the day Laurie disappeared."

Renee gulped down a mouthful of coffee from the chipped Dodgers mug Connor had handed her when she'd first arrived, leaving a peachy-pink lipstick smear on the rim. The coffee must have been cold by now and she winced slightly before continuing.

"It was just like any other day," she said. "Laurie went down to the beach to do some sketching in the morning, something she did often for inspiration. She'd usually be back at the studio by lunchtime. On this occasion, she sent a text asking Elizabeth if she'd be okay to look after the shop for the rest of the day, said she had some stuff to take care of. They weren't busy so Elizabeth was happy to hold the fort, didn't quiz Laurie on what her plans were.

"I speak to Laurie on the phone most evenings and I received a text from her that afternoon saying she was super busy with work stuff and she'd give me a call tomorrow. Of course, she never did. Her van was found on the shoulder of the Twentynine Palms Highway, out by Joshua Tree National Park, the next day."

Connor got up from the table and walked over to a map of Los Angeles and the surrounding areas Scotch-taped to the wall. A yellow pin was stuck in the Westside next to a patch of blue, presumably the location of the agency. He traced his finger from the pin to the spot where Laurie's vehicle had been found. Turned to them both with a frown. "That's a hell of a distance. Must be, what, a couple hundred miles?"

"Almost 160 miles," Renee confirmed. "Around three hours' driving time."

"Quite a journey. And you've no idea what she was doing out there in the desert?"

Renee shrugged helplessly and dropped her eyes to the table. "None at all," she said. "We paid for a missing person ad on a billboard close to where her van was found. Offered a ten-thousand-dollar reward but we had to withdraw the cash after the tips line was inundated with cranks."

"Yeah, I'll bet it was." Connor returned to his seat.

"Were her personal effects recovered from the vehicle?" Jessica asked. "Purse, wallet, cell phone?"

"All missing."

"There was nothing left behind at all?"

"Just the paintings."

"What paintings?"

"They found them in the back of the van," Renee said. "They were both Laurie's own. Wrapped up in brown paper like they were sales. But there were no appointments in her planner and her sales transactions usually take place at work. I don't know if it's significant. The police didn't seem to think so."

"Where are the paintings now?"

"At her apartment."

"May we take a look around her apartment?"

"Of course."

Renee fished in her purse and came up with a bunch of keys. Slipped one off the ring and handed it to Jessica. "Here's the spare. I don't have one for the workspace but Elizabeth can show you around."

"Was there any sign of a struggle or foul play?" Jessica asked.

"None. No blood. No damage. The van doors weren't even left open." Renee laughed bitterly. "That's why the cops did precisely nothing when we reported Laurie missing. She's an adult so apparently that means she has the right to walk away from her life, and everyone who loves her, without any sort of an explanation, and they won't do a damn thing about it."

It wasn't a crime to be a missing person, so Jessica knew the police's role in situations like this was often limited. Unless foul play was suspected or the individual was a critical missing—regarded as endangered due to medical problems or life-threatening situations—there wasn't a whole lot the cops could do with regards to an investigation. Especially in a place like Los Angeles, where up to three hundred people a month were reported missing. That's where folks like Jessica and Connor came in.

"We'll do everything we can to bring Laurie home, Renee," Connor said. "Is there anything else before we finish up?"

Renee chewed on her bottom lip. "I should probably tell you about the others. It might be nothing but it might be something."

Jessica and Connor glanced at each other, then they both stared at Renee.

"The others?" Jessica asked.

"What others?" Connor said.

"The other missing women."

2

DEA—1990

"Girl Most Likely to Succeed."

It was at times like this—fingers red raw and wrinkled, the stench of bleach making her eyes sting—that Dea Morgan would think about that silly yearbook prediction and she would laugh.

If she didn't laugh, she'd cry.

And no way was she going to allow that to happen. Not right now anyway. Maybe later when she was at home, trying to snatch a few hours' sleep on the lumpy sofa, she'd let the tears fall. Quietly so Buddy wouldn't hear in the next room. But she would not cry in public and definitely not at work. She didn't have a whole lot of self-respect left, but she still had some.

Looking back, it was easy to see why she'd been voted "Girl Most Likely to Succeed" in her senior year at Brodie High School. Dea had never been the prettiest girl, or the funniest, or the biggest flirt, or the best dressed. But she'd definitely been the smartest. Student council president, class president, member of the debating team, straight "A"s without really trying. She'd been accepted to a much-coveted Ivy League school that should have changed her life.

And, boy, did her life change that summer.

Just not in the way she'd expected. One night—not long after graduation—had changed everything.

If her classmates had had a crystal ball back then, had been able to glimpse into the future, their predictions might have been somewhat different. Something along the lines of:

"Most Likely to Be a Single Mom."

"Most Likely to Have Two Jobs that Still Barely Pay the Rent."

"Most Likely to Wind Up Living in a One-Bed Mobile Home."

Or how about . . . her personal favorite?

"Most Likely to Scrub the Shit off Strangers' Toilet Bowls for a Living."

No, that wasn't quite right. It wasn't a stranger today. It was much worse than that. Someone from her past, from Brodie, who didn't need a high school reunion to find out exactly how things had turned out for the "Girl Most Likely to Succeed."

Dea didn't know who was more shocked and embarrassed when she'd shown up for her new cleaning job and Kristy Jensen had opened the door.

Kristy Jensen a.k.a. the "Girl Most Likely to be Happy."

Judging by the huge McMansion on one of the best streets in Yucca Valley and the gleaming Ford F-150 parked in the driveway, so shiny you could fix your makeup in the reflection on the paintwork, Dea figured her old classmates might just have called that one right.

Eight years on and, as well as the house and the car, Kristy Jensen still had the same size two figure, perky blonde ponytail and toothpaste commercial smile she'd had in high school. The smile had definitely faltered when she'd spotted Dea Morgan standing on her doorstep in her cleaning scrubs with her plastic caddy stuffed full of bleach and rags and furniture polish.

"Oh, hey, Kristy," Dea had said brightly. "I didn't know you lived in Yucca Valley too. What a coincidence. Small world, huh?" Fake laugh. "Mr. Jenner—that's your husband, right?—hired me to clean the house. I guess he saw my ad in the Post Office window and, well, here I am!"

She'd been aiming for the sweet spot between nonchalance and cheerfulness. Had sounded borderline manic instead.

"Dea! How great to see you!" Reciprocal fake laugh from Kristy. "Yes, Derek mentioned someone would be coming round to help with the cleaning. He wants to make things a little easier for me, you know? Come on in."

Make things a little easier? What the hell was so hard about Kristy Jensen's life?

Two minutes later and Kristy's truck was spitting gravel as she'd headed for the nearest Ralphs to pick up some groceries, leaving Dea to her cleaning duties.

Dea had wondered meanly why Kristy's husband didn't just pay someone to do the grocery shopping too. Then she'd realized the other woman was probably trying to save them both any further embarrassment by not sticking around while Dea dusted and scrubbed and polished. A quick peek inside the fully stocked cupboards and over-stuffed fridge-freezer had confirmed her suspicions.

Dea pushed herself up from the tiled bathroom floor now and groaned as the bones in her knees cracked. Jeez, she was only twenty-five but she felt like she was 105. To be fair to Kristy, her toilet bowl had already been pretty clean. No shitty residue like some of Dea's other clients. Sometimes, rich people could be filthy pigs. She pegged Kristy as one of those women who felt the need to clean before the cleaner arrived, in case the hired help thought badly of her.

Dea bent down and pulled the liner out of the tiny stainless-steel pedal bin and replaced it with a fresh one. Was just about to tie a knot in the used liner when she felt something hard and plastic amongst the soiled face wipes and used cotton buds. Intrigued, she pulled out the item. It was a pregnancy test. One line in the tiny window. A negative result. Dea wondered if Kristy had been sad or relieved.

She flashed back to an August day eight years ago. Both of her parents at work. Cold faucet running in the bathroom to help make her pee. The sharp edges of the plastic toilet seat biting into Dea's skin as she'd shifted awkwardly to hit the tip of the stick just right when the flow finally did come. Skinny legs shaking as she'd waited the longest three minutes of her life for the result.

Two lines in the tiny window.

From virgin to teen mom just like that.

She returned Kristy Jensen's pregnancy test to the used trash bag and knotted it. Turned her attention to the mirrored medicine cabinet above the sink. She never could resist a peek inside the lives of the people she worked for. One of the very few perks of the job. And this one told her a fair bit about the Jensen-Jenners.

There was the usual boring crap—razors, over-the-counter painkillers, zit cream, cold cream. Some Men's Rogaine hidden right at the back. Ouch. That was fast, assuming Derek was of a similar age to Kristy. There was a half-empty box of tampons and two more pregnancy test kits, still in the cellophane packaging. A bottle of Xanax with the sticky label in Kristy's name.

Maybe the class of '82 had gotten that one wrong after all.

Dea twisted the top off the anti-anxiety meds and shook one out. Placed it on her tongue. She did that sometimes. Took little things she knew wouldn't be missed—a lipstick to help make her look good, a little dinosaur bookmark from the kids' room for Buddy, some hand cream to soothe the dried skin, a tiny blue pill to help her get through the rest of the day. She wasn't a thief. She'd never help herself to cash or jewelry or anything big. She just wanted a little bit of what everyone else had.

As she closed the medicine cabinet door, the pregnancy kits caught Dea's eye again and it struck her then that she had something Kristy didn't have. Something Kristy desperately wanted. Fuck having the big house and the perky ponytail and the brand-new set of wheels. So what if Dea didn't have two spare dimes to rub together? So what if she was exhausted from working late shifts in the bar and cleaning other folks' homes during the day?

She had Buddy and that made her the luckiest woman in the whole damn world as far as she was concerned.

Things might have turned out differently had she told her mom and dad the truth about what happened that summer's night. Maybe they wouldn't have kicked their only child out onto the street like a dog, with a few hundred bucks in her pocket, to make her way alone in the world. Maybe they wouldn't have let the townsfolk wonder what had happened to star student Dea Morgan, rather than just dealing with the shame of everyone knowing the pastor's seventeen-year-old daughter had gotten knocked up.

But they would never have let her keep Buddy in a million years—and life without her little boy was simply unthinkable.

Dea felt a sudden, almost overwhelming, surge of love for him. Decided when she picked him up from school later that she'd treat him to McDonald's for dinner. One of those Happy Meals, with the free toy. Maybe some ice cream too. Dea would go without, hopefully pick up some food at the bar later. The portions were huge and there were usually some leftovers to nibble on after clearing away the customers' plates.

She made her way downstairs to vacuum the carpets before Kristy got home.

Dea didn't know if it was thinking about Buddy, or the effects of the little blue pill kicking in, but she suddenly felt like she was floating. Felt happier than she had done in months. Dea and Buddy—they'd be okay. They just needed to catch a break. She smiled to herself.

Dea knew their luck would turn soon. She could feel it in her weary bones.

3

JESSICA

Jessica stepped out of the office straight onto the sidewalk and lit a Marlboro Gold.

MAC Investigations was a small shopfront on Washington Boulevard, wedged between a bike rental place and a deli, on a tiny drab block the color of cold cappuccino that seemed at odds with the vibrancy elsewhere in the neighborhood. The agency's name was stenciled on a square of pebbled glass on the front door and a blue canvas canopy shaded Jessica from the mid-morning sun.

She smoked the cigarette and thought about the two women Renee Simmonds had told them about before she'd left.

Amanda Meyers was a legal assistant at a lawyers' firm in Downtown LA. She'd been reported missing two years ago by her parents, who lived out of town, after they'd been unable to reach her and she'd then failed to show for work. She was thirty-three when she disappeared.

Mallory Wilcox was a married stay-at-home mom. Then forty-eight years old, she had two young kids and resided in the town of Whitewater over in Riverside County. She'd been missing for eighteen months.

The last known whereabouts of both women was the Twentynine Palms Highway.

Jessica took a final draw on the cigarette, crushed the butt on the lid of a nearby trash can and dropped it inside. The Culver CityBus whooshed past and the towering palm trees on either side of the street shivered in the light breeze. She popped an Altoid and headed back inside.

Her laptop was set up on the conference table, where they'd had the meeting with Renee, and which was also doubling up as Jessica's desk. She thought about getting a pen holder or a framed photo or a plant, something to make the space more personal. Then again, she might not stick around long enough to keep a plant alive.

"What do you have?" she asked, slipping back into her seat.

Connor looked up from his computer screen, where he'd been reading press cuttings on Mallory Wilcox. He occupied the only desk in the office, a cheap white fiberboard thing that looked like it'd come from a Swedish flatpack store. In fact, everything in the room—the shelves, magazine files, filing cabinets, two-seater funky-patterned sofa—looked like they'd been purchased at IKEA.

"Mallory told her husband she was attending a candle party at a friend's house and not to wait up," Connor said. He looked at Jessica. "What the fuck is a candle party?"

"I believe it's when a bunch of middle-aged women get together and drink wine and, um, buy some over-priced candles," Jessica said. "You know, like Tupperware parties. Only with candles."

"Sounds like a blast. Anyway, when hubby realized the next day that Mallory hadn't come home, he tried her sister. The sister knew about the candle party but hadn't heard from Mallory. The husband tracked down the friend, who had no idea what party he was talking about, so he called the cops. They found out Mallory's credit card had been used at a gas station on the Twentynine Palms Highway the previous night. CCTV footage from the gas station confirmed it was Mallory who'd used the card. She'd bought some snacks and booze and then driven off. No one else was in the car with her. There were no more sightings of her—she just vanished."

"Anything else?"

"An article in one of the tackier newspapers hinted at marital problems."

Jessica raised an eyebrow. "Aha. An affair?"

"Maybe. It's one theory. Probably the one the cops liked."

"Photos?"

Connor turned the computer monitor around so Jessica could see the screen. As well as a series of CCTV stills from the gas station, there was a big, full-color shot of Mallory Wilcox. She had a plump, pretty face with deep dimples as though someone had poked a finger into each cheek. Big blue eyes and long lashes that could've been stolen from a porcelain doll. Her brown hair was styled in a blunt bob with the bangs cut short above her eyebrows.

"Nothing like Laurie Simmonds," Jessica noted.

"Nope." Connor got up from his chair and stretched. His t-shirt rode up a little, showing just a hint of the toned body underneath. Jessica quickly looked away. "You want a coffee?" he asked. "I don't know about you, but I sure could do with a caffeine hit."

They'd stayed at Larry's bar drinking whiskey and beer until midnight the night before and Jessica was also feeling the slump. "Sure," she said.

Jessica watched as Connor retreated to the small kitchenette. His dark hair was shorter than it had been when they'd first met six months ago, no longer curling at the nape of his neck, but those green eyes were just as intense. Dressed in blue jeans and a classic white tee, he looked more like a guy from a cologne commercial than he did a PI.

"You want cream and sugar?" he called from out back.

"No thanks!" she yelled.

He returned a few moments later with two steaming mugs. Handed Jessica the Dodgers one that Renee Simmonds had drunk from earlier—thankfully minus the peachy-pink lipstick—and sat down across from her. Before she could reach for the coffee, Connor leaned over the table and placed a hand on top of her own.

"You sure you're okay working this case?" he asked. "After everything that happened?"

Jessica stared at his hand. Tanned skin, tiny sun-bleached hairs, short, clean nails. Anyone else, and the gesture might have seemed friendly, brotherly even. A guy like Matt Connor, it almost felt like foreplay. She snatched her hand away.

"Of course I am," she snapped. "It's not like it's the first missing persons case I've worked since all that shit happened last year. And this one is totally different anyway."

"Good."

The sexy, crooked grin was the same as she remembered too.

She took a sip of coffee and swallowed even though it was too hot. Spun the laptop around so Connor could see it. "Amanda Meyers," she said. "Very different in appearance to both Mallory Wilcox and Laurie Simmonds."

Connor nodded his agreement.

If Mallory was soft lines, Amanda was all sharp angles. Long, straight nose and severe features. Blonde hair professionally colored at a decent salon and the kind of hard-earned skinniness that suggested a Big Mac hadn't crossed her glossy lips for at least a decade. Her choice of attire was a navy power suit. She looked like Melanie Griffith in *Working Girl* but without the shoulder pads.

"What's her story?" Connor asked.

"Last seen on a Friday night two years ago," Jessica said. "She checked into the Tranquility Motel on—yep, you've guessed it—the Twentynine Palms Highway, having already pre-booked the room earlier in the day. Stayed a couple hours and then left. No visitors that the manager was aware of. She usually spoke with her mom on the weekend. When she didn't call home Saturday, her folks were a little concerned but not overly so. When they tried to reach Amanda at her office on the Monday morning, and she hadn't shown for work, alarm bells started ringing."

"Amanda's motel and Mallory's gas station are both in the same county?" Connor asked.

"Yep. San Bernardino County."

"But Mallory lived in Riverside County so her husband would've called the local cops when she didn't come home."

"Right," Jessica said. "Likewise, Amanda and Laurie were both likely reported missing to the LAPD to begin with. So, potentially, three different county police departments involved, paperwork all over the place, and no one quite sure which jurisdiction should be taking responsibility. It's unlikely a link was established between all three women until Renee Simmonds joined the dots for them. That is, if they *are* all connected. Sounds like the cops aren't convinced. Only the location links them, and that highway—also known as State Route 62 by the way—is over 150 miles long and covers two counties. Yes, I checked already."

"You don't think there's a connection?"

Jessica hesitated, shrugged uncomfortably. "I really don't know."

"The victimology—if they have all been victims of a crime—is pretty varied. Different age range, physical appearance and background. Nothing in common, as far as we can tell, other than all three being Caucasian females."

"Yes, but . . . something just feels off to me."

Connor nodded. "I agree."

"You think they're dead?"

"Shit, I really hope not. For Renee's sake, and the other women's families too. Mallory Wilcox has two young kids, for Christ's sake."

"Best case scenario? If there is a link between them, I mean."

Connor thought for a moment. "They're still alive but being held against their will someplace?"

"Maybe. Or how about they all joined a secret community hidden out in the desert?"

Connor snorted. "What, like some sort of cult? Like the Manson Family?"

Jessica rolled her eyes. "Yeah, but without the experimental drug-taking, weird Beatles conspiracies and, you know, going around murdering folk."

Connor still didn't look convinced.

Jessica went on, "What I meant was a commune, where people go to disconnect and escape from modern life for a while. Get away from stressful jobs and marriage problems, and over-protective parents."

"But, surely, if that was the case, they'd at least let their families know they were safe and well?"

Jessica sat back heavily against the seat with a sigh. "Yeah, that's the part that doesn't make any sense."

They were silent for a few moments, both of them deep in their own thoughts.

Finally, Jessica said, "So, what's the plan, boss?"

Connor laughed, then turned serious. "I say we do a bit of digging into the Meyers and Wilcox women, as well as Laurie Simmonds. What harm can it do?"

"My thoughts exactly," Jessica said. "Because if there's someone out there, luring women out to the desert, he might already have the next one lined up."

4

BURDEN

Burden had figured out very quickly just how much you could learn about a person's life simply by watching them.

Give it a few days, and you'd know what time they left for work each day, what their Starbucks order was, and which newspaper they liked to read on the morning commute. A few weeks, and you'd also know where they worked out, shopped, and ate. If they liked to party or favored early nights. If they were married or single. If they were screwing someone they shouldn't be.

If you were willing to spend several months observing your subject? Well, that's when things got really interesting.

Social media made it even easier. Facebook, Snapchat, Twitter, Instagram, Tinder, Grindr. Birthdates, anniversaries, holiday destinations, parents' names, maiden names, the kids' school, place of work, allergies, pets, pet hates, single, divorced, it's complicated, red or white wine, celebrity crush, real life crush, favorite movies, music, and TV shows.

It was all right there, in the public domain for anyone to find, if you were prepared to look hard enough. But garnering information from behind a keyboard wasn't enough for Burden.

He liked to get right up close and personal too.

So close he could smell the coconut shampoo from their morning shower, feel the heat radiating off their body. Sometimes, he'd allow himself to touch them. A gentle graze of the shoulder in a crowded bar or an accidental collision in the freezer aisle at the grocery store.

Routine made it possible to infiltrate the lives of complete strangers—and Cara Zelenka was definitely a creature of habit.

Yesterday was Monday, which meant laundry night. As usual, she'd visited the strip mall just off Vine, a plastic basket stuffed full of clothing balanced on a hip, plenty of coins in her pocket. Burden had watched her through the telephoto lens of his camera from his regular spot, parked in front of a Thai massage place, a few units down from the coin laundromat.

Cara was tall and slim with small breasts and long legs and fingers. Her straight dark hair hung to her elbows and she had thick bangs that got in her eyes. She looked like she'd stepped straight out of a '70s movie, like a young Ali MacGraw or Jaclyn Smith. Her choice of outfit was always the same—jeans slung low on narrow hips, tight tank top or tee, battered sneakers. Some might call her a tomboy but Burden knew from observing her through the big window, while she loaded the machine, that the casual clothing hid lacy bras and tiny panties in shades of black and red and shocking pink.

Like a present waiting to be unwrapped, Burden thought. Their little secret.

He knew she made the weekly trip to the laundromat because there wasn't enough room in her tiny apartment for a washer-dryer. And he knew this because he'd found an old rental listing online that had included a floor-plan of her studio apartment, which was situated in what the rental firm had referred to as "a prime location" just a few blocks south of Sunset.

He had watched last night as she'd sat cross-legged on a bench and read a book while the dryer went through its cycle. At one

25

point, she'd set the paperback down and stared at the clothes being whipped around, as though hypnotized by the motion or deep in thought about something.

Burden had really wanted to know what she was thinking about at that exact moment.

Then, suddenly, she'd turned and looked out the window, as though feeling the weight of his gaze upon her, and he had slid down in his seat, heart thumping like he'd just run a fast mile. He'd waited a full minute before risking another look. She was reading the book again. He could see the cover now. *A Clockwork Orange*. Always contemporary classics for Cara.

After a while, she'd gotten up from the bench, opened the dryer door and pulled out jeans and tees and underwear from the machine. Folded them all neatly, stacked them in the plastic basket, and made her way outside to where her yellow VW Bug was parked right next to the front door.

He'd then followed at a safe distance to her studio apartment on Afton Place and parked across the street in his usual spot. Her apartment was on the ground floor of a two-story, ten-unit complex, with tuck-under parking and a tiny patio out front. It was dark now but he knew in daylight the building was piglet pink with pistachio trim. It looked pretty from a distance but showed wear and tear upon closer inspection, mold smudges ruining the paintwork like sooty mascara tears on flushed cheeks.

Her windows were to the side and rear so he couldn't tell if her lights were on or off. As always, he'd waited until midnight, when he guessed she'd be in bed, wearing only an oversized t-shirt and panties. No pajamas. He'd never once seen any in her basket at the laundromat. He'd started the car and driven the few blocks to his own rental place. The one he'd chosen specifically to be close to her.

Tonight, Cara was where she always was this time of week.

Of course she was.

The jazz bar on the corner of Vine and De Longpre had live music every Tuesday and the place was always busy. Cara had arrived to find all the tables taken but had managed to grab a vacant high stool at the bar. Burden was already there, occupying one of the coveted candlelit tables in the rear of the room.

He watched now as she placed a drinks order and knew it'd be for a beer because she couldn't justify the fourteen-dollar cocktails and even the wine was too expensive. The bartender placed a stubby bottle of Red Stripe on the counter in front of her and she took a pull and spun the stool around so she had a good view of the performance area. She'd have two, maybe three, beers over the course of the evening. He'd never seen her properly lit. For Cara, it was all about the music, not the booze.

Burden hated jazz. It was too messy and improvised. The scat singing was the worst of it, a bunch of no-word nonsense syllables that gave him a headache. But he liked the way Cara looked when she was lost in the music. He took a sip of his California Cabernet Sauvignon—the most expensive red they had on the menu—and watched her over the rim of the glass.

Eyes closed, a small smile on her lips, fingers tapping the side of the beer bottle along with the erratic beat.

He saw her but she'd never notice a guy like him. Long, unwashed hair and a hipster beard he could never quite get used to. Wire-rimmed glasses, even though his eyesight was perfect. Padding under a plaid shirt to give the impression of a middle-aged spread and disguise his hard muscles.

He reluctantly dragged his gaze away from her and turned his attention back to the four-piece band, pretended to be interested in the glissando, stabs, and swung rhythms that were drawing appreciative "oh yeah"s from the crowd.

Burden realized he had grown rather fond of Cara Zelenka over these last few months.

But it didn't change what he had to do to her.

5

JESSICA

Jessica decided to kick off the Laurie Simmonds investigation in the missing woman's Venice Beach neighborhood, while Connor took a closer look at Mallory Wilcox and Amanda Meyers.

Venice was the second largest tourist attraction in California after Disneyland. Jessica thought it was kind of like a theme park for adults, what with the touristy t-shirts, garish knick-knacks and fast food stalls—just with more tattooists, weed, and bare-chested men in tiny shorts on skateboards. She hoped she might fit in here, with her nose piercing and tattoos.

Jessica took the scenic route to Laurie's workspace, setting off down Washington in the direction of the glittering blue ocean a couple of blocks ahead. The sidewalk was crowded with bikes and scooters for sale or rent and the air was filled with the tempting aroma of garlic rolls and melted mozzarella from a nearby trattoria that made Jessica's stomach growl. She hooked a right at the Venice Whaler onto Ocean Front Walk. Strolled past sidewalk markets, with their plastic sunglasses, floppy hats, tiny neon bikinis and cheap jewelry on display. Passed henna artists, fortune tellers, and hot-dog and gyros stands. She bought a cheeseburger and soda at one and ate her lunch while watching wannabe Arnies pumping iron at Muscle Beach.

Jessica was five-five and slim but she was soft with it. Almost thirty, she knew she should be factoring regular workouts into her routine. Pilates or running. Some light weights. Add a bit of muscle tone and strength and definition. Maybe give up smoking and cut back on the booze and cheeseburgers while she was at it. She trashed the burger wrapper and soda can. Figured there was probably more chance of her winning the Mega Millions or saving Leonardo DiCaprio from eternal bachelorhood than there was of her managing such a dramatic lifestyle overhaul.

She found the 2Women gallery on a side street off the Boardwalk, just like Renee Simmonds had said. It was a small building the color of uncooked shrimp, with the name in a cube of hot pink neon that was unlit during daylight hours but was probably very cool after dark. An old-fashioned bell chimed as Jessica pushed open the door, announcing her arrival.

"Be right out!" she heard a woman call from through the back.

"No rush, take your time!"

Jessica took in her surroundings. The east wall was dominated by oil on canvas paintings of various sizes, all of which depicted beachy landscapes in a modern, abstract style. The west wall's shelves were filled with ocean-themed sculptures of sea turtles and dolphins and tropical fish. A counter straight ahead housed a retro cash register and some mugs and folded tote bags printed with the same artwork hanging on the wall. Jessica studied Laurie Simmonds' paintings while she waited.

"Sorry to keep you."

Jessica turned to see a young woman emerge from a doorway behind the counter. She was the same age as Laurie but a gap between her teeth when she smiled made her look more like a mischievous kid. She wiped dirty hands on black denim overalls and pushed dark curls off her face, leaving a clay smudge on her cheek.

"Elizabeth Mann?"

"That's me. Can I help you with anything or were you just browsing?"

"My name is Jessica Shaw. I'm a private investigator."

The gap-toothed smile disappeared. "This is about Laurie, right?"

"Right. Renee Simmonds told me where to find you."

"Let me just close up and we can talk out back."

Elizabeth flipped the "open" sign in the front window to "closed" and twisted the key in the lock. Gestured for Jessica to follow her into a big, bright studio. The midday sun flooded in through large skylights in the ceiling, acting as a spotlight for the works in progress. An easel was set up, holding a half-finished painting. Others were stacked in a corner. A paint-splattered radio played "Good Vibrations" with the volume down low. Elizabeth switched it off.

"Can I get you something to drink?" she asked. "Coffee, soda, water?"

"I'm good thanks."

They both sat on a battered Chesterfield sofa that looked like it had been rescued from a dump.

"Renee always said she'd hire a PI if Laurie wasn't home for her birthday," Elizabeth said sadly. "I guess here we are."

"Can you talk me through what you remember about that day?"

"Laurie spent the morning at the beach sketching while I manned the shop. It was something she did often, didn't like to be stuck indoors for too long. She'd usually bring us both some sandwiches for lunch and we'd lock up for a half hour and eat them through here. I didn't see her at all that day. She sent a message saying she had some stuff to do. I didn't think it was weird at the time. Maybe I should have."

"Did she have plans for later in the evening? Maybe she was meeting someone or heading out someplace?"

"I don't think so." Elizabeth's brown eyes glistened with tears. "God, if I'd known it might be the last time I ever had any contact with her . . ." She shook her head, didn't finish the sentence.

"What about a boyfriend?" Jessica asked. "I know Renee said she was single but was there a guy she was interested in, someone she might've been dating, who her folks didn't know about?"

"Laurie hadn't dated in months. She was really focused on work and her career. You know her folks pay rent on this place, as well as her apartment? She felt she was at an age where she wanted to stand on her own two feet, without their help, so all her time and effort went into her art. Romance was definitely on the backburner."

"No chance she'd hooked up with a guy she didn't tell you or her parents about? You know, someone you wouldn't approve of? A married man, maybe? Someone she might've run off with?"

Elizabeth was shaking her head before Jessica had finished asking the questions. "Uh-uh. No way. Don't get me wrong, Laurie's the romantic type. Believes in fate and thunderbolts and all that stuff. But she's not flakey. She wouldn't just run off and leave everyone worried sick about her like this. And she'd never get involved with a married man. That's just not her style."

"What about work? Any appointments or meetings scheduled around the time she disappeared?"

"There was nothing in her planner for that day. Like I said, she spent the morning at the beach and then took the afternoon off. No clients."

"You mind if I take a look at her planner?"

"Sure thing. It's right over here."

31

Elizabeth got up and walked over to a scarred wooden table covered with sketchbooks and pencils, mason jars filled with brushes, and tubes of paint rolled up like toothpaste. She picked up a brown leather planner and returned to the sofa. Handed the file to Jessica. She found the date when Laurie was last seen. Sure enough, it was blank. She went back a week before the disappearance, two weeks, a month. Nothing stood out. Mostly reminders to pick up supplies from the art store or collect mugs and tote bags from the printer. She thumbed forward to the days after Laurie vanished and found an entry for three days later.

"Who's Randal?"

"Who?"

Jessica showed Elizabeth the page. A noon appointment. Just a name. Could be a first name or a surname. No cell phone number or any other information. Elizabeth's blank expression gradually gave way to faint recognition.

"Oh, I think he's the guy she met at a local art festival a few months back. He bought a couple of her paintings for his private collection. Owns some trendy gallery in New York."

"A regular client?"

"No, but she hoped he might become one. He'd told her he was interested in featuring some of her work in an exhibition showcasing up-and-coming Los Angeles artists. He must've been planning another visit to LA and wanted to discuss potential pieces for the exhibition in person."

"You remember the name of the gallery he works for?"

"I'm sorry, I don't. But I do remember Laurie showed me his website and the gallery seemed quite impressive. She was excited about the possibility of an exhibition and some big sales."

"Did he show for the appointment?"

"No, I would have remembered."

Jessica frowned. "That's odd."

Elizabeth shrugged. "I guess so. Maybe he tried calling her cell phone to cancel or rearrange and couldn't reach her? Or he read about Laurie being missing and decided not to make the trip after all."

"I doubt it. An adult from Los Angeles, who'd been missing just a few days, wouldn't be news in New York. Do you have a landline here in the shop?"

"Yes, it's out front on the counter."

"And this Randal guy would've been able to find out the number easily enough?"

"Sure, it's listed and it's on our website. In fact, I'm sure Laurie said they swapped business cards at the fair so the shop number would've been on her card."

"Where does Laurie keep all of her paperwork?" Jessica asked. "Things like sales transactions, invoices, client details."

"Not here. Most likely the desk in her apartment."

"Great. I'll check it out." Jessica got up from the sofa. The butt of her skinny jeans was sweat damp from the crinkly old leather. She jotted down her own number on the cover of a sketchpad. "Thanks for your time, Elizabeth. If you think of anything, please give me a call."

She followed the other woman back into the shop and paused in front of one of Laurie's paintings. The brilliant white foam of a crashing wave contrasted beautifully with the intense turquoise, teal, and azure of the ocean. Jessica didn't know the first thing about art but she thought Renee Simmonds was right—her daughter did have talent.

"It's a stunning piece, isn't it?" Elizabeth said from behind her. "Although, none of Laurie's paintings are for sale until she comes back—you wouldn't believe the number of rubberneckers I had in here after she made the local papers. Some of her older paintings were selling for more than double on Craigslist."

"What do her paintings usually go for?"

"Anything from five hundred to five thousand. Although the bigger sales are quite rare."

Jessica smiled. "A little out of my price range." She picked up a mug from the counter display, one with the wave print on front. It was way nicer than Connor's chipped Dodgers one. Jessica was a Yankees fan in any case. "How much for this?"

"No charge," Elizabeth said. "Just find Laurie and bring her home to us."

6

CONNOR

Connor spent the morning making calls and feeling mostly like he was hitting his head against a load of brick walls.

First, he'd tried the detective who'd worked the Mallory Wilcox case and discovered he was now retired. Then he'd left a message for the cop in charge of Amanda Meyers' disappearance. He'd also gotten the machine for Amanda's parents after finally tracking down an address and contact number for them in Bakersfield.

He'd then gone through all the usual checks for missing persons: local hospitals and homeless shelters, the "Inmate Locator" website, websites for the County Coroner and County Morgue. He'd tried Los Angeles, then San Bernardino, and then Riverside. Knew they would all have been checked already but also knew he had to give them another go in case a Jane Doe matching the descriptions of Mallory or Amanda had turned up recently. Had hoped, if that was the case, he'd find her in jail, rather than the morgue. No dice. Blanks all the way. Jessica had gone through the same list searching for anyone who might be Laurie Simmonds, before heading out to speak to Elizabeth Mann and having a look around Laurie's apartment.

Jessica.

His brain had been fried since she'd shown up out of the blue at Larry's the night before. He'd sent her a text a while back, one night when he'd been drinking, telling her he'd been thinking about her.

Yeah, real smooth, Connor.

When she hadn't replied, he'd assumed he would never see her again. That thought had hit him a whole lot harder than he'd expected it to. He'd only spent a matter of days in Jessica's company but she'd left her mark on him, that was for sure. He hadn't been lying when he admitted in the text that he'd been thinking about her a lot. So, when she'd walked into the bar, casual as anything, he'd thought he must be seeing things. Wondered how strong the whiskey was he'd been drinking.

When she'd asked him for a job, he'd known straightaway he should say no. It was a bad idea. A *terrible* idea. He'd pissed her off once before and the voice inside his head was telling him it would all end badly again. He would buy her a drink, let her down gently, then walk away. No harm done. Maybe they'd even keep in touch this time. Then he'd looked into her eyes, seen the vulnerability under that tough exterior, and he'd heard himself saying yes.

Connor sighed now. He picked up the phone and punched in the number for Terence Wilcox, Mallory's husband. It rang and rang at the other end and Connor was just about to hang up when the call finally connected.

"What?" barked a male voice impatiently.

"Can I speak to Terence Wilcox, please?"

"Which one?"

"Huh?"

"Which Terence Wilcox? There's three of us."

"Um, the one who's married to Mallory Wilcox."

"That'd be Terence Wilcox II. Just as well 'cos the other two ain't available. Terence Wilcox I is six feet under in Riverside

36

Cemetery and Terence Wilcox III is at school. Or at least, he damn well better be."

Connor thought the guy might be drunk.

"Are you Terence Wilcox II?"

"Depends who's asking. What're you selling?"

"I'm not selling anything."

"Reporter?"

"Nope."

"But this is about Mal, right?"

"Right. My name is Matt Connor. I'm a private investigator."

"I didn't hire no private dick."

"No, but someone else did."

"Someone hired you to find my Mal?"

"Not exactly. I'm looking for another woman. Your wife's disappearance may be connected. I was hoping I could ask you a few questions?"

"Is it gonna cost me?"

"No, sir."

There was a long silence on the other end. Connor could hear the canned laughter from a daytime TV show in the background.

Eventually, Wilcox spoke again. "Stop by the house whenever you want. I'm home most days. You know my phone number, so I'm assuming you know where I live too." The words were slurred. Definitely drunk. "Then you go find that bitch and bring her home to look after her goddamn kids."

There was a click.

Wilcox had hung up.

Connor stared at the receiver, shook his head, and replaced it in the cradle.

He tapped his pen on his notepad and thought about what to do next. Decided Terence Wilcox II could wait. He pulled up a Google search page on the computer and looked up an address, jotted it down, and grabbed his car keys.

◆ ◆ ◆

Amanda Meyers had worked in one of the most eye-catching buildings in Downtown LA's Theater District.

The thirteen-story glossy turquoise, terracotta, and gold-trimmed Art Deco building stood out on the corner of Broadway and Ninth like a vintage jewel in a pawn shop window display. Crowned with a four-sided clock tower, even the surrounding zigzag and chevron-patterned terrazzo sidewalks were fancy. Once the headquarters of the Eastern Outfitting Company and the Columbia Outfitting Company furniture and clothing stores, it was now home to a mix of luxury condos, office suites and retail outlets.

Connor took the elevator to the floor occupied by the offices of Haywood, Dunne & Smith. The doors slid open soundlessly to reveal a stylish reception area with expensive-looking modern art on magnolia walls, a plush black leather couch, and carpet so thick his feet almost disappeared into the deep pile. The intimidating contemporary styling seemed at odds with the '30s charm of the rest of the building.

An attractive black woman sat behind a big glass desk, holding a phone to her ear with one hand, while tapping on a computer keyboard with the other. She was a burst of color in the otherwise monochrome surroundings: a red dress that showed off her curves while being office-appropriate, rouged lips, and dark curls dipped in rust. She eyed Connor as he approached, her gaze traveling from his face all the way down to his Adidas sneakers. She silently held up a finger topped with a scarlet nail, indicating she'd be with him in a minute. He suddenly felt underdressed in his jeans and t-shirt.

This place was only a half hour from Venice, but it might as well have been a million miles away.

The receptionist murmured something into the phone, hung up, and gave him the once over for a second time. Very slowly and deliberately. He realized he should be feeling undressed, rather than underdressed.

"Can I help you, sir?"

"I sure hope so. My name is Matt Connor and I'm a private investigator. I was hoping to speak to someone about Amanda Meyers."

The woman looked surprised, then hopeful. "Have you found Amanda? Is there news?"

"No, no, nothing like that, I'm afraid." Her face fell and he felt bad, wondered if they'd been friends. "I'm just following up on some potential leads."

"Oh, okay. I guess you'll be wanting to speak with Mr. Dunne in that case. Amanda reported directly to him and they worked very closely together. But . . . I know you don't have an appointment because I don't remember making an appointment for anyone half as exciting as a private eye."

He grinned. "You got me. No appointment. Guilty as charged."

She winked. "This is a lawyer's office, Mr. Connor. We don't use words like that here. Now, why don't you take a seat over there and let me see what I can do?"

She picked up the phone again and Connor wandered over to the window, rather than the couch. He was nowhere near high enough for a panoramic view of the city but he spotted the Orpheum Theatre and the Broadway Bar and dozens of tiny people going about their business on the sidewalk below. It sure beat what he saw from his own office window.

His reverie was broken by the sound of the receptionist's voice.

"Mr. Dunne has some meetings this afternoon but he can spare ten minutes right now."

Connor turned away from the view. "Perfect."

"Head on down the hallway." She pointed a red talon and he shuddered, thinking about the damage those things could do. "Third door on the left."

"Thanks . . ." He smiled. "Sorry, I didn't catch your name?"

The receptionist smiled back. She had a great smile. "My name is Vanessa. Now scoot. Nine and a half minutes."

Connor followed Vanessa's directions and found a polished oak door with a silver name plate on front which read "Zachary Dunne, Partner." He rapped a knuckle twice.

"Come on in."

The office was spacious and bright, thanks to its corner position in the building, with natural light streaming in from south- and west-facing windows. There was a smaller version of the leather couch he'd seen in the waiting room, a conference table that could seat six, and a big sturdy desk topped with a bunch of fat files, a banker's lamp, leather blotter, and some framed photos.

Zachary Dunne was around fifty, bald, bespectacled, and twenty pounds overweight. He wore navy pants with a white pinstripe, a white shirt with the sleeves rolled up, and a Homer Simpson tie. Connor couldn't see his feet behind the desk but guessed there might be novelty socks too.

He tried not to roll his eyes.

One of those guys.

Connor took a seat and explained how he'd been hired by the family of another missing woman and was looking into the possibility that Amanda Meyers' disappearance might be connected somehow.

"What can you tell me about Amanda?" he asked.

Dunne steepled his fingers and puffed out some air. Cocked his head slightly to the side, like a schoolkid puzzling over a particularly tough question in a pop quiz.

"Okay, Amanda. Let me see now. Amanda worked for the firm for, uh, almost three years, I think. She joined in a junior role and earned a promotion after a year or so. She was hardworking, tenacious, punctual, ambitious. Very popular with her fellow coworkers. A big loss to Haywood, Dunne & Smith when she . . . um . . . now that she no longer works here."

Connor thought the speech sounded rehearsed, like Dunne was dictating a reference for a résumé, rather than talking about someone he'd known, who'd been missing for two years.

"She's been replaced, then?"

The other man sighed. "We tried to manage as best we could without Amanda in the days and weeks after. Then we brought in a temp to pick up some of the workload. Eventually, after six months, we had to officially terminate her contract and find a permanent replacement."

"What happened to her things?"

"She mostly had work files in her desk. The few personal items were boxed up and mailed to her parents."

"I've not been able to get hold of them yet."

"I'm not sure they'll want to speak to you."

"No?"

"I heard there was some kind of breakdown. The mother, I think. Her parents took it very badly."

Connor nodded. "You mentioned Amanda was popular with her coworkers. Did she have friends here? Did she socialize much outside of work hours?"

Dunne frowned. "I don't think so. Of course, she would attend the Christmas party, office leaving drinks, things like that.

Otherwise, no, I don't think she spent much time with any of the staff outside of regular working hours."

"What about you?"

The lawyer looked startled. "What about me?"

"The receptionist out front said you worked together a lot," Connor said. "Were you close? Would you say you were friends?"

Dunne twisted a gold class ring on his left pinky finger. No wedding band, despite the wedding photo on the desk.

"Yes, I guess you'd say we were friendly." He nodded toward the conference table wistfully. "We'd often grab lunch over there while working on a case."

"Late nights too?"

"Sometimes, if the work demanded it."

"You ever drop her home after work?"

"No. She usually had her own car. Or sometimes she'd take an Uber."

"Did she live nearby?"

"A rental in Victor Heights." Dunne picked up a pen, twirled it in his fingers, dropped it back on the desk. "That's what she told me anyway. I'd never been there obviously."

"Obviously," Connor said. "Do you have the Victor Heights address for Amanda on file? Would save me a job looking it up."

Dunne's eyebrows bunched together into a single line of confusion. "Why do you need her address? She hasn't been there for two years. I'm sure there must be another tenant in her apartment by now."

"Might be worth speaking to the neighbors." Connor met his gaze. "See if they remember anything useful."

"I don't think it would be appropriate for me to give out personal information on our members of staff."

"You said Amanda's contract had been terminated."

Dunne twisted the pinky ring again. "Even so."

Connor shrugged. "Fair enough. What about the days leading up to her disappearance? Did Amanda seem different at all? Upset? Distracted? Like she had something on her mind?"

"Nope. Not that I recall."

"Any idea why she'd be at a motel out on the Twentynine Palms Highway?"

"None whatsoever."

The lawyer glanced pointedly at his Breitling watch.

Connor took the hint, got up from his chair.

"Thank you for your time, Mr. Dunne." He pulled a business card from his back pocket, slid it across the desk. "In case you think of anything else. I'll see myself out."

Connor strolled back down the hallway to the reception area, tossed a wave and a smile at Vanessa, and turned toward the elevator.

"Mr. Connor?"

He turned to see the receptionist holding up a square of neon-yellow paper.

He walked over to her. "What's that?"

"Amanda's address. I pulled it from the files. I thought it might be useful."

Connor grinned and pocketed the note. "You're a star, Vanessa."

"Don't I just know it." She hesitated. "Look, there's something else you should know."

"What's that?"

She glanced down the hallway. "Not here."

"Okay. Tell me where?"

"I get off at six. Hank's is my go-to for a post-work Scotch and soda. I'll meet you there."

7

JESSICA

It was a short stroll from the gallery to Laurie's apartment.

Jim Morrison gazed down from the corner of 18th and Speedway, the huge infamous Rip Cronk mural, one of several decorating the buildings around the beach town. Speedway was a narrow back street lined with apartment blocks tagged with graffiti and daubed with slogans and song lyrics. A blaring horn made Jessica start and she jumped out of the way just as a young guy raced past on a scooter, whooping and jeering, a fist pumping the air.

"Jerk," she muttered.

Laurie's apartment was on the first floor of a modest drab building with a street-facing balcony. Jessica climbed the stairs and raised a hand to knock on the front door out of habit. She shook her head, lowered her hand. No one would be answering. She found the spare key Renee had given her. Unlocked the door and hesitated before crossing the threshold. The idea of stepping inside a complete stranger's home without their knowledge or consent felt very weird.

It felt even more weird once Jessica was inside.

The door opened straight into an open-plan living, dining, and kitchen area. The place had a *Mary Celeste* vibe about it. Not quite the table set without any crew to be found but not far off it. A wine glass and a plate were stacked on the drainer next to the kitchen sink, probably washed and left to dry after dinner the night before Laurie disappeared. A half empty bottle of red with a stopper in the top stood on the counter. There was also a smaller plate and a coffee mug in the sink, likely used for breakfast on that last day. A glossy magazine lay open on the coffee table, two TV remotes were on the arm of the couch, a light sweater had been tossed onto an overstuffed armchair, and a pair of sneakers had been kicked off next to the front door.

Jessica ran a finger over the surface of a big wooden sideboard. No dust. She noticed the mail had been piled neatly on top, next to a sea turtle sculpture and some coffee table art books. Renee had clearly dusted and sorted through the bills in Laurie's absence but had otherwise left the apartment as it was the last time her daughter was home. As though she might walk through the door again at any moment.

The thought prompted a stirring of unease in Jessica. Her skin prickled and the tiny hairs on her arms stood on end. She suddenly had the feeling of being watched, as though someone's eyes were on her. She turned around slowly, almost expecting to find Laurie standing there, demanding to know who this stranger was poking around in her apartment. But, of course, there was no one there. Jessica was alone.

She pulled open the sliding door next to the sideboard and stepped out onto the compact balcony. It was dominated by a rusting wrought-iron bistro set and some potted plants and lanterns. There wasn't even a hint of a sea view, or any view at all really, unless neighboring buildings and fire escapes and tagged dumpsters were your kind of thing. But Laurie had made an effort all the same with the table and chairs and accessories.

Maybe she used to sit out here with a glass of wine and the sun on her face and watch the world go by. Might be nice if you didn't mind the exhaust fumes and the marijuana smoke drifting up from the street below. Despite the lack of view and the unpretentious surroundings, Jessica figured a two-bedroom apartment this close to the beach would still cost a hell of a lot of green. A lot more than the average struggling artist would be able to afford. Did Laurie appreciate what she'd had? Or did she grow to resent it?

Jessica went back inside.

She went into the master bedroom next. The bed was made although slightly rumpled, as though someone had sat on it. Cheap jasmine and patchouli-scented candles in jars cluttered the bedside table. Fairy lights were twisted around the bedframe. A turquoise and purple dream catcher hung above the bed. Jessica knew they were traditionally used to protect sleeping people from bad dreams and she wondered if Laurie's life had somehow become a waking nightmare a couple of months back despite the talisman. She opened the closet doors to find tank tops and tees folded on the shelves, sneakers and flat sandals in messy pairs on the floor. Floaty skirts, rainbow-colored maxi dresses, jeans, and the black dress from the birthday photo hung on the rail. A few of the wire hangers were empty.

There were more candles in the bathroom, as well as the kind of stuff you'd expect a young woman to keep in there. Tampons, hand cream, bubble bath, a spare roll of toilet paper. Jessica made a mental note of what she saw—as well as what she didn't see. No shampoo or conditioner. No toothpaste or toothbrush. No shower gel. She went back through to the living room and found another closet next to the front door. Inside was some luggage. One of those matching sets that comes in threes—except there were only two suitcases. The smallest one was gone, a dusty rectangle showing where it had once been stored next to the others.

It looked a lot to Jessica like Laurie Simmonds had been planning a trip. Not a long one. Maybe an overnighter. Two days at most. Certainly not two months. Had Renee also picked up on the missing items? Jessica thought she probably had, wondered why Laurie's mother had neglected to mention it in their meeting earlier. She decided it might be a good idea to pay a visit to the Simmonds' place sooner rather than later. Jessica and Connor still had to speak to Laurie's father in any case.

She wandered through to the second bedroom, which had been turned into a smaller version of the studio at 2Women. Tons of natural light and paints and brushes everywhere. An easel was set up holding an unfinished painting, just like the space Laurie shared with Elizabeth. Jessica felt another chill creep down her back, that icy finger on her spine once more. The idea of a life unexpectedly and abruptly disturbed, waiting to be resumed again at any time. She spotted two canvases stacked in a corner. They were wrapped in brown paper, which had been ripped down the front, exposing the artwork inside.

The two paintings found in Laurie's van.

Jessica bent down on her haunches for a closer look. Like the paintings on display at the shop, they were both beach scenes and both impressive. Large in size. The five-grand price range, Jessica guessed. She got up with a groan, feeling the burn in her thighs, and made her way over to a large whitewashed bureau.

It looked like an old thrift store find that had been upcycled into the kind of trendy shabby chic piece of furniture you'd see on carefully curated Instagram feeds. The lower cupboard was used mainly to store art supplies but the pull-down top was more promising. It revealed shelves and drawers housing stationery, correspondence, and paperwork. Jessica found sales invoices, receipts of payments, proof of purchase for art materials, statements for Laurie's business account, a check book and check slips, cell phone statements.

All of the woman's business documents had been filed meticulously until two months ago. Jessica scanned the most recent bank statement and noticed a cash deposit of $2500 had been made by Laurie herself around a month before she'd vanished. Jessica opened one of the drawers and saw that it held pens and pencils and envelopes. The other drawer had more stationery junk. In among the paperclips and staples and Post-it notes and Scotch tape, Jessica found a little silver case with a black tourmaline stone glued to the front. The crystal was often used for protection and Jessica's mind flashed to the dream catcher in the other bedroom. Laurie Simmonds had appeared to surround herself with trinkets and talismans to protect her from bad things yet had somehow ended up with a stranger rooting through her stuff, searching for clues as to what had happened to her.

Jessica opened the little case and saw it was a business card holder. One pocket held Laurie's own cards, the other was for cards she'd been given by potential clients. Jessica flipped through them until she found what she was looking for.

A business card for a New York art gallery.

She turned it over. Jessica had never bothered with business cards of her own, preferring to scribble her digits on scraps of paper or palms of hands. But she could see this one was a quality product. Thick cream paper with "The Grand Street Gallery" in raised gold foil lettering. Underneath was an address in Brooklyn and a website address. A cell phone number and "Randal" were written on the back.

Jessica returned to the living room and rifled through the mail on the sideboard. The most recent cell phone statement showed no calls or texts. Maybe Renee was keeping the contract going in the hope Laurie would suddenly start using her cell again. The second to last statement—the one documenting the last calls and texts the missing woman had made—was also there. Laurie hadn't called anyone on the day she vanished but she'd sent five texts. Two were presumably to Elizabeth Mann and Renee Simmonds. The other three were to a single cell phone number.

The same number as the one written on The Grand Street Gallery business card.

Jessica pulled her own cell phone from her bag and tapped in Randal's number. Got a recorded message telling her the call could not be connected. Next, she pulled up the internet app and typed in the address for the gallery's website, the one that had impressed Elizabeth Mann. It redirected to a domain company holding page. She called directory assistance and asked for information on the business at the address on the card. The operator told her it was a pizza delivery place. Jessica disconnected the call and confirmed what she'd been told with a Google Street View image of the premises on Grand Street in Williamsburg. Finally, she did an image search for "Randal" from The Grand Street Gallery.

There was nothing.

Nada.

Zilch.

Randal was a ghost. It was like he had never existed.

And the only person who could say otherwise—Laurie Simmonds—was nowhere to be found either.

8

LAURIE—TWO MONTHS AGO

It was the kind of day Laurie Simmonds loved. One of those days where nothing could possibly go wrong and only good things were allowed to happen.

The heat of the mid-morning sun pleasantly warmed her bare arms and legs but wasn't so hot that she had to worry about her fair skin turning pink. It'd be another month before she'd have to break out the high-factor sun cream and her big floppy hat. The Pacific Ocean shimmered and the waves were just high enough to keep the surfers and paddle-boaters happy. Laurie dug her toes into the warm sand and put the finishing touches to the sketch she'd been working on, before lighting the joint she'd rolled earlier.

"Mind if I join you?"

She glanced up to see who had spoken to her, the bright glare forcing her to squint and shade her eyes. Laurie almost fainted when she saw who was standing there.

"Randal! Hi! Yes, please come sit." She instinctively swapped the joint to her left hand and lowered it out of view, while patting the sand next to her with her right hand. Pot wasn't illegal in California but Laurie wasn't sure the owner of a fashionable New

York gallery would approve. After all, their relationship was a fledgling business one and impressions—first or otherwise—were always important when working with new people.

Randal lowered himself onto the sand and crossed his legs. He was dressed casually in a short-sleeved Tommy Hilfiger shirt, chinos, and deck shoes with no socks. He reminded Laurie of her old high school boyfriend, Miles McCaw, although Randal was blond and Miles was dark. Like Miles, Randal's style was laid-back preppy, while hinting at plenty of cash in the bank.

The sweet smell of the joint was embarrassingly noticeable over her lavender perfume and Randal leaned across and eyed it pointedly. "Are you going to share that or what?"

"Um, sure." She passed him the joint. "Sorry, I didn't think it'd be your kind of thing."

"When in Rome, right?" Randal took the joint, inhaled deeply, and handed it back. "Anyway, you don't seriously think I spent four years at art school without smoking some weed, do you?"

Laurie laughed. "Good point." She licked her finger and pinched the lit end of the joint. Dropped it in her purse for later. "What're you doing here, anyway? I thought our meeting was next week? Or did I get the days mixed up?"

Laurie had first met Randal a month earlier at a Venice art fair. The two-day event provided local artists with the opportunity to showcase ceramics, jewelry, paintings, and sculptures for the general public to browse and purchase. Randal had made a beeline for her stall on the first day and had talked passionately, and knowledgeably, about her work. Laurie had been thrilled when he'd offered to buy two of her paintings for $1000 each, cash in hand, right there and then, for his private collection. And she was even happier when he mentioned he was a gallery owner who was interested in including more of her work at an upcoming exhibition in Brooklyn.

They'd swapped business cards and Laurie had immediately checked out the website address listed on his card. To say she was impressed by what she saw was an understatement. The Grand Street Gallery was housed in a beautiful, ornate old building on a bustling Williamsburg street. It had once been a bank in a previous life and, while the outside was classic nineteenth-century architecture, the interior was minimal, modern and ultra-trendy, with strategically placed sculptures and paintings contrasting wonderfully with the stark decor.

She'd excitedly told Elizabeth all about Randal, and the paintings he'd purchased, and his interest in including her work at an exhibition in New York.

"New York!" she'd squealed. "Can you believe it?"

Then she'd shown Elizabeth the photos of the gallery on the website, and her friend had tried to look pleased for her but Laurie could tell there was a hint of envy behind the smile, and she'd felt bad for bragging, knowing Elizabeth had endured a disappointing fair with almost no sales.

Randal had written his cell phone number on the back of the card he'd given to Laurie, and they had texted and emailed several times since their first meeting.

A few days ago, he'd told her he was planning another trip to Los Angeles and wanted to come down to Venice and visit the gallery space she shared with Elizabeth, to discuss potential pieces for the exhibition.

She'd made a date in her diary for Monday at noon. Today was Friday.

Randal smiled reassuringly. "Nope, you didn't get the days mixed up. There's been a change to my schedule, which is why I came looking for you. Do you have any plans for this weekend?"

"Nothing important. Why?"

"Fantastic. I have an exciting proposition for you."

"Sounds intriguing."

"Oh, it is. It involves your best paintings, a road trip, and this." He reached into his back pocket, pulled out a neon wristband and handed it to her. "It's going to be lots of fun—and very beneficial for you."

Laurie took the wristband and read the words printed on the soft fabric. Her eyes widened when she saw what it was for. "Are you serious? This is for me?"

"It sure is. It's where all the action will be happening this weekend and I'd love for you to be there to meet some people I know. Some very influential people. It'll be a great chance to show them how talented you are. Trust me, they're already interested."

"I don't know what to say." She regarded the wristband again. "These things are definitely not cheap."

"Just say yes. It's my treat."

Laurie smiled. "What's the catch?"

"No catch," Randal said. "Although I do think it should be our little secret for now."

9

CONNOR

Victor Heights was a small obscure corner of LA comprising a bunch of hilly residential streets hidden between Echo Park and Chinatown. So obscure that it wasn't found on Google Maps and Connor had never heard of it until today despite living in the city for the whole of his forty-one years.

After finally losing all faith in his Ford pick-up's GPS to find the address scribbled on the yellow Post-it stuck to the dash, he pulled over and asked an elderly Chinese man for directions. Connor was beginning to wonder why an ambitious career girl like Amanda Meyers would choose to reside in such an esoteric little neighborhood when he turned onto her street and immediately knew the answer. Stretching out majestically before him from the peak of the hill was the most magnificent view of Downtown, rivaling even that of the vista from his seat at Dodger Stadium. So taken was he by the dramatic and unexpected appearance of the city center skyline, that he didn't notice the sudden flash of color until it was almost too late.

Connor slammed on the brakes.

The truck screeched to a halt.

For the second time in the space of a few seconds, he was stunned by what he saw in front of him. He leaned on the steering wheel and peered through the windscreen, his mouth hanging open.

"What the . . .?"

There, in the middle of the street, stood a peacock, its long tail fanning out behind in a blur of blue and green and turquoise. It appeared to stare back at Connor for a long moment, before unleashing an almighty squawk and continuing on its journey. He watched in amazement as it strutted down the side of a fourplex and disappeared round the back.

Connor shook his head with a laugh and restarted the truck. He found Amanda Meyers' old apartment complex—a three-story putty-colored building with a red stucco-tiled roof—a half block away and parked up outside.

He quickly ruled out calling on whoever now resided in her old apartment on the basis that they'd be unlikely to know anything about the previous tenant or her disappearance. He made his way up to the top floor and knocked on the doors of Amanda's two nearest neighbors instead and completely struck out. No answer from either apartment. It was mid-afternoon and Connor figured the occupants of both apartments were probably at work. Not the best time of day for an impromptu canvass of the neighborhood.

He took the stairs down to the middle floor and banged on the first door he came to. Was just about to give up and move on to the next apartment when he heard a shuffling movement from inside. The door opened to reveal a young skinny guy with mussed-up hair and boxers and a creased t-shirt. He looked like he'd just woken up. The hallway behind him was dim and he squinted in the light from the landing.

"Yeah?"

Connor didn't know if the guy was a stoner or a student or a night-shift worker trying to grab some sleep.

"Sorry to bother you. I'm looking to speak to someone who might be able to tell me about Amanda Meyers. She used to live upstairs."

The guy pressed the heel of a hand into his eyes. Blinked a couple times. "Uh, she's the chick who went missing, right?"

"Right."

"Must be, what, a year ago?"

"Two years."

"Whoa. Really? Time sure flies, man."

"It sure does."

The guy suddenly seemed more alert, much more cautious.

"Hey, you're not a cop, are you?"

Stoner, Connor decided.

"No, I'm not a cop. I'm a private eye, looking into her disappearance." Stoner's eyes narrowed and Connor added quickly, "I'm not looking to cause any trouble for anyone. I'm just after some information on Ms. Meyers."

"Look, dude. I wish I could help but I didn't really know her at all. Not even to say hello to. I offered to help carry her groceries upstairs once and she looked at me like I'd just grabbed her ass." Stoner shook his head, his expression a mixture of hurt and confusion. "Man, I was only trying to help. Be courteous, you know?"

"That sucks big time, bud," Connor agreed. He gestured vaguely in the direction of the other doors. "Is there anyone else likely to be around right now who'd be happy to talk?"

Stoner shook his head. "Nah. Not in this building anyways. You want information on what goes on around here, you'll be wanting to speak to Mrs. DuBois. She's the block captain."

"Block captain?"

"Yeah, it's a Neighborhood Watch thing. Means she gets to spy on folks all hours of the day and night and it's legit somehow because she was voted in or something. I even heard a rumor she uses binoculars." Stoner laughed and it turned into a wheezy cough. "Can you believe that shit, man?"

"Is that so?" Connor had to stop himself from punching the air. Neighborhood Watch. The best friend of the private eye. "Where exactly do I find this Mrs. DuBois?"

The answer to Connor's question was right across the street in an ivy-covered Spanish-style bungalow. A red-and-white Neighborhood Watch sign starring "Boris the Burglar"—a shady noir villain silhouette—was nailed to a streetlamp outside. Connor thought he saw the curtain in the big front window twitch as he approached the front door and, again, had to suppress the urge to punch the air.

He pressed the doorbell and heard the chimes echo inside the house, along with the excited yip of a small dog. A shadow appeared behind the stained glass window of the front door, which opened a few inches to reveal wary eyes behind a taut security chain.

"Yes, can I help you?"

"Mrs. DuBois? One of the residents across the street suggested I speak to you. I'm a private investigator looking into the disappearance of Amanda Meyers."

"I.D. please?"

He pulled his PI license from his messenger bag and showed it to the woman.

The door closed over and he heard the scrape of metal on metal as the security chain was unlatched and the door opened fully to reveal Mrs. DuBois.

She was old but alert. Five foot nothing in her no-brand sneakers but not frail. Heavy makeup and wild, wispy pink hair that brought to mind freshly spun cotton candy at a funfair. She had the crepey tan skin of a lifelong sun worshipper and wore lots of gold jewelry and she was holding a small silver handgun. An octogenarian sparkplug. She eyed Connor appraisingly.

"Well, aren't you a tall drink of water on a hot day?"

Connor laughed nervously, his eyes on the gun.

Mrs. DuBois followed his gaze. "Can't be too careful these days, young man. Now, why don't you come on in and I'll fetch you some iced tea and cookies while we chat?"

He waited in the front room, while she busied herself in the kitchen. The place smelled of home baking and his belly rumbled loudly. A blond pug looked up from where it was lying on a cushioned dog bed and then lay down again, clearly deciding Connor wasn't interesting enough to bother getting up for. He stepped over to a big bay window, which offered a fantastic view of the street, and spotted his own dark green Ford parked outside Amanda Meyers' building. A set of expensive, military-style binoculars sat on the windowsill next to a notebook.

"Here we go." Mrs. DuBois placed a tray with a pitcher of iced tea, two highball glasses and a plate of cookies on the coffee table. "The cookies were already cooling on the rack. Your timing is impeccable."

Connor was relieved to see the handgun was gone. He poured himself a drink and picked up a couple of cookies from the plate. Bit into one and groaned with pleasure. "Chocolate chip," he said, between bites. "My absolute favorite. And, I gotta say, these cookies are something else."

Mrs. DuBois beamed. "Best in the neighborhood. Or so I'm told."

"Can't argue with that." Connor nodded in appreciation. "Speaking of the neighborhood, I hear you're the local block captain? I'd heard of Neighborhood Watch but I'd never come across that particular phrase until today."

Mrs. DuBois took a sip of iced tea and replaced the tumbler on the coffee table. "That's right," she said. "I've been a resident of Victor Heights half my life and block captain for more years than I care to remember." She laughed and it was a deep throaty sound. "I guess you could say I got involved because I'm nosy as hell."

Connor grinned. "I like your honesty, Mrs. DuBois." He inclined his head toward the binoculars. "And you certainly have some serious equipment there."

"Necessary for the job these days. My eyesight isn't so sharp now and I'm not getting any younger either. You saw how steep that hill is outside. Me and Coco here like to get out as much as possible but the years are catching up with us both and neither one of us is as active as we used to be. A lot of the time, that front window is my observation point."

"And what did you observe about Amanda Meyers?"

Mrs. DuBois sighed, shook her head. "Such a tragedy what happened to that young woman. Every time I pass by her apartment block, I wonder what became of her. I can't say she was the friendliest—and this is a friendly community—but she was a respectable enough tenant from what I could gather. Took the trash out on time, no reports of late-night parties, never rolled up drunk and boisterous at all hours, didn't have a string of young men in and out the place all of the time."

"So, no boyfriend, then?"

"That's not what I said. What I meant was she wasn't a trollop who entertained a different man every night of the week. But she did have one regular gentleman caller, as far as I could tell."

"Oh yeah?"

"Older than her, smartly dressed, but podgy. Not a looker. In my opinion, she could have done better for herself, even if she did look like she could do with a few decent home-cooked meals to fatten her up a bit."

"Was she involved with this man for a while?"

"Oh yes. He was on the scene for a little over a year, right up until the day she disappeared. Sometimes they'd arrive together in her car, other times he'd visit in his own vehicle."

"I don't suppose—"

She cut him off. "I noted down details of the car? Of course I did. The other vehicle too."

"What other vehicle?"

"The mystery truck. I know every set of wheels in this neighborhood. All the ones that belong here and all the ones that don't. So, when I see something unfamiliar, it catches my attention. This one appeared suddenly one day, parked a block away from Ms. Meyers' building, on the other side of the street. For three months, it was there. Two or three times a week, different hours of the day and night. The driver was always in the car, always wore a baseball cap. He had an untidy beard. One day, I tried to get a closer look at him while out walking Coco. He saw me coming and drove off in a real hurry."

"What makes you think the truck had anything to do with Amanda Meyers?"

"I never saw it again after she went missing."

"And you have records of both of these vehicles?"

"I sure do. Let me go find my book from two years ago."

She returned with a leather-bound journal and a Ziploc freezer bag. Flicked through the pages until she found the right one, folded back the spine and handed it to Connor.

"See those two highlighted entries? Those are the details of the vehicles you're interested in—Ms. Meyers' gentleman friend and the mystery truck."

Connor was impressed. Mrs. DuBois had documented the make, model, color, and number plate of both cars, as well as time of arrival, where exactly they'd been parked, and how long they'd stayed for. There were also entries for an upturned trash can and a busted streetlight.

"Did you tell the police about these two vehicles after Amanda's disappearance?"

"Sure did. I have regular meetings with Senior Lead Officer Zhao. He's the one in charge of this Basic Car Area. Nice fella. Big fan of my cookies too."

Connor nodded. Each of the city's nineteen geographic areas were served by a community police station, and each station was apportioned into small neighborhood units, which were known as Basic Cars.

"And what was the outcome of that conversation?"

"Officer Zhao said he passed the information onto the Missing Persons Unit. I never did find out if what I told them was any help though."

Connor pulled out his cell phone and opened the camera app. "You mind if I   ?"

"Not at all. You go right ahead."

While Connor photographed the details from Mrs. DuBois' journal, the old woman lifted the plate and slid the remaining cookies into the freezer bag and zipped it shut. She handed the bag to him with a wink.

"For later. Enjoy."

He grinned. "Thanks, Mrs. DuBois. I certainly will."

Twenty minutes later, Connor was at a table inside a nearby family-run deli, eating the best meatball sandwich he'd had in his entire life. He wiped his hands and mouth with a paper napkin and scrolled through the numbers stored in his cell phone. He found the one for his contact at the DMV and waited for the call to connect. Asked his contact to run the two number plates provided by Mrs. DuBois and was told he'd have both drivers' names by the end of the day.

Connor killed the call.

He already had a pretty good idea who one of them would be.

◆ ◆ ◆

Connor had always thought of Hank's, a dive bar right next door to the Stillwell Hotel, as a little piece of heaven in the heart of the city. Dark and narrow with dim lighting casting everything in a red glow, the booze was cheap and the music was good. The kind of place you visited to drink your drinks, rather than take photographs of them, unlike some of DTLA's other, shinier, establishments.

He ordered a Scotch and soda for Vanessa and neat bourbon for himself and found a table in the back corner. Hank Williams played on the jukebox. After speaking to Mrs. DuBois, and his late lunch in Victor Heights, Connor had driven back to Venice, showered and changed into fresh jeans and a black shirt, before hopping back on the 10 for the 6 p.m. meet. He checked the time on his cell and noticed he had a text from his contact at the DMV.

As predicted, the Mediterranean-blue BMW 4 Series convertible—belonging to the man Mrs. DuBois had referred to as Amanda Meyers' "gentleman friend"—was registered to Zachary Dunne, her boss.

The mystery truck—a gray Dodge Dakota—remained a mystery. The DMV search had drawn a blank. Connor guessed the pick-up must have had fake, unregistered plates.

He fired off a text thanking his contact and looked up to see Vanessa approaching the table. She was taller than he'd first thought, having only seen her from behind a desk before. Long legs made longer by skyscraper heels. The playful, flirty smile from earlier was gone. She dropped into the seat facing him.

"You changed your clothes," she said.

"I did."

"And you ordered already. Thanks for the drink."

"No problem."

"I'm So Lonesome I Could Cry" ended. There was silence for a beat, then "Only the Lonely" by Roy Orbison started up. Connor thought whoever was feeding the jukebox must be going through a tough break-up.

Vanessa took a big gulp of Scotch. She appeared troubled.

"Look, I think I made a mistake coming here," she said. "I've been thinking about it since you left. I've worked for the firm for more than a decade and I can't afford to lose my job. That's why I didn't say anything to the cops at the time. I don't want my name anywhere near this mess." She took another drink and shook her head. "Damn. It's just that . . ."

"Amanda and Zachary Dunne were having an affair," Connor supplied. "They'd been screwing around for at least a year."

Vanessa stared at him in surprise. "You already knew. How?"

"I suspected as much after speaking to Dunne. Didn't know for sure until about a minute ago."

"Well, I'll be damned. I guess you wasted a journey and the price of a drink."

"Not at all. You can still help me fill in a few blanks."

The troubled expression returned. "I don't know . . ."

"Completely off the record," Connor added quickly. "Your name won't appear in any of my reports for the Simmondses."

"The Simmondses?"

"The family of another missing woman. The ones who hired me."

Connor opened his messenger bag and pulled out a photo. Laurie Simmonds was sitting on the beach with a sketchbook, squinting slightly against the sun. He showed it to Vanessa.

She shook her head, handed it back to him. "Nope. I don't recognize her. Sorry."

Connor returned the photo to the bag and swapped it for his notepad and pen. "Tell me about Amanda and Zachary Dunne."

Vanessa emptied her glass and Connor finished his bourbon. He caught the bartender's eye and signaled for two more drinks.

"Okay, but I should start off by saying none of this is fact," she said, leaning in closer and lowering her voice. "Just my own impressions of what I think was going on. I never walked in on them or caught them in the act or anything like that. Another reason I never spoke to the cops."

"I understand. But anything you can tell me will be a big help."

"At first, it was just a shift in the air, a change of atmosphere when they were together. Like something had changed between them. It's hard to explain what I mean exactly. It just felt different when they were together."

"Sure, I get what you mean."

The bartender placed the fresh round of drinks in front of them.

Vanessa said, "There were knowing looks. They were more tactile with each other. Amanda started spending a lot more time in Mr. Dunne's office. They began working more cases after hours too. Again, it was all just speculation on my part at this point. Then, I came across more solid evidence of an affair."

"Uh-huh. What'd you find?"

"I take care of Mr. Dunne's expenses, as well as those of the firm's other two partners. I started noticing some, um, irregularities, I guess you'd call them. The occasional overnight stay in a hotel that didn't tally with any client cases he was working on at the time. Receipts for gas stations out by Echo Park, close to where Amanda lived, but nowhere near Mr. Dunne's home in Beverlywood. Then there was the apartment."

"What apartment?"

"You know there are luxury condos in the same building as the office, right? Very nice. Rooftop pool, the works. Johnny Depp used to own the penthouse. Well, Mr. Dunne rents one of the apartments. He'd stay over when he was working late or had an early breakfast meeting. One time, I dropped off some papers at the apartment before finishing up for the evening and Amanda answered the door. Don't get me wrong, she was dressed, wasn't wearing just lingerie or a robe. But she had this smug expression on her face when she snatched the file off me, like she'd bagged the boss and that made her special somehow. Other mornings, she'd come out of the elevator right after it'd traveled down from the condo's floor, rather than up from the ground floor. Back then, Mr. Dunne used the condo occasionally. Now he stays there full-time."

"Marriage problems?" Connor asked. "I noticed he wasn't wearing a wedding ring."

Vanessa took a sip of her drink and nodded. "I assume so. When Amanda disappeared, Mr. Dunne took it bad. He tried to hide it from the rest of the staff, of course, but I could tell his mind wasn't on the job. He'd show up late. Oftentimes, he appeared hungover. Once or twice, I was sure he was drunk at work. About a month or so after, he took some time off for 'complications with a burst appendix.' He was signed off sick for months. I suspected a breakdown. Others did too."

"Dunne said Amanda's mother had suffered a breakdown."

"I guess she wasn't the only one. When Mr. Dunne finally did return to the office, the wedding ring was gone. That's when he moved into the condo permanently."

"His wife found out about the affair?"

Vanessa shrugged. "Again, I can only speculate. What I can tell you is, I think he was way more into Amanda than she was him. Call it women's intuition. The way he looked at her at times, he was like a little lovesick puppy. I don't think there was much love on her part. I think her relationship with Mr. Dunne was more . . . strategic. She was extremely ambitious."

"You think she had someone else?" Connor asked. "Another lover she might've been meeting out at that motel in the desert?"

Vanessa smiled sadly. "That I can't help you with. The only person who knows what happened that night is Amanda Meyers."

10

AMANDA—TWO YEARS AGO

Friday afternoon and the city was in the grip of a relentless summer. It was hotter than hell outside and not so much fun inside either, with stuffy work areas and sticky armpits and desktops fans pointed at damp faces.

Amanda Meyers was absolutely fine though.

She had the AC cranked all the way up to the kind of temperature an Arctic explorer would find chilly and she was enjoying the coolness, and the quiet, as she worked through the last of the week's paperwork. Zach was out at meetings all day, so she'd decided to take advantage of his absence and use his office instead of her own desk on the overheated main floor. One of the perks of sleeping with the boss.

Her cell phone vibrated and a message flashed up on the screen from a number she didn't recognize.

New burner. Save this number xx
Zach.

He always signed off with two kisses, just like a teenage girl would. Amanda used to find it cute, now she found it irritating. A lot of things about Zach irritated her these days, such as the nonsense with the burner phones. When they'd first hooked up, they'd agreed she wouldn't contact his regular cell phone after office hours, so he'd purchased a burner. Fair enough. Then he'd started replacing the burner every few months after his wife found the first one and he'd had to convince her the phone belonged to a client in the middle of a messy divorce. It was boring now. So was staying home alone on the weekend when Zach had plans with Stephanie.

As if he'd been reading her thoughts, another message arrived from him.

I want to see you tonight. Let's spend all weekend in bed together. Fancy packing a bag? xx

Amanda tapped out a reply: What about S? x

She didn't want to spend all weekend in bed with Zach. This thing, whatever it was, had run its course. Amanda had some interviews lined up for rival firms in the coming weeks. As soon as she quit her job here, she'd quit Zach too.

Her phone lit up again. S thinks I have a business trip. What do you say? xx

Amanda knew Zach was crazy about her. That's why he showered her with expensive gifts, including a sports car. He'd even started making noises recently about leaving Stephanie. He'd probably picked up on Amanda's growing indifference toward their relationship and mistaken it for frustration that they weren't an "official" couple. It didn't matter either way. Zach would never end his marriage. Stephanie would make his life hell, and then take him to the cleaners, if he even tried.

In any case, Amanda knew she could do way better than Zachary Dunne. Someone richer, and more powerful, and definitely better looking. Zach had served his purpose. She'd gone as far as she could at Haywood, Dunne & Smith. The sex wasn't great and she didn't even enjoy kissing him. Not that he was a bad kisser, not really, but she hated the way his glasses pressed against her face and the feel of his bald leathery scalp beneath her fingers. Amanda liked to run her hands through thick hair when she was making out. Liked the feel of a hard, toned body on top of her own, not a flabby, middle-aged gut.

She picked up her cell, intending to text back letting him know she had made plans already.

But.

Another perk of sleeping with the boss was that he *did* always choose the best hotels and restaurants when they spent time together away from the office. Only the finer things in life for Zachary Dunne. It was the reason why he'd hit on Amanda. If he was planning on taking her someplace fancy for the weekend, then maybe she'd meet him after all. They didn't have to spend the whole time in bed together. She could relax in the spa, maybe have a massage, definitely order some nice food, and drink the best champagne the hotel had on offer.

Okay. Where? x

Zach replied straightaway. The Tranquility on Twentynine Palms Highway. Can you phone ahead and book the room on your card as usual? Here's the number. Will give you the cash tonight xx

Amanda: Am I meeting you there? x

Zach: Yes. Ask for room 25 and use the private parking spot round back. And wear something sexy! xx

Amanda smiled at his last comment. She imagined him imagining her in a hot little number, getting all frisky in between his boring meetings.

She phoned the number and booked the room. It sounded like the guy who answered said "motel" rather than "hotel" and it was a lot cheaper than she expected. Must be desert prices, she told herself. Zach wasn't cheap and he always gave her the cash back straightaway whenever she put anything on her card, which was another precaution against Stephanie finding out about the affair. Further proof he'd never leave his wife.

Amanda returned to the client file she'd been working on. Stared at the page for a full five minutes before realizing she hadn't read a single word. Her mind was elsewhere, already fantasizing about an outdoor hot tub, with a panoramic view of the Mojave Desert, and an ice-cold glass of fizz in her hand.

Yes, Amanda and Zach would have one final weekend together and then she would tell him it was over between them.

11

JESSICA

The sun dipped into the horizon and the sky looked like it was on fire as Jessica eased her Chevy Silverado through the tight twists and turns of Mulholland Drive.

Way down below, the lights of the Los Angeles Basin began to twinkle like a million stars reflected on a still lake. Jessica had been born in this city but, having grown up in low-rent apartment blocks among the grime and noise and bustle of New York, she was still trying to get used to the place she now called home. She didn't know if native Angelenos took such views for granted but, to Jessica, the scene was pure Hollywood. Even more so than the famous sign and the studios and the A-list stars.

She turned off the two-lane highway onto a winding paved driveway leading to an elegant six-foot gate with an intercom to the side. It wasn't much of a deterrent for any intruder determined enough to gain access to the grounds but it did provide the place with the kind of gated estate feel folks in the neighborhood clearly coveted. Jessica leaned out the truck's window and pressed the button. A short pause was followed by a low buzz as the gate slid open.

The driveway led to an imposing peach Tuscan-style house perched proudly in an elevated position amongst the flora and fauna and shale of the hillside. Jessica thought the property might be the same size as the entire block where she had once shared a house in Blissville with her dad, Tony. Definitely worth a few million at least. Several cars, all showroom new and sparkly, were parked in front of a triple garage. Jessica pulled up next to a Porsche 911 and shut off the engine.

She got out of the truck and stood for a moment, enjoying the feel of the warm evening breeze ruffling her short blonde hair and the intoxicating sight of the blood sunset over the Santa Monica Mountains. The neighborhood's grand properties were all impressive in their own way but they couldn't begin to compete with the rugged landscape when it came to the wow factor. Jessica headed for the Simmonds residence—and stopped dead in her tracks when she spotted the twin-pillared front entrance.

"You have got to be kidding me."

She suddenly felt very inappropriately dressed in her stripe tee, skinny jeans and Converse—and not because of the lavish surroundings. Renee's diamond rock, the regular financial handouts for Laurie, the exclusive Mulholland address, Jessica had been prepared for the wealth that would be on show. It didn't bother her. She hadn't been prepared for what else she saw.

Huge gold and silver "two" and "four" balloons, banners, and streamers adorned the front of the house. The muted sound of conversation and music drifted through an open window.

A party. And not just any party. A birthday party.

For missing Laurie Simmonds.

Jessica had texted Renee earlier in the day, said she wanted to speak to both her and Trey. She'd assumed Connor would join her at the Simmonds' place but he'd been out all day digging into Amanda Meyers' background and said he'd arranged a meet with one of the woman's former coworkers. It sounded to Jessica like the interview was taking place in a bar. She was sure she could hear a Bob Dylan song in the background as well as lots of barroom chatter.

Jessica felt irrationally pissed at Connor. While he was out mixing business with pleasure, she was stuck gatecrashing a weird party with no guest of honor.

Before she had the chance to change her mind, back out, and return to her truck, the door opened and Renee stood there, swaying slightly, a glass of white wine in her hand, her eyes a little too wide and wild.

Chardonnay drunk.

Great, Jessica thought. This evening was just getting better and better.

"Jessica!" Renee cried as though greeting an old friend, rather than someone she'd met for the first time earlier that day. She stumbled onto the gravel and leaned forward to give Jessica a quick demi-hug and air kiss, the way rich people do when they don't want to make actual physical contact.

"Hey, Renee. Apologies if I'm interrupting. I didn't realize you were having a party."

"Nonsense! Come on in and meet everyone."

Renee led the way rather unsteadily on her high heels into a living room tastefully decorated in hues of cream, white and beige. Music played softly from unseen speakers. Jessica decided she'd speak to Renee about the missing luggage and the mysterious Randal when the woman was sober. Figured Trey Simmonds might be a better bet tonight.

There were eight other guests at the party. Three couples from the neighborhood—introduced as the Hunts, Goldmans, and McCaws—were scattered along a giant L-shaped leather sofa. The men nursed whiskeys, the women clutched wine glasses, and they all looked like they'd been dressed from the spring-summer Ralph Lauren collection. Laurie's best friend, Elizabeth Mann, pretty in a navy jumpsuit and her hair down around her face, stood with a guy around her own age. Preppy-handsome in a polo shirt, chinos and boaters, Miles McCaw was apparently Laurie's old high school boyfriend.

Everyone looked as awkward as Jessica felt.

The other person in the room was Trey Simmonds. Jessica didn't need Renee's introductions to figure that one out. His fair hair was turning gray but he shared the same pale blue eyes and freckled complexion as Laurie, who had clearly inherited her all-American looks from her father. Jessica shook his hand—a cool, firm grip—and quietly asked if she could speak with him away from the others.

"Of course," he said. "Can I fix you a drink first?"

"A Scotch would be great, thanks."

"I keep the good stuff in my study. Let's talk in there."

Jessica followed him out of the living room. As they passed Renee, she said brightly, "Don't forget about the fireworks!"

Fireworks?

Simmonds led Jessica into what could only be described as a proper study. It was just like the ones you'd see on old TV shows, the kind she imagined all wealthy businessmen to have in their plush homes. Dark wood, floor-to-ceiling bookshelves housing tomes no one ever read, a matching pair of oxblood Chesterfield sofas, a substantial mahogany desk. Framed photos on the walls showed graduation ceremonies, diplomas, a college group shot, Trey and Renee on their wedding day, Laurie at various stages from baby to young woman.

Simmonds went over to a drinks trolley in the shape of a vintage globe and lifted the lid to reveal a selection of high-end liquor and crystal tumblers. He poured two Scotches, handed one to Jessica, and gestured for them to sit on the sofas.

"I'm sorry for dragging you away from your friends," she said. "But I had a look around Laurie's apartment today and have a few questions. I'll try not to take up too much of your time."

"Please, don't apologize," he said. "I was glad to escape. No one thinks this damn party is a good idea other than Renee."

"It is a little . . . odd."

"Yes, that's one way of putting it." Simmonds swallowed some whisky. "What did you want to ask me about?"

Jessica told him about the luggage, clothing, and toiletries that were all missing from the apartment on Speedway. How she'd reached the conclusion Laurie had been planning some sort of trip. Her confusion as to why Renee neglected to pass on this information when they'd met at the detective agency earlier.

"Of course, we already knew about Laurie's missing personal effects," Simmonds said. "Spotted the items were gone as soon as we searched the apartment. The police are also aware. But I'm not surprised Renee didn't mention it. Sometimes, I think she'd rather think the worst, than face up to the most likely scenario."

"Which is?"

"Laurie took off for a while. And the reason she took off is Renee."

"Why would Laurie do that?"

Simmonds sighed. "I don't wish to criticize my wife, Miss Shaw, but it's important you understand the background here. Renee is a good person and she's a great mother. She adores Laurie. But I know Laurie finds her love to be stifling at times. She's twenty-four now. She wants to be independent. But Renee won't allow it. She needs Laurie to need her mother."

"Even so," Jessica said. "Two months with no contact? It doesn't worry you?"

"Sure it does," he said. "Don't think I haven't thought about it plenty. Renee isn't the only one who's been affected by this whole thing. I've had sleepless nights too. Why would Laurie put us both through this hell? Why wouldn't she let us know she's okay? I've asked myself those questions every single day since she's been gone."

"And?"

Simmonds shrugged helplessly. "Maybe Laurie's worried she'll be guilt-tripped into coming home if she does call."

"Okay," Jessica said. "Let's assume you're right. Where do you think she went? Do you believe she's on her own or with someone else?"

Simmonds finished his drink in one big gulp. "I have no idea." He gestured toward Jessica's own Scotch. "You want another?"

"Thanks, but no." She'd barely touched her drink. "I have to drive back to Venice tonight."

He walked over to the globe-bar and she studied him while he poured himself a refill.

Simmonds was tall and in good shape for his age. He had a strong jawline and thick head of hair. A nice summer tan. All the ingredients required to be handsome but not quite succeeding somehow. Maybe it was the dullness behind his eyes. No doubt the result of months of worrying about Laurie. Despite his insistence his daughter had simply taken a trip someplace, Jessica thought Trey Simmonds looked like a man who was feeling the strain.

They both started as a sudden ear-splitting bang ripped through the calmness of the evening. It sounded like gunfire and panic flashed across Simmonds' features. Then the dark night sky outside the window exploded into a riot of color, followed by whistles and more bangs.

"Fireworks." Simmonds shook his head and returned to the sofa with the topped-off drink. "Renee hired a guy to put on a display in the back yard."

"Yeah, she mentioned something about fireworks earlier, didn't she."

"It's Renee's answer to everything." Simmonds laughed bitterly. "Something needing done? Hire a guy to do it. And usually a young, good-looking one. Pool guy, lawn guy, fireworks guy. Missing daughter? Hire a guy to find her." He smiled at Jessica. "Or woman. Sorry."

She returned the smile. "Renee actually hired my boss, Matt Connor. We're both working the investigation."

Simmonds opened his mouth to speak. Closed it again. Paused a beat. Then he said, "Can I be straight with you, Miss Shaw?"

"Sure. Please do."

"Hiring a private eye—or two private eyes—to look for Laurie was Renee's idea. And it's not one I agree with. I don't like the idea of complete strangers rooting around in my daughter's business and personal life. But Renee insisted so I signed off on the check. It doesn't mean I like it, though. Like I said before, I believe Laurie will come home when she's good and ready."

Jessica wasn't offended, or even surprised, by Simmonds' reticence. It wasn't the first time she'd encountered family members who disagreed over hiring professional investigators to look for their loved ones.

She did have more questions though.

"What about the other missing women?"

A shadow crossed Simmonds' face. "Laurie doesn't have anything to do with those women," he said. "The cops don't think so either."

"No? You don't think it's strange they all vanished from the same place?"

"The circumstances are very different. The only thing they have in common is that damn highway."

"You don't think it's worth exploring?"

"Honestly? No. This is all just Renee obsessing. Trying to whip folks, like yourself, into a frenzy over a conspiracy that doesn't exist. My wife literally spends hours online every single day scouring the internet for anything to do with Twentynine Palms Highway. It's how she found out about those other two women. But it's a long stretch of road and dozens of things have happened out there over the years, mostly a lot of road traffic accidents. It doesn't mean any of it is connected to Laurie."

"What about Randal?" Jessica asked. "Do you think he has anything to do with Laurie's disappearance?"

"Who?" Simmonds shot Jessica a look. "I've never heard of him. Who is he?"

Jessica told him what she knew about the art gallery guy—his interest in Laurie's paintings, the appointment at the shop he never showed for, how he now appeared to be a ghost who couldn't be traced in any way.

Simmonds nodded slowly. "I do remember Laurie being quite excited about some potential big sales, possibly an exhibition, but she didn't go into details. Didn't mention anyone by the name of Randal. I don't know . . . Perhaps their business relationship turned into something more and they both took off together for a while?"

"What about the disconnected cell phone number?" Jessica asked. "The website that no longer exists? The wrong address in New York?"

Worry was etched all across Simmonds' face as he considered her questions. Then he shook his head, as though dismissing Jessica's concerns.

"Maybe this Randal guy wanted to disappear from his own life for a while too?" he said. "Maybe the pizza place took over the gallery premises after he left?"

Jessica was doubtful, thought Simmonds was desperately grasping at straws, but she didn't say anything.

He went on, "What you have to remember is Laurie made the decision to leave—the missing luggage and personal effects, the texts to say she wouldn't be at work. My daughter will be home soon, when she wants to come back. I'm sure of it."

"What if you're wrong, Mr. Simmonds?"

He fixed Jessica with a hard stare. "I have to believe I'm right," he said. "Because the alternative simply doesn't bear thinking about."

12

JESSICA

Jessica didn't have a home and that was exactly the way she liked it.

She didn't think of herself as homeless or transient or down on her luck. The lack of a permanent address was a lifestyle choice, rather than falling on hard times. After the death of her dad, Tony, from a heart attack almost three years ago, she'd taken to the road and vowed never to return to New York and its painful memories.

Now, after six months living in a tin can trailer out in the desert, Jessica was glad to be back where she was happiest—in low-rent motels. The Venice Motor Inn suited her just fine. She could've opted for one of the tourist hotels closer to the beach—the sale of the house she'd shared with Tony in Blissville and his small life insurance policy meant she had more than enough cash in the bank—but proper hotels just weren't her thing.

The forced politeness every time she passed the front desk, muzak in the elevators and lobby, the temptation to empty the over-priced mini-bar every night. No thanks. She much preferred to come and go as she pleased, with a door leading directly to her own room, no one to judge or question the hours she kept, a decent full-size bottle of Scotch compensating for the lack of expensive miniatures.

She'd paid two nights in advance when she'd first landed in Venice, unsure whether Connor would agree to giving her the job. Now he had, she'd book an extended stay. Didn't want a rental someplace, didn't want to think too far ahead about the future.

Jessica picked up her cell phone and found the photos she'd snapped yesterday of the iconic Venice sign strung across the intersection at Pacific and Windward, selected her favorite one, and texted it to Jason Pryce and his daughter, Dionne. The caption on both texts read: Home Sweet Home.

Pryce, an LAPD detective, had been childhood friends with her father and knew stuff about Tony and Jessica no one else knew. Without her even realizing it, he had been in her life since she was a kid, but it was only in the last year she'd grown close to Pryce and his family. He was a connection to the past, as well as providing hope for a future where she didn't have to be on her own.

Jessica threw back the bedsheet, got up and showered, towel-dried her hair and applied some eye makeup. She pulled on yesterday's jeans and selected a gray t-shirt from her suitcase. She always traveled with two cases: one for warm weather, one for winter. Also stored in the truck's covered flatbed was a carton holding the rest of her personal belongings. Not a lot to show for almost thirty years in the world but Jessica figured her heart held what really mattered: her memories. Watching old '80s movies and drinking beer with Tony, game nights at Yankee Stadium, discussing cases with her old boss Larry Lutz over breakfast at the Clinton Diner—you couldn't just box up stuff that precious.

Jessica checked her cell and saw she'd received responses from Pryce and Dionne while she'd been in the shower. A reporter for the school newspaper, Dionne had big plans to study journalism at Berkley once she graduated high school. Having read some of her articles, Jessica knew the girl was a talented writer but, when it came to texts and social media, she was just like every other teen her age.

Dionne: Venice?? Coooooollll!! Let's meet for lunch at The Rose soon . . . Luv ya!

Jessica replied with a row of thumbs-up emoticons.

Pryce's response to her photo was both cautious and to the point. Typical Pryce style.

Pryce: Venice? Matt Connor??

Jessica: Yes. He gave me a job. We're working a MP case. It's interesting.

Pryce: Glad you're back in LA. Just be careful.

Jessica: I have worked plenty of MPs in the past you know!

Pryce: I wasn't talking about the case.

Jessica dropped the cell phone into her bag, along with her Glock. She left the room and walked out into hard sunlight and salty air. A guy in a gray truck parked up next to a sweating vending machine was reading a newspaper and drinking coffee. She thought about grabbing a coffee or a soda from the machine but she was pushed for time and didn't want to be late on her second day. The caffeine hit would have to wait until she arrived at the office.

The journey to MAC Investigations took less than ten minutes and, sure enough, Connor had a cup of coffee waiting for her in the chipped Dodgers mug. She produced the new one with the art print on front from her bag and held it up for him to see.

"Got my own mug," she said. "From Laurie Simmonds' shop. You do know I'm a Yankees fan, right?"

Connor made a face.

Jessica poured the contents of the Dodgers mug into the art one.

"Don't get too comfortable," Connor said. "We're going on a road trip."

"Do I even need to ask where we're going?"

He grinned. "Nope. Drink your coffee and let's go."

Jessica offered to drive, was eager to get out on the open road again, so they took her truck.

After a quick stop at her motel to pick up some things, she hopped on the 10 heading east and joined Highway 60 at Boyle Heights. East LA and Montebello and Hacienda Heights flashed by in a blur as she filled Connor in on what she'd found out about Laurie so far: the missing luggage, the appointment with the elusive Randal, Trey Simmonds' belief that his daughter had simply taken off for a while and had possibly hooked up with someone. Connor told Jessica about Amanda Meyers' affair with her boss, Zachary Dunne, and the man's apparent extreme reaction to her disappearance, according to his off-the-record contact.

"And this contact insisted on meeting in a bar?"

"That's right."

"Female?"

"Yup."

"Attractive?"

"Very."

Jessica glanced at him and shook her head with a grin. "You're such a douchebag."

Connor spread his hands out in front of him. "Can I help it if women want to open up to me?"

She laughed. "Anything else?"

"One of the neighbors, Mrs. DuBois—who's eighty if she's a day before you say anything—spotted an unfamiliar vehicle in the street in the months leading up to Amanda's disappearance. The plates aren't registered with the DMV."

"Interesting." Jessica shook a cigarette out from the pack. "You don't mind if I smoke, do you?"

"Yes, I do. If I have to die young, I'd rather it'd be from something more exciting than second-hand smoke inhalation."

"Don't tempt me." Jessica buzzed down the window a crack and lit the cigarette. "Feel free to walk if you're not happy with the ride."

Connor's cell pinged with a text before he could respond. He read the message and shut off the phone without replying. A few minutes later, it pinged again. He glanced at the screen with a sigh. When the alert sounded for a third time, he flicked the tiny switch on the side of the phone to silent.

"Sounds like someone's real keen to get hold of you," Jessica said.

"Yeah. I'll answer her later."

Her?

They drove in silence for several miles. Passed at least three homes with speedboats in their driveways despite being miles away from any water.

Jessica could feel Connor's eyes on her. Not a heavy stare so much as a light gaze. Eventually, he spoke again. "Look, speaking of texts . . ."

Jessica groaned inwardly. She knew exactly where this conversation was headed. "It's fine," she said. "We don't have to talk about it."

About a month ago, Connor had sent her a message saying he'd been thinking about her a lot. At the time, she'd been living and working in the desert town of Hundred Acres, about an hour north of LA. Connor hadn't known she was still in the state.

"We probably should talk about it if we're going to be working together. It wasn't the smartest thing to do. But I'd been drinking . . ."

"I guessed as much."

"And then you didn't reply."

"I thought about it. Typed out a response a million times. Decided it was a bad idea."

"Why?"

"I was seeing someone."

"Was?"

"It didn't work out."

84

"I'm sorry."

"Don't be. I'm not."

Connor opened his mouth to say something else when his cell phone screen lit up with an incoming call. This time, he swiped to answer.

"This is Connor."

He listened for a second, then met Jessica's eye with a raised eyebrow.

Who is it? she mouthed.

"Detective Valdez," he said. "Thanks for returning my call."

Connor switched to speakerphone so Jessica could also hear the conversation.

"I just picked up your message," Valdez said. "So, you're looking into Amanda Meyers' disappearance? Her folks up in Bakersfield hire you?"

Connor hesitated. "Not exactly."

"What does that mean?" Valdez huffed impatiently. "They either did or they didn't."

Jessica rolled her eyes.

"I was hired by the parents of another missing woman," Connor said. "Laurie Simmonds. They believe there may be a connection between her disappearance and what happened to Amanda Meyers. Also, another missing woman by the name of Mallory Wilcox."

Valdez laughed. "Renee, huh? Like a dog with a bone, that one."

"You think there's anything in what she says?"

Valdez said, "Look, it's not my case anymore. We picked it up because Amanda was last seen on our turf. Once we'd exhausted all leads out here, the case was transferred to the agency which has jurisdiction over the missing person's residence. That's LAPD."

"Who took over the case? You got a name?"

"Not off the top of my head."

"Anything you can tell me about your own investigation?"

"Officially, no. I shouldn't be discussing the case with you. And Laurie Simmonds is someone else's case too, by the way."

"Unofficially? Just some broad strokes?"

There was nothing but static silence in response.

"I'm trying to help," Connor pointed out. "Amanda has been missing for two years now and I'm guessing you guys and the LAPD don't have a whole lot of time or resources to make her a priority. Totally understandable, especially after all this time. The thing is, I *can* make her a priority. Surely any new information we can turn up has to be a good thing?"

Valdez sighed. "Okay, off the record. This doesn't come back to me, understood?"

Jessica gave Connor a thumbs-up.

"Of course. No comeback."

Valdez said, "When Renee Simmonds came to me with her theories, I checked out the MP reports for both her daughter and Mallory Wilcox. I also spoke to Jim Weiss, who worked the Wilcox case before he retired. That one seems fairly straightforward, you ask me. Her husband, Terence Wilcox, is a drunk who's quick to use his fists. He has a record for drunk and disorderly, minor assault. Mostly bar brawls."

"He ever hit Mallory?" Connor asked.

"If there were any bust-ups at home, they were never reported by the wife or any of the neighbors. Doesn't mean it didn't happen though.

"When Wilcox reported Mallory missing, Jim's men did a canvass of the neighborhood. The lady who lives right across the street said she'd spotted a young, good-looking man calling on the Wilcox residence at least twice during the day while Terence was at work. That information never made the newspapers, by the way. What you do probably know is she was last seen buying snacks and booze at a gas station. The kid on duty said she was kind of 'giddy.' That's the word he used. It all points to a woman who'd finally had enough of her bullying husband and ran off with a younger man."

"She has two young kids, though," Connor said. "You really think she'd just leave them behind? Especially if Wilcox is as bad as you say he is?"

"According to Jim, the kids spend most of their time at Mallory's sister's place. His theory is she'll come back for them once she's properly set up someplace."

"Okay, let's say you and Jim Weiss are right about Mallory Wilcox," Connor said. "What about Amanda and Laurie? On the surface, they're not alike at all but, when you take Mallory out of the equation, maybe not so different after all. Both young, blonde, single, career-focused."

"Again, Laurie Simmonds isn't my case," Valdez pointed out. "I'm only going by what I read in the MP report. Like Mallory Wilcox, there's evidence to suggest Laurie left of her own free will."

"My fellow investigator at the agency had a look around Laurie's apartment," Connor said. "She noticed luggage and some clothing was missing. This was confirmed by Trey Simmonds, the girl's father. She also thinks Laurie might've been in contact with a gallery owner from New York, by the name of Randal, around the time Laurie vanished. My investigator is having a hard time trying to track down this Randal guy."

"Randal?" Valdez said. "The name isn't familiar. What I can tell you is, the weekend Laurie Simmonds' van was found out by Twentynine Palms, a big music festival was happening nearby in Indio. When I say big, I mean huge."

Jessica shot a look at Connor.

"We didn't know about the festival."

Valdez went on, "I'm too old for all that shit, and it's never been my scene in any case, but I figure not a lot has changed since the Woodstock days—kids getting high or drunk, getting 'lost in the music,' having lots of sex. Hell, it's not unheard of for folks to run off and get married after hooking up at these festivals."

"You really think that's what happened with Laurie Simmonds?"

"Who knows? But they found some paintings in her van, right? My guess is, she took a bunch of paintings out to the festival, sold a few, and decided to live a little off the proceeds."

Jessica glanced at Connor. No one had mentioned the festival until now. It sounded plausible to her.

"What about Amanda?" he asked. "I know it's not your case anymore but what do you think happened to her? Gut feeling?"

"That one ain't so easy to tie up in a nice neat little bow," Valdez said. "Great job, nice apartment, close relationship with her family but enough distance not to feel stifled by them. No real reason to go off-grid. Nothing like Mallory Wilcox or Laurie Simmonds. When we pulled Amanda's cell phone records, there were several text messages to another cell phone number on the day she disappeared. We weren't able to trace the number. Probably a burner phone. Also worth noting, this number only appeared on her records the day she was last seen, which is also the last day her cell picked up any pings. So, likely a brand-new contact."

"Burner phones usually mean someone has something to hide," Connor said. "Like an affair."

"As far as we know, Amanda wasn't in a relationship at the time of her disappearance."

Jessica glanced at Connor and raised her eyebrows. The cops didn't know about Zachary Dunne.

Valdez said, "Like I already told you, her file is still open and I'm sure LAPD will keep on looking for her and we'll follow any leads that come up out here. But . . ."

"But what?" Connor prompted.

"I hope to God I'm wrong but, if I was a betting man, I'd put money on Amanda Meyers being six feet under somewhere."

13

DEA—1990

Dea winced as the screen door slipped from her grasp and slammed hard against the wooden frame. She listened for any sounds of movement from inside the mobile home. Satisfied Buddy hadn't been awakened by the noise, she made her way to her tan '84 Chevy Chevette parked under the communal carport she shared with two neighbors.

She hated leaving her little boy home alone. When he was younger, Mrs. Rivera would let Buddy sleep over in her trailer while Dea worked late shifts at the bar. The old woman loved having a kid around again now that her own grandchildren were all grown, wouldn't dream of taking so much as a cent in babysitting cash. When Mrs. Rivera passed almost a year ago, Dea couldn't afford proper childcare, and she didn't trust anyone else in the mobile home park to look after Buddy for free, so she'd had no choice but to leave him asleep in his bed while she was out at work.

She'd swapped the bar nearby for one in Twentynine Palms so the locals wouldn't know Buddy was being left on his own three nights a week. He was real smart, and mature for his age, and Dea had made him memorize both the telephone number for the bar where she worked and 911 in case anything ever went wrong. But it still broke her heart every time she walked out of their home and left him asleep with his favorite stuffed dinosaur tucked under his arm while she kept old desert rats and the latest recruits at the Marine base suitably refreshed.

Despite the shade of the carport, the inside of the car was hot and stuffy. Within seconds, the bare flesh of her legs felt slick against the cheap vinyl seating. She popped a Def Leppard cassette into the deck. They weren't one of her favorite bands but the tape had been left behind in the car when she'd bought it second—or possibly third—hand. Dea yanked down the window and stagnant, warm air flooded the car.

Once on the main highway, it was a straight shot of less than thirty minutes to Twentynine Palms. The breeze now cooling the sweat on her skin was a blessed relief. The mobile homes and tumbledown ranch houses of Yucca Valley soon gave way to the sandy dirt and resolute flora of the savage desert for several miles before the tattoo parlors and gun shops and diners of Twentynine Palms appeared on the horizon. The Desert Heart bar was at the far end of town, on the lonely stretch of road heading east toward the tiny airport.

It was Friday night but quiet. Just five patrons. Soon after Dea arrived, her boss, Freddy Diltz, asked if she'd be okay manning the bar herself and then locking up. His wife and kid were both sick and he didn't feel too good himself. She relished the extra responsibility for the first time, so she told Diltz to go home early. Assured him she could handle the customers, no problem at all.

And she did. At least, in the early part of the evening.

An hour into her shift, she noticed, with an excited flutter in her belly, the cute guy who'd been drinking in the bar the last few weekends was back. He was sitting on a stool at a beer barrel table under the wall display of battered number plates, every one of them picked up from the highway right outside the bar where the vehicles they had once belonged to had hit a bump in the road that had never been smoothed out.

His dark hair was cropped short, and he had big brown eyes, and biceps so huge they strained the material of his sports jacket. Did Dea have a type? If she did, this guy was it. He was maybe a few years younger than herself and, other than taking his drinks orders, she'd never spoken to him properly. Didn't know if he was a student at The Palms University or a military guy from the nearby Marine Corps base. She didn't even know his name but she knew he liked to drink Pabst on tap. Tonight, he'd also ordered the larger portion of chicken wings and fries for an extra dollar but had left at least half of the meal untouched.

"Not to your liking?" Dea cleared away his plate and cutlery and used napkin.

"No, it was great." He grinned and patted his stomach, "I guess my eyes were just a little bit bigger than my belly."

She nodded and headed through to the back with the plate. Her mouth was wet with saliva and her belly rumbled painfully. She'd lost another few pounds and her thrift store skirt, which fit perfectly a few months back, now hung off her hips. Dea tore feverishly at the leftover chicken and stuffed a handful of fries into her mouth. She was still chewing, jaws aching, when she heard a voice call out from the bar.

"Hey, any chance of a goddamn drink in this place?"

Dea sucked the grease off her fingers, and wiped her hand across her mouth, and then again on the back of the skirt. She picked at her teeth to make sure there were no telltale bits of chicken stuck in there. Then she plastered on a smile, her best game face, and headed back out front to where a customer was waiting with an impatient scowl on his face. His fist clutched an empty beer schooner. A cigarette burned between two nicotine-stained fingers of the other hand, the ash drooping precariously over the counter she'd cleaned just ten minutes ago. She didn't know his name either and didn't want to. He was a mean, sloppy old drunk.

Dea filled the glass, deliberately ensuring it was topped off with a thick head of foam that slopped over the sides. He dropped some bills onto the counter and she handed him his change. He didn't appear to notice his refill resembled a milkshake. His thin, cracked lips pulled back to reveal pointy yellow teeth in what Dea guessed was supposed to be a smile.

"Have one for yourself too, sweetheart," he said, pushing a couple of single dollar bills toward her, the ash finally dropping on the bar top.

"Thanks for the offer but we're not allowed to drink on duty."

The sloppy drunk leaned in close in a conspiratorial kind of way. Dea caught a whiff of Hai Karate and halitosis.

"Don't see the boss around," he stage-whispered. "I won't tell if you won't."

The smile on her face felt fixed and fake. "Even so," she said through gritted teeth. "Rules are rules. No drinks from patrons but we do have a tips jar that gets shared between the staff."

Sloppy Drunk snatched up the singles from the counter. "Forget it. Just trying to be courteous is all. You don't want my hospitality, that's fine."

He grabbed his beer and returned to his table. Dea met Cute Guy's gaze and he shook his head and rolled his eyes. She smiled and gave a small shrug of the shoulders in a "what you gonna do?" kind of way.

The rest of the shift passed without much incident, other than Sloppy Drunk making another failed attempt to buy her a drink. As she pulled beers, and poured whiskey, and wiped down the counter, and restocked the refrigerator, Dea's thoughts turned to her folks.

Over the years, she had returned to Brodie a number of times. At first, she would stand across the street from her old house, Buddy in her arms, and wait for a glimpse of her mom and dad. Later, she'd sit in her car, her son in the passenger seat next to her. More than once, Dea almost got out and spoke to her parents. Convinced herself if they met their grandson, even once, they'd love him just as much as she did, that they'd realize they still loved her. Then her mom would say something to her dad, and they'd laugh and look happy, and Dea would realize they didn't need—or want—her or Buddy in their lives.

She shook her head and told herself for the millionth time that she and Buddy didn't need anyone else.

Dea rang the old brass bell and called last orders.

Cute Guy finished off his drink and tossed her a wave and a shy smile as he made his way to the exit. "See you soon," he said.

She returned the smile. "I'll look forward to it."

It was a little flirtatious but what the hell.

Sloppy Drunk was still at his table, a third of his beer remaining. She asked him to drink up and leave. He drained the schooner and strolled toward the bar. "Night's still young," he said. "Why don't you and me have ourselves a private party?"

Dea was very aware that they were the only two people left in the place. "No can do," she said. "Diltz will be here any minute to lock up. If he finds customers still in the bar, he won't be happy."

Sloppy Drunk stood there for a long moment, swaying slightly, watching her through narrowed eyes. She thought he wasn't going to buy the lie but eventually he placed the schooner on the counter.

"Well, we wouldn't want you getting into no trouble now, would we?"

Dea followed him to the exit and breathed a sigh of relief as she locked the door behind him. She spent the next twenty minutes washing and drying the last of the glassware and cashing out the register before turning off the lights and locking up.

Outside, the midnight sky was as dark as blue velvet. There was no traffic. The highway was an empty, black ribbon. Any other night when she finished a shift, Diltz would still be in the bar. The big neon sign on top of the building—and the smaller beer signs behind the grilled windows—would flash blue and red and green as she made her way to her car. Not tonight. Dea could only just make out the shape of the Chevy from the dull glow of a single streetlight further along the highway.

She hurried to the parking lot. There was a chill in the air and she shivered in her short sleeves. Despite the cold, exhaustion hit her as though she'd been stabbed with a tranquilizer dart. She yawned big and loud. Another half hour and she'd be home, would be able to sneak into Buddy's room and give him a hug, before collapsing into her own bed.

Dea had almost reached the car, keys in hand, when she became aware of a presence behind her. She turned to see Sloppy Drunk standing there, hands on his hips, beer gut hanging over the belt of his slacks. He licked his dry lips and his beady eyes crawled over every inch of her body.

"Well, looky what we have here. What are the chances of bumping into you again tonight?"

Pretty fucking high when you hang around parking lots stalking folk.

"Yeah, what are the chances?" Dea muttered.

Other than her own car, the lot was empty. No one around other than Dea and Sloppy Drunk. About a half mile along the highway, another bar was open later than the Desert Heart but she couldn't hear any music or chatter or laughter all the way back here.

"Looks to me like we might be having that party after all," Sloppy Drunk said.

Panic began to blossom in the pit of Dea's belly. Not a good situation. Not good at all. When she'd agreed to lock up, it'd never even crossed her mind that she might not be safe on her own.

Not until now.

"No party," she said. "I'm going home."

Dea had two options—remove the can of pepper spray she kept in her purse and hit him right between the eyes. Or avoid a confrontation and get into the safety of the car as quickly as possible. She turned her back on the man to insert the key into the lock and realized immediately she'd made the wrong choice. The sudden, nauseating mix of bad breath and cheap cologne told her he was now right behind her. Her fingers shook as she tried to find the lock in the gloom. The keys fell onto the dirt. Before she could bend down to find them, Sloppy Drunk pushed her hard against the car door, his body pressed tight against her back, pinning her to the station wagon.

"Don't you think it's about time you started being a bit friendlier to old Merv?"

His breath was hot and moist against her ear. So close, she could identify the brand of cigarettes he smoked. Dea tried to push back against him but he was stronger than he looked and clearly fueled by booze and lust. She could feel his hardness against her.

"Get off me, you fucking asshole."

He laughed. "A fighter, huh? I like that in a woman." He pulled her hair to one side and kissed her wetly on the back of her neck. Dea tried not to throw up.

"I said, get off me."

"Is it money you want?" he growled. "Is that it? Always going on about tips in the bar. You want cash, you little whore? Okay, I'll give you cash and then you gotta play nice with old Merv."

He produced two crumpled ten-dollar bills and stuffed them roughly down the front of her top. Then snaked a hand up her skirt and tore at her underwear, while trying to nudge her legs apart. Dea heard the metal jangle of his belt buckle being undone. She flashed back to another night. Another drunk. Another car.

"*NO!*"

"You heard the lady."

Dea felt Merv being pulled roughly off of her and turned to see him sprawled on the dirt on his hands and knees. Standing over him was the cute guy from the bar. The older man struggled to his feet and squared up to Cute Guy, who was several inches taller and a whole lot of muscle stronger.

"Butt out, son. You ain't got no business here."

Cute Guy's response was a sharp right hook which caught Merv square on the face. He fell to his knees again. Cute Guy dragged him up by the lapels and punched him a second time. Blood snaked a red river from Merv's nostrils and down his chin.

"You broke my fucking nose."

"I'll break your legs too if you don't get out of here right now."

Merv glared at his younger opponent for a long moment. Then he spat blood onto the dirt at Cute Guy's feet, pulled himself to a standing position, and shambled off toward the highway before being swallowed up by the night.

Cute Guy watched him go, then turned to Dea. "You okay?"

Dea smoothed down her skirt, suddenly embarrassed by how much flesh had been on show. She pulled the dollar bills from her top and ripped them into tiny pieces. She might be broke but she'd need to be beyond desperate to keep Merv's cash.

"Yeah, I think so. Thanks."

"Any time."

Cute Guy bent down and scooped up her car keys from where they'd fallen in the dirt. He unlocked the door and held it open for her. She noticed the knuckles on his right hand were grazed as she climbed inside.

"Hopefully that jerk-off won't bother you again," he said. "If I see him back in the bar, I'll be making it clear he isn't welcome."

"I dread to think what would've happened if you hadn't shown up when you did."

"Try not to think on it too much." He smiled. "I'll see you around."

He slammed the car door shut and headed off in the same direction as Merv.

Dea sat behind the wheel for a moment, waited until she'd stopped shaking before inserting the key into the ignition. Then realized she didn't even know her savior's name. She started the car and pulled out of the lot, leaving a cloud of dust in her wake as she turned onto the smooth two-lane. She looked around for the young man who had come to her rescue.

But there was no sign of the cute guy, or Merv, or any other vehicles.

Other than Dea Morgan, and her old '84 Chevette, the Twentynine Palms Highway was dark and empty.

14

CONNOR

Connor slammed the Silverado's door shut and squinted against the glare of the midday sun. It was bright and fierce after the coolness of the truck's cab. He leaned on the sill of the open window. "I'm not sure how long this is going to take," he told Jessica. They had stopped off in Whitewater so Connor could speak to Terence Wilcox II. While he was interviewing Mallory's husband, Jessica would continue on to Twentynine Palms to follow up on Amanda Meyers' disappearance. "Could be an hour or could be five minutes." Connor thought of the abrupt phone call with Wilcox. "I'd guess five minutes is more likely."

Jessica turned to face him and smiled. A lock of short blonde hair fell over one eye, like he'd noticed it often did, and Connor almost reached out his hand to brush it away. She tucked the hair behind her ear and slipped on a pair of shades and started the engine. "Text me when you're done and I'll come pick you up."

"No, don't come all the way back out here. I'll get an Uber or Lyft or whatever cab service they have in town."

"It's an hour from here to Twentynine Palms. That's going to be quite a cab fare."

"That's what expense accounts are for. Catch you later."

Connor watched as the truck disappeared around a corner at the end of the street. Then he opened a creaking gate in a chain-link fence surrounding a mobile home with duck-egg blue siding set in a lot of about a quarter of an acre.

The Wilcox property had likely once been well cared for, when Mallory was still around, but appeared to have fallen into disrepair recently. The paintwork needed refreshing and the gravel front yard was filled with junk. The one thing it did have going for it was an impressive view of the mountains. Connor wasn't sure if he was looking at the San Bernardino Mountains or San Jacinto Mountains but, either way, they were vast and snow-capped and made him feel small and insignificant in comparison.

He hadn't even reached the three steps of the tiny wooden porch when he heard a low growl, followed by loud, guttural barking.

"Holy shit!"

Connor instinctively jumped away from the noise and noticed, for the first time, an ugly silver-gray Canary Mastiff had been shading itself from the sun under the porch stairwell. The mutt strained against a metal chain looped around a leg of the porch. Connor liked dogs a lot but not ones with sharp teeth and dripping saliva that would relish tearing him apart from limb from limb.

He quickly climbed the steps and knocked on the screen door. The dog kept right on barking.

Connor leaned over the porch railing. "There, boy." He nervously wondered just how strong the metal chain was, while trying to soothe the dog. After what seemed like forever, the front door opened to reveal a disheveled and pissed-looking middle-aged man.

"What do you want?" he snapped from behind the ripped mesh of the screen door. It was a carbon copy of yesterday's phone call greeting.

Terence Wilcox II.

The guy was mostly skinny but had a bowling ball belly that his tight dirty wifebeater and open plaid shirt did nothing to disguise. The top button of his stained jeans was undone. He had thinning gray hair that hadn't seen a barber or shampoo in months, and the sallow skin and loose jowls of a really old person, even though he couldn't have been older than fifty.

"Matt Connor." Connor had to shout over the incessant barking of the dog. "We spoke on the phone yesterday."

Wilcox squinted and cocked an ear in Connor's direction, like he hadn't heard right. Then realized the reason why he wasn't hearing properly. He threw open the screen door, leaned over the porch railing, just as Connor had, and glared down at the dog.

"Would you shut up with that goddamned barking?" he yelled.

The mutt shut up as instructed, whimpered, and lay down under the porch stairwell. The sudden silence was deafening and Connor's other senses sprang into action. He could smell beer and mustiness coming off of Wilcox in waves.

"Matt Connor," he repeated. "The private investigator."

Wilcox gave him a hard stare for a long, uncomfortable moment. The man was only slightly less intimidating than the dog. The sleeves of his plaid shirt were pushed up to the elbows, revealing crude, blurred tattoos. The type you'd get in prison or in the backroom of a dive bar. Connor spotted the three symbols of a college Greek letter organization; Mallory's name eternally inscribed in a sweeping ribbon across a red love heart; a fluttering Old Glory; and two others so faded by time he couldn't even guess at what they were supposed to be.

Eventually, Wilcox said, "So, you're serious about trying to find my Mal, huh?"

"Yes, sir."

"You'd better come on in then."

Connor followed the other man into a living area so dimly lit he felt like a cinemagoer trying to feel his way to his seat after the main feature had already started. Only the tiniest amount of day-light slipped through the closed slatted blinds, casting the room in the sepia glow of an old photograph.

Wilcox settled onto a worn, tan faux-leather recliner—like a La-Z-Boy but without the price tag—and popped out the footrest. He grabbed a can of beer from a six-pack on the floor next to a pile of used cardboard pizza boxes. Cracked open the booze and sucked up the foam. Two beers were left in the pack.

"Want one?" Wilcox offered.

"Thanks, but I'll pass," Connor said. It was just after noon. "It's a little early for me."

"Suit yourself." Wilcox shrugged. "It's happy hour somewhere in the world right now, that's what I always say." He laughed and it was a horrible, humorless sound. "Hell, it's always happy hour round here now I don't have Mal nagging at me all day."

Connor looked for somewhere to sit. The couch appeared to be covered in a load of stuff. He peered into the gloom and realized it was about two dozen knitted dolls.

What the fuck?

A cot bed, with a rumpled sheet and a limp pillow, was set up next to the couch. The only other available seating was an armchair, with white lace doilies on the arms, in the same faded floral design as the couch.

Wilcox gestured to the armchair. "That's Mallory's seat but it's okay if you want to sit there." He said it like it was a big deal to give permission to sit on Mallory's chair. "Those dolls haven't been moved from the couch since Mallory left. Don't want to mess up her stuff."

"I see," Connor said, trying not to show how creeped out he was by the dolls.

"Those dolls are also the reason why the dog spends all her time out in the yard. Mallory never wanted a pet. So, six months after she left me on my own, I bought myself one."

Wilcox was trying to come off as all defiant, like a kid disrespecting his mom. Connor wondered if the real reason for the dog was a yearning for companionship, an attempt to fill the void left by an absent wife. Especially now Wilcox's own kids seemed to spend most of their time at their aunt's home.

Wilcox went on, "The problem with that damned dog is she ripped apart one of Mal's toys within two minutes of being let inside the house. And not just any old doll—the Las Vegas Elvis one." Wilcox shook his head mournfully. "It was Mal's favorite pastime. She made the dolls and sold them at local craft fairs—Christmas, St. Patrick's Day, Easter. Elvis, The Beatles, Cher. You name it, she made it. When Dolly destroyed one of Mal's favorites, it was unforgivable. Now she stays outside in the front yard or the kennel I built out back."

Dolly?

Connor thought of the hundred pounds of muscle and sinew and sheer aggression chained up in the front yard and didn't think the dog could have been any more inappropriately named. Maybe Wilcox was a fan of the country singer but still.

"Mal would sit in the chair you're sitting on right now and we'd watch *Jeopardy* together," Wilcox said. "Her knitting needles would be clicking and clacking so fast together that I didn't think it was even possible she could be concentrating on anything else. Then she'd shout out one of the answers—and usually one of the tricky ones. She's real smart, my Mal."

Connor thought Wilcox's eyes might be wet but he couldn't be sure in the dim light.

An awkward silence followed and Connor gazed around the room. More of Mallory's knitted dolls filled the shelves of a bookcase. Only one shelf wasn't stuffed full of them. He got up and went over to the shelf for a better look. This one housed a baseball bat, as well as some other college memorabilia. Most of the stuff was emblazoned with the slogan: *Go Hawks!* It was clearly Wilcox's shelf.

"Did you play?" Connor asked, trying not to sound too surprised.

"Sure did," Wilcox said proudly, sitting up a little straighter in the chair. He seemed animated and alive all of a sudden. "Best in the county for my age group. Earned me a fully paid-up scholarship to college. Folks were comparing me to Babe Ruth back in the day. Freshman year was when I met Mallory too. Best year of my life."

"Did you play professionally or semi-professionally?"

"Nah," Wilcox said, deflated again. "I'd dropped out by the end of first semester my sophomore year. My playing career was over. Done. Kaput."

"Injury?" Connor asked.

"Nope. Nothing physical, anyways." Wilcox tapped the side of his head. "Mind went, didn't it? Focus was fucked. The confidence just disappeared. There one day, gone the next."

"How come?" asked Connor.

Wilcox shrugged. "Just did." He took a long pull of beer, crushed the can, and dropped it at his feet. Popped the tab on another.

Connor returned to Mallory's armchair. "What are you going to do with all them toys?"

"They stay right where they are until Mal comes home. There's another dozen or so on the bed we shared. Ain't no one touching Mal's stuff, that's for sure. It's why I sleep on the cot bed now. Mal wouldn't want me disturbing her toys. She has them all sorted by theme and color. Annual holidays, pop stars, and so on."

"So, you do think Mallory is coming home?"

"Course she is."

"It's been eighteen months," Connor said. "Where do you think she's been all this time? What do you think happened to her?"

Wilcox sucked on the fresh can of beer. Then said, "I don't need reminding how long my wife has been gone. She needed a break is all."

"A break from what?"

"A break from me," he snapped. "From the boys. From everything."

"Why?"

Wilcox sighed. "Young Terence is twelve now and Wade is nine. They're quieter now, since their mom left. But, back then, they were both little shits. Cheeky little bastards. As for me, I'm the first to admit, I'm not always the easiest to live with either. I guess I can understand why Mal felt like she needed to go away for a while. Don't get me wrong, I'm still real pissed she upped and left the way she did. But I understand why."

"Where do you think she went?"

"Not a clue."

"She used a credit card at a gas station the night she disappeared. Has she used it again since?"

"Nope. That card is for a joint account. I see all the statements. She hasn't touched another cent."

"Did she have a separate bank account she could be using? Access to other funds someplace?"

"Not that I know of. Only the cash she made from selling the dolls, which she kept in a cookie jar in the kitchen cupboard."

Connor didn't think a cookie jar stash sounded like much to survive on for eighteen months. Then again, Mallory Wilcox's productivity levels appeared to be pretty impressive based on the stock at home.

"Did she take the money from the cookie jar with her?" he asked.

"No, it's still there. Or at least, it was." Defensiveness crept into Wilcox's voice. "I need to keep this place running, don't I?"

"You don't have a job?"

"Not anymore. My boss gave me some compassionate leave when Mal first left. After a while, he stopped feeling quite so compassionate so I told him where he could stick his job. Can't work anyways, can I? Not with my anxiety and depression after all that's happened."

"What do you think Mallory is doing for cash?"

"Her interfering sister gave her a loan, didn't she? Lucinda denies it, claims she has no idea where Mal is. But I reckon she knows exactly where my wife is."

"Mallory's sister lives here in Whitewater? What's her full name?"

"Lucinda Dawkins. You should be asking her where my Mal is."

"I plan to. Can you give me her phone number?"

Wilcox recited the number while Connor tapped the digits into his cell phone and saved the new contact. "Could Mallory be with someone?"

Wilcox leaned forward in the recliner suddenly, the footrest snapping back into place. He glared at Connor in the same way he'd glared at the barking dog earlier. "What you trying to say, boy?"

"There's a suggestion Mallory could have had a 'friend' who visited her once or twice before she vanished. Could she be with him?"

"You been talking to that nosy bitch from across the street?"

"I haven't spoken with any of the neighbors, Mr. Wilcox. But I understand a witness saw a young man enter your home on a couple of occasions."

"A young, good-looking guy in my home? Load of BS, that's what that is." Spittle flew from Wilcox's mouth and landed on his whiskers. He jabbed a finger in the direction of a picture frame on the mantelpiece. "Take a look at her. She ain't no looker. Ain't the type to be screwing around with no young gigolos."

From where Connor was sitting in the dark living room, the photo could have been of Mallory Wilcox or Marilyn Monroe. But he thought Wilcox was being unfair. The picture in the newspapers had shown a woman who was pretty in a wholesome kind of way. Maybe Wilcox just couldn't deal with the idea of an affair.

"She bought snacks and booze at the gas station," Connor said. "That sound like Mallory?"

Wilcox popped the footrest on the recliner up again, laid back, and took a gulp of beer. "She likes her candy."

"Red wine and beer too?"

Wilcox downed some more of his own beer and belched loudly. "Probably needed some Dutch courage to walk out on her family the way she did."

"Her car has never been traced."

"Still driving it, isn't she? Got herself some fake plates. Don't forget, she's real smart. Like I said before, knows all the answers on *Jeopardy*. Speaking of TV shows, *Newhart* is about to start and I don't like to miss my programs."

Wilcox picked up a remote control from the armrest and switched on a huge TV mounted on the wall above the mantelpiece. Bob Newhart and Mary Frann, circa 1985, filled the screen. In contrast to the TV show, the flat screen looked new and expensive. Probably less than eighteen months old. Connor wondered if Mallory's cookie jar savings had been spent on the TV, rather than household bills.

"One last thing," he shouted over the too-loud volume.

Wilcox hit the mute button. "You think you're Columbo now? What?"

"I told you on the phone that I'm investigating the disappearances of two other young women who may be connected to Mallory." Connor removed two photos from his messenger bag and handed them to Wilcox. "Their names are Laurie Simmonds and Amanda Meyers."

Wilcox fired a sharp look Connor's way. "Simmonds?"

"Yes, Laurie is the one on the beach. Do you know her?"

Wilcox stared at the image of Laurie Simmonds for a long time, before handing both photos back to Connor. "Nah. Don't know either of them."

"You sure you don't know Laurie Simmonds?" Connor pressed. He thought the woman's name and photo had gotten a reaction from Wilcox.

"Positive." The other man picked up the remote again, unmuted the sound, and turned his attention back to the old rerun. "I'll see myself out."

Wilcox ignored him. Connor heard him laughing along with the canned laughter as he closed the door behind him.

Outside, Dolly growled but didn't get up as Connor rushed down the porch steps and along the path. Once safely beyond the yard's gate, he pulled his cell phone from his jeans pocket. He'd been inside the Wilcox residence for thirty-five minutes.

He tapped out a text to Jessica: All done here. Seems plausible that Mallory took off with a lover, like Valdez and Weiss said, and is living off the proceeds of a million creepy knitted toys (will explain later). But also seemed to me like Wilcox recognized Laurie's name and photo although he denied knowing her. Speak to you soon.

Connor glanced at the homes across the street but he had no idea which one belonged to the neighbor who'd spotted the young, attractive visitor calling at the Wilcox place. Wouldn't know which door to knock on. He pulled up the new contact for Lucinda Dawkins on his cell and hit the call connect button.

A woman answered after several rings. "Hello?"

"Lucinda Dawkins?"

"This is she." She sounded a little uncertain, like she was concerned she might be talking to a telemarketer.

Connor introduced himself and explained the reason for the call. Told Lucinda he was in Whitewater and asked if they could meet for a chat.

A long pause. Then, "I don't think that's a good idea."

"No? Can I ask why not?"

"I don't care what Terence told you. I don't know where Mallory is and I didn't give her any money. I told the police everything I know. All I can do for my sister now is look after her boys as best I can."

"You have no idea where Mallory might be?"

"I don't. Look, I have to go . . ."

Time to cut to the chase, Connor decided. "Was Mallory having an affair?"

There was dead air for a long moment. Finally, the woman said, "Please don't call me again."

Lucinda Dawkins ended the call before Connor could say another word.

15

JESSICA

The Tranquility Motel was a roadside motor inn on Route 62, about two miles from a smoke shop and used bookstore to the west, and four miles from the city of Twentynine Palms to the east.

The place had a kind of rustic charm about it, an oasis in the middle of the desert, quiet and very isolated. Jessica figured that was the whole point. After all, you weren't going to find a hell of a lot of tranquility in the middle of a bustling town.

Given the name and location, Jessica had been expecting to find an ageing hippie behind the front desk, like the ones who made pottery and painted at remote artists' retreats out in the desert. What she got instead was a fat guy with Coke bottle lenses flicking through the kind of reading material usually found on the top shelf of a newsstand wrapped in black plastic. He quickly shoved the magazine under the counter as Jessica approached and nudged the glasses back up his nose.

"Afternoon, Miss. You after a room?"

"Nope."

The guy laughed nervously. "Uh, well, I guess you're in the wrong place. That's kind of what we do here. Rent out rooms. Are you lost or something?"

He was about a decade older than Jessica and wore a green t-shirt with a grease stain above one man-boob and a plastic nametag pinned above the other. The nametag read "Ralph."

"I'd like to speak to whoever was on duty the night Amanda Meyers stayed here. She's the woman who went missing two years ago."

"I was on duty myself that night." Ralph eyed Jessica up and down with interest. "You a cop?"

"No."

"A reporter?"

"No."

"Rubbernecker?"

"No."

"It's fine if you are."

"I'm not."

"Family member?"

"No. You're getting colder and this is getting boring."

"So, who are you?"

"I'm glad you asked, Ralph, otherwise we might have been here all day. I'm a private investigator."

"Is that so?" Ralph's eyes, already magnified by the thick lenses, widened. "Like Jim Rockford or Magnum PI?"

"Yes, except they're fictional characters, whereas I'm a real person."

"That's very cool."

Ralph pushed back from the desk on his swivel chair and reached for a wooden cubby hole unit behind him. His t-shirt rode up, displaying too much of a belly that was big and round like that of a pregnant lady in her third trimester. Except his gut was likely down to too much beer and fried chicken. He pulled out a key from a cubby hole with the number "25" painted above it.

"Okay, let's go."

"Go where?"

"The Amanda Meyers Room. You do want to see it, right?"

The Amanda Meyers Room. Like it was a specially named suite or something.

"I guess so."

"We can talk while we walk," Ralph said excitedly. "I have lots of questions."

"It's supposed to be the other way around," Jessica muttered, as she followed him outside into the blazing early afternoon sun.

The Tranquility was a corridor-style motel, with twenty-five rooms stretching back behind the office, heading away from the main highway. The dappled cream concrete structure contrasted prettily with red stucco-tiled roofing and brightly painted green doors. Some rooms had a bench outside, while others had a small round table and two chairs.

"Is Amanda Meyers dead?" Ralph asked. "She's dead, isn't she?" Jessica thought he sounded almost hopeful.

"I don't know," she said. "I hope not. She's still missing."

"So, there are no new developments? They've not found a body or anything?"

"No."

"Ah, okay."

Jessica frowned. "You sound kind of disappointed, Ralph."

"Look, if something bad happened to that gal, that's real sad. But so is the state of my bank balance. I've got a business to run here. All I'm saying is, a bit of renewed interest in the case might increase footfall at the motel and boost my turnover. And nothing grabs the public's interest like murder. I figure that room could become a tourist hotspot. You know, like Joshua Tree National Park or the Sky's the Limit Observatory. But for true crime fans."

Jessica stared at him in disbelief. "Are you serious? You really want to use Amanda Meyers's disappearance to attract ghouls out here?"

"Damn straight I do. True crime is big business these days. Netflix, podcasts, books—you name it, people can't get enough of it." Ralph shook his head sadly. "But, other than a few weirdos in the month after she went missing, the interest here never really took off. I figure the Meyers woman wasn't glamorous enough or famous enough or dead enough."

"Huh?"

"Take Elizabeth Short, for example. Better known as the Black Dahlia. A beautiful starlet, a brutal murder, an enduring unsolved mystery. Now, that story had everything. I guess a missing lawyer ain't exciting enough for the true crime nuts. Too boring."

"She was a legal assistant," Jessica said. "Not a lawyer."

"That's even worse."

Jessica shook her head.

They passed an old man with long white hair and skin that was brown and tough and wrinkled like bull hide. He was sitting on a bench smoking a cigarette.

"Hey, Bill," said Ralph, with a mock salute.

"Ralph," said the old man by way of acknowledgment.

The motel owner jutted a thumb at Jessica and grinned. "She's a private eye. Can you believe it? Wants to have a look at the Amanda Meyers Room."

"Is that so?"

Jessica rolled her eyes at the old man and an amused smile tugged at his lips. She heard splashing and squealing and guessed there must be a pool out back. The Amanda Meyers Room was right at the end of the block. The most secluded room in a secluded motel. Beyond room 25 was nothing but miles and miles of open yellow scrubland, pockmarked by an occasional cluster of flora.

Ralph unlocked the door and pushed it open. He stepped aside and made a sweeping gesture with his hand in an "after you" kind of way. Jessica hesitated a beat and then stepped over the threshold. The first thing she noticed was the welcome coolness of the room after the merciless heat of the desert sun. The second thing was the room was pretty much like every other motel room she had ever stayed in while on the road.

Twin queen beds with quilted floral bed covers dominated the main space. Faded art prints in cheap frames hung above the beds. A coffee machine was stacked on top of a microwave, which was stacked on top of a refrigerator. Overly starched towels hung in the bathroom. Ralph hovered in the doorway as Jessica looked around.

"Amanda Meyers asked for this room specially," he said. "Room twenty-five."

The room was basic but clean. Nothing out of the ordinary. Nothing special. Jessica assumed it was a carbon copy of the other twenty-four rooms.

"Do your guests usually request specific rooms?"

"Nope. Mostly, it's just what's available."

"And you're sure Amanda asked for this exact room?"

"Yep. That's why I remember, because it's kind of unusual. It's not like this place is a fancy hotel with a penthouse suite. The only exceptions are the regulars, like Bill outside, who always stay in the same room. But the Meyers woman wasn't a regular. I'd never laid eyes on her before that night."

"So, why did Amanda Meyers want this particular room?" Jessica muttered to herself, gazing around again.

She pushed past Ralph and surveyed the surroundings outside the front door. Miles and miles of nothing to the south, other than some mountains far off in the distance. The Twentynine Palms

Highway up ahead to the north, traffic zooming past in both directions. She turned the corner at the end of the building. Nothing but packed dirt and some tire tracks.

Ralph followed her. "Additional space for parking," he explained. "Hey, I guess that's one reason why room twenty-five might be popular."

"But there's enough space in the lot out front for two vehicles," Jessica pointed out. "Just like every other room. Why would Amanda need to make use of the dirt lot out back?"

The most secluded room in a very secluded motel.

This far from Los Angeles, any room in the motel would've provided enough privacy for an illicit tryst with Zachary Dunne, or anyone else Amanda might've been planning to meet out here in the desert. So, if even more isolation was the reason for requesting room 25—then why?

Jessica walked back round the front of the building and sat on one of the chairs outside the room. Ralph took the seat facing her on the other side of the table. The stucco roof extended out just enough to shade them both from the sun. Jessica pulled a pack of Marlboro Golds from her bag, shook one out, and lit it. She offered one to Ralph and he leaned across the table so she could light his cigarette for him.

Jessica took a long draw, then said, "Talk me through what happened that night."

Ralph said, "The Meyers woman called earlier in the day to make the booking. She wanted a two-night stay, both the Friday and Saturday. Asked for room twenty-five. I was real pleased, told her I loved to see guests returning to my motel. She replied, rather curtly I thought, that she'd never stayed at the Tranquility before. She provided her payment details and then hung up. Checked in a little after 9 p.m. I know this for sure because her arrival interrupted one of my favorite TV shows."

"You have any security cameras?" Jessica asked.

"Nope."

"Why not?"

"Not worth the expense," Ralph said. "We never really get any trouble out here."

"What if you get robbed one night?" Jessica asked. "It could happen. This place is pretty isolated."

"Yeah, and if it does happen, they'll be wearing masks or stockings over their heads and would most likely shoot out the cameras anyways, so why bother?"

"Fair point. Not a great deal of help to the cops searching for Amanda Meyers, though. Speaking of whom . . . Please, carry on."

"She showed up looking like she was dressed for a date."

"How so?"

"All dolled up. Sexy dress, high heels, lots of makeup. Pretty nice if you like that sort of thing. Way too skinny for me, though. I like my ladies with a few more curves. But I'd say the gal was definitely dressed to impress. I remember asking if she was expecting some company but she didn't answer. Just signed the guest book and snatched the key from me. Then she went back outside to her car and carried on to her room at end of the block. I didn't expect to see her again that night. Turned out, I saw her another couple times."

"Go on," Jessica prompted.

"About an hour later, she marched right on past the office, all the way to the side of the highway. I could see her, clear as anything, from the front window. She was holding her cell phone aloft like she was trying to get a cell signal." He chuckled. "I see that a lot."

"There's no cell signal in the motel?"

"Depends on the network," Ralph said. "But, mostly, it's patchy at best."

Jessica stubbed out her cigarette in an ashtray on the table and pulled her own cell phone from her bag. Checked the screen. Sure enough, no signal.

"You don't offer Wi-Fi? For folks who want to get online or FaceTime or WhatsApp or whatever?"

"Nope. Not in the guest rooms anyways. The whole point of the Tranquility Motel is to get away from it all. Relax in the pool, meditate on the deck, go for a long walk. It's not the kind of place where you come to spend hours on a cell phone or laptop. The only Wi-Fi is in the office and that's for customer payments and records."

Jessica's mind flashed back to the magazine Ralph had been reading earlier. "Sure, customer records."

Ralph ground the butt of his own cigarette. "I'd say the Meyers woman must've spent a good ten minutes waving that damn phone around. Then another five minutes just standing there, hands on hips, watching the highway."

"Like she was expecting someone?"

"Exactly like she was expecting someone. Even though it was full dark by then and she wouldn't have been able to see much. But I figured she was probably one of those impatient folks who thinks a kettle boils faster if you stare at it hard enough. Finally, she marched right on past the office again and went back to her room."

"You said you saw her a couple times that night?"

"Uh-huh. That's right. Around forty-five minutes later, she was back again. This time, she stormed into the office and demanded to use my phone."

"Did you let her?"

"Did I hell," Ralph snorted. "Who's left to pay the bill? Me, that's who. We have a pay phone that guests are welcome to use. I offered to sell her a preloaded phone card. She purchased one of those and made a call."

"How did she seem?"

"Angry. And, I'd say, a little drunk by then."

"And she made just one phone call? Did you hear any of it?"

"It was hard not to—the way she was yelling down the phone. Although, it sounded like she was leaving a voicemail, rather than speaking to someone. If it was a conversation, the guy on the other end wasn't getting a word in edgeways."

"What makes you think it was a guy?"

"She called him Jack. Or Zach. Something like that. Told him she was done with being let down and made a fool of. That she was too good for him and they were definitely finished this time. Then she hung up. Slammed the receiver so hard, I thought she'd broken my damn phone."

Zach.

Zachary Dunne.

A cloud passed over the sun momentarily and Jessica shuddered. "Can you remember if she consulted her cell phone or a scrap of paper when keying in the number? Or if she knew the number from memory?"

"From memory," Ralph answered without hesitation. "She stabbed the number in hard and fast. Definitely a woman scorned."

"Did you tell the cops about the phone call?"

"No."

"Why not?"

"They didn't ask. Just wanted to have a look in her room, and to know when she arrived, and left, and if I had any video footage. Seemed to lose interest when I told them we had no security cameras."

"Anything else you remember?"

"Not really. She left around fifteen minutes later. Zoomed past real fast in her sexy little Maserati. I got to say, when the cops showed up a few days later, and said she was missing, my first thought was she'd been in a crash. Real pissed, a little drunk, driving too fast." Ralph shrugged. "But, apparently, there were no road traffic accidents around here that weekend. I don't think they ever did find the Maserati. I guess it's a real mystery what happened to that gal, huh?"

"It sure is."

"Hey, why the interest in Amanda Meyers now, after all this time?"

"I'm looking into the possibility Amanda's disappearance may be linked to two other missing women."

"Yeah? No shit! *Three* missing women? Now that's a story, right? You think Netflix will make a documentary about it? You think they'll want to film here?"

Jessica hesitated, then showed him the photos of Mallory and Laurie. "You ever see either of these women at the motel?"

Ralph snatched them from her and eyed them eagerly. Stabbed a finger at Mallory. "I've definitely seen the brunette before. She was a guest here. No doubt about it. Maybe the blonde too."

"When did the brunette stay here?"

"Not recently. A year ago, maybe two."

Jessica didn't know if Ralph was telling the truth or thinking about his starring role in a future Netflix documentary. "Okay, thanks for your time." She got up and started off back toward the office, where her truck was parked up outside.

"Let me know if the cops find any bodies," Ralph called after her.

Jessica ignored him. Kept on walking and thinking.

16

BURDEN

Burden consulted his watch.

The digital display read 18:23. Any moment now. He tapped his fingers lightly on the steering wheel.

One minute.

Two minutes.

There it was.

The yellow VW Bug emerged noisily from the underground parking lot and turned onto the street, the *put-put-put* of its old engine shattering the early evening calm like a round of fire from a machine gun. Both car and driver were 1979 models but Cara Zelenka was wearing the years a hell of a lot better than the heap of junk she drove.

Burden didn't follow her this time. Not like he'd done when she'd visited the laundromat.

He already knew where she was headed—an evening class at a local community college—and what route she would take. A straight run east on Sunset through Little Armenia, before dropping south onto Vermont into East Hollywood. A fifteen-minute journey, give or take, depending on the traffic.

From what he could tell, the beginners' photography class was more than just a new hobby. It was a possible fledgling career, a belated attempt to make something of herself. Cara worked the day shift at a twenty-four-hour drive-in diner, a retro Googie-style building on the Strip that he knew, from personal experience, served the best breakfast in town. He also knew her tips could be the difference between Cara making the rent that month or the shame of begging for an extra few days to make the payment.

Cara's folks had money—and lots of it—but she was too proud to ask them for handouts. He admired that about her, even if it was completely misguided. She'd moved from her hometown of Indio to Hollywood to be closer to her lover, a wardrobe assistant at Paramount Studios by the name of Gina Scervino. They'd split six months ago, leaving Cara with a bruised heart and an apartment she couldn't really afford.

Single and broke and the wrong side of forty.

He suspected Cara thought of herself as the fuck-up in the family, the underachiever, the disappointment.

If she did, she was wrong.

Very wrong.

Not even close.

The class began at seven and lasted for three hours. The journey back to West Hollywood meant she'd arrive home sometime between ten-fifteen and ten-thirty. Burden had plenty of time.

He pulled out his cell phone and checked Cara's social media feeds for updates. Unsurprisingly, Instagram was the one she used most. It was early days but, scrolling through her photos, he wasn't convinced she had the talent to be the next Annie Leibovitz. She wouldn't be attending class anymore anyway.

He waited until the day gave way to dusk and streetlights began to flicker on along the sidewalk. Then he slipped his cell phone into one of his pants pockets, a screwdriver into the other, snapped on a pair of latex gloves, and pulled the hood of his dark sweater up over his head. He got out of the truck, closed the door quietly, and jogged across the street toward the pink and green building. There were plenty of trees to provide shade on a hot day and cover for someone like Burden who didn't want to be seen at night.

He'd found out several weeks ago there was no AC in apartment 2. The old wooden ceiling fan was busted and Cara didn't hold out much hope of what she referred to as the "useless super" fixing it any time soon. All Burden had to do was wait patiently for the warmer weather to arrive. Sure enough, now the early days of summer were here, and the temperature was edging toward three figures, she'd started leaving the windows open just a crack to let in some air. One of the windows overlooked an alley behind the building, where the trash cans were kept. All of the windows were covered by old ornate metal grilles.

He ducked down the east side of the building and round the back. He'd watched the place enough times to know there was little chance of being disturbed by a neighbor taking out the trash so late in the evening. He pulled the screwdriver from his pants pocket, trained the cell phone's flashlight on the window, and got to work.

It took more than fifteen minutes to loosen the rusted screws enough to remove the grille. He was blinking sweat out of his eyes by the time he was done and his hands were damp inside the latex gloves. He placed the grille carefully on the gravel. Then he slid his fingers into the small air gap and pushed up on the sash window, muscles straining as the old wooden frame stubbornly inched up just enough for him to haul himself up onto the sill and slip inside. He switched on a floor lamp, shut off the flashlight, and surveyed his surroundings.

Cara was messy and lived modestly. Unmade bed in the middle of the main room, with underwear and t-shirts piled on top of an easy chair. Crumbs on the kitchenette counter and jars of peanut butter and jelly left out with the lids off. The door to the small bathroom was open and he could see a cheap plastic shower curtain and empty cardboard tube in the toilet roll holder.

The studio apartment smelled like her. Not her perfume, or her body spray, or her hair lacquer. Her own unique scent.

He checked the time on his watch.

21:28.

Time to get to work.

Burden searched in cupboards and closets, sifted through junk mail and unpaid bills, rifled through the drawers in the dresser. Eventually he found what he was looking for, slipped between the pages of a dog-eared copy of *The Catcher in the Rye* for safe keeping.

After taking several photos on his cell phone, Burden returned the piece of paper to the book, and the book to the shelf, and then he climbed out of the window, pushed the frame down to its original position, and replaced the ornate window grille. He retraced his steps back to the truck. Removed the gloves, stuffed them in the glove compartment, and started the engine. As he turned onto Vine, he passed the familiar little yellow car and he smiled to himself.

The next stage of the plan was beginning to take shape in his mind.

17

JESSICA

Connor had booked a couple of rooms at a motel in Twentynine Palms—but thankfully not the one owned by Ralph.

Jessica went for a swim and a nap in the afternoon, while Connor worked some other client cases. In the evening, after they'd both freshened up, they ordered in pizza for dinner, then went to a nearby bar for drinks. The night was still warm and the sky was a deep blue, tinged with soft pink and peach tones, providing the perfect backdrop for the inky silhouettes of the surrounding palm trees.

Fine Line Cocktails was located on the other side of the highway. The bar was housed in a green cinderblock and siding building with red trim and had a ton of character, thanks to its quirky railroad theme. Not fancy but friendly so long as you didn't bring a dog or a concealed weapon onto the premises, according to the signs nailed outside the front door. Jessica was glad she'd left her Glock locked in the truck's glove compartment. Inside, there was a pool table, jukebox and shuffleboard, and a whole lot of people having a good time. Jessica and Connor both ordered three-dollar domestic beers and whiskey shot chasers.

They found a relatively quiet table in the back of the room and Jessica filled Connor in on what she'd found out at the Tranquility Motel. How Amanda Meyers had specifically requested a room right at the end of the block that seemed to have no benefit other than additional space for parking that couldn't be seen from the highway or the office or any of the other rooms.

"Was it the reason Amanda wanted that exact room?" Jessica said. "I don't know. What I *do* know was who Amanda was planning on meeting at the motel that night."

"Zachary Dunne?"

"Got it in one. The motel's manager overheard a phone call she made to someone called Jack or Zach. Sounded like he was supposed to meet here at the Tranquility and never showed. If her 'date' was with Dunne, it leads to a whole other bunch of questions."

"Such as?" Connor asked.

"Why didn't he show? Where was he instead? Did he have an alibi for that night? Was he involved in her disappearance? Or did Amanda cross paths with someone else?"

"We need to speak to Zachary Dunne again."

"Yes, we do," Jessica agreed. "But no softly-softly approach. This time, we challenge him on his affair with Amanda and their planned rendezvous out in the desert the night she disappeared."

"What if he won't speak?" Connor asked.

"If he won't talk to us, he'll have to talk to the cops instead. It's his choice. Valdez, and whoever is looking after the LA investigation, clearly don't know about the affair or the phone call Amanda made—at least not yet."

"Okay, let's speak to him tomorrow once we're back in the city."

"Another drink?" Jessica asked.

"Sure. Same again."

Jessica weaved her way through a crowd of sweaty bodies to the bar and placed the order. As the bartender fixed the drinks, a well-refreshed woman next to Jessica nudged her hard in the ribs. "Bag yourself a handsome guy and you might go hungry but at least you'll always have something nice to look at. That's what my momma always said."

"Excuse me?"

The woman nodded toward the table where Connor was sitting watching two young guys whoop and cheer as they pushed pucks down the wooden shuffleboard table. "That's one fine-looking man you got yourself there, sweetheart. I'd hold onto him tight if I were you."

Jessica didn't respond, just handed over the cash to the bartender, and picked up the tray of drinks. When she returned to the table, she asked Connor about his visit with Mallory Wilcox's husband. "What's all this about knitted dolls?"

"It's apparently what happens when a hobby turns into an obsession. Mallory's obsession, that is, not Wilcox's. There are dozens of the creepy little fuckers all over the house." Connor smiled sadly. "The thing is, it was those dolls that convinced me Wilcox really does love his wife."

"Huh? How'd you figure that out?"

"He treats them like revered objects," Connor said. "Won't even sleep in the bed he used to share with Mallory because she has a load of dolls displayed on it. So, he sleeps on a cot bed in the living room instead. The dolls are all over the couch too. Wilcox acted like it was a big deal allowing me to sit on Mallory's armchair."

"Valdez painted Wilcox as a real asshole," Jessica pointed out.

"Oh, he's an asshole all right. No doubt about it. I'm not saying Mallory had the best life with him, and I very much doubt he showed her a great deal of affection. But I don't think he was violent toward her, like Valdez was insinuating. Even after walking out on him—if that's what she did—I'd say Wilcox still cares deeply for her."

"Maybe Wilcox killed her and those dolls are now sick trophies?" Jessica offered. "Or her death was accidental and his guilt means he can't bring himself to get rid of them the way he had to get rid of his wife's body?"

Connor nodded slowly. "An interesting, if rather gruesome, theory." Then he shook his head. "I just don't see it somehow. Wilcox seems convinced Mallory will come home one day, and he also claims her sister—the one who looks after the kids now—gave her the cash to get away from him."

"We need the sister's take on it."

"I already tried. She wouldn't speak to me, other than to say she knows nothing about Mallory's disappearance."

"What about Laurie?" Jessica asked. "You said in your text you thought Wilcox recognized her?"

"Seemed to me like her name was familiar to him and he spent a long time looking at her photo. But he was adamant he didn't know her."

"You think Laurie and Mallory knew each other?"

"Maybe. I don't know. It seems unlikely they'd be friends."

"Yeah, I agree."

They were both silent for a few minutes. Sipped their drinks while folks chatted noisily all around them. A band began to set up their equipment.

"I just found the whole visit to Whitewater really sad," Connor said eventually. "Here's a guy who can't be much older than myself but looks old enough to claim his ten percent seniors' discount at the grocery store—if he ever eats anything other than take-out pizza, that is. He was also halfway through a six-pack of beer before noon. Then he tells me he was a college baseball star. Met Mallory his freshman year too. Must've thought he had the world at his feet back then."

"Wow. What happened?"

"Sounds like he had some sort of mental breakdown. Too much pressure, I guess. He was a frat guy too. I swear, you'd never guess his past, looking at him now."

"How'd you know he was a frat guy?"

"He had a tattoo with the Greek symbols. There was something familiar about it but he didn't belong to the same fraternity as me."

"You were a frat guy?" Jessica asked, amused. "Actually, I don't know why I'm surprised. Of *course* you were a frat guy."

"Sure was—and don't say it like it's a bad thing! Lambda Chi Alpha at USC. The best fraternity at the school. 'Every man a man.'"

"Oh, jeez." Jessica shook her head and took a slug of beer.

"What about you?"

"What about me?"

"Sorority sister?"

Jessica snorted. "What do you think?"

Connor stuck out his bottom lip in mock sympathy. "Aw, did those mean girls not let little Jessica join in the fun?"

Jessica grinned and drained her beer. "You're such an asshole, do you know that?"

Connor laughed. "You say the nicest things. Another drink?"

"Sure, why not?"

◆ ◆ ◆

They listened to some songs by the band, a local three-piece by the name of DirtBoys, and ordered some more drinks at the bar, and then decided to return to the motel shortly before midnight.

"Nightcap?" Connor asked. "I have some Wild Turkey."

"No Scotch?"

"This is America, sweetheart. Nothing wrong with some good old Kentucky bourbon."

"I guess. Your place or mine?"

"Poolside?"

"Sounds like a plan."

Connor went to his room to fetch the bottle, while Jessica made her way to the pool area. Underwater lights cast the water in a weird turquoise alien glow. Palm trees flapped gently in the breeze outside the perimeter mesh fencing. Jessica got comfortable on a plastic chair. Connor appeared with the bourbon and two stubby glass tumblers. Poured them each a generous measure, then settled into a chair of his own. He put a playlist on his iPhone and placed it on the table between them, the volume down low enough so as not to disturb the other guests.

"What a beautiful night," he said.

He was right. The moon was huge and bright and there were so many stars it would take a lifetime to count them all.

"Yeah, it's not bad. Not bad at all."

They were quiet for a while, just drinking and lost in their own thoughts and the music. A Tom Petty song gave way to a Robert Plant number and Connor asked Jessica what she was thinking about.

"Those three women," she said. "Laurie, Mallory, and Amanda. I was wondering if a midnight sky, just like this one, was the last thing they ever saw. Or if they're happy someplace, completely oblivious to the pain and suffering their absence is causing those who love them."

"That's what we're going to find out, Jessica," Connor said. "We don't give up until we know the truth."

He topped off their glasses. Picked up both tumblers and set them down by the edge of the pool.

"What're you doing?" Jessica asked.

He turned to her and wiggled his eyebrows. "Water looks real tempting."

"You're not seriously suggesting going for a swim at midnight? I'm pretty sure it's against the motel's rules."

"Since when did you care about rules, Miss Shaw?"

"I can't even if I wanted to. My bathing suit is still drying in my room after my swim earlier."

"Who said anything about bathing suits?"

Before she could respond, Connor had slipped off his sneakers, pulled off his t-shirt, unbuckled his belt and stepped out of his jeans, and was standing in only his boxer shorts. He dropped his watch onto the little mountain of clothing and dived into the water. When he resurfaced, he looked at Jessica with that now familiar sexy, crooked grin.

"Come on in. The water's lovely."

"Nope. I'm fine right here."

"What, are you scared or something? I can't believe Jessica Shaw is a candy-ass!"

"I am not a candy-ass."

"Prove it."

"If you must know, I'm not wearing a bra."

Connor put his hands over his eyes. "I won't peek. Promise."

Jessica laughed. Before she could change her mind, she stood up and stripped down to her panties. Hoped her waterproof mascara and eyeliner was as good as the packaging promised. She jumped in and let out an involuntary squeal. The water was cold, much colder than she remembered from her swim earlier under the brutal afternoon sun.

"Holy shit! It's fucking freezing!"

Connor took his hands away from his eyes and pressed a finger to his lips. "Shhhh. You want to wake up the whole motel? You want the other guests to see your boobies?"

"Please don't ever say the word 'boobies' to me again. We're both adults, not little kids. They're called breasts."

"And very nice breasts they are too."

"Jerk." Jessica splashed him on the face with water and swam over to the side of the pool where her bourbon was sitting on the tiles. Connor joined her and took a sip of his own drink and then ran a finger along Jessica's arm. Goosebumps popped out all over her flesh and had nothing to do with the cool temperature of the water.

"You never did tell me the story behind all those tattoos," he said.

Jessica had first got inked—an anchor tattoo—just hours after they put her dad, Tony, in the ground. It was her way of dealing with the pain of his loss. She shrugged. "Not much to tell."

Connor's finger stopped on a tattoo of a pair of open hand-cuffs. "What about this one?" he asked. "Is this to symbolize your dark, criminal past?"

Jessica smiled. "No, it's a reminder to stay away from bad men."

Connor waited for her to elaborate. She didn't. Took a long drink of bourbon instead and winced at the burn.

"And?" Connor prompted.

"And what?"

"You can't just leave it at that. What bad guy? Why handcuffs? C'mon, spill the juicy deets. What's the story?"

"You wouldn't believe me if I told you."

"Try me."

She sighed. "Okay, a few years back, when I was still in New York, I was dating a guy. A cop. His name was Tommy and he was older than me. A little rough around the edges. Not classically good-looking but sexy. He worked NYPD Homicide and was great at what he did. It wasn't just about his clearance rate, Tommy really seemed to care about getting justice for the victims and their families. I guess I looked up to him a lot." Jessica side-eyed Connor. "And he was great in the sack too."

"I hate him," Connor said. "Go on."

"We never lived together or anything but it got very serious very fast. Of course, our jobs meant it wasn't a conventional relationship. Weekends away together were few and far between. Dates would be cut short or cancelled at short notice. But the time we did spend together, it was great. We dated for six months, which doesn't sound like very long, but I thought it was the real deal, that me and Tommy would get married. Maybe even have kids one day."

"Wow. I never pegged you as the settling-down type."

"I'm not. Not anymore."

"What happened?"

"A woman came into the agency one day. A potential client. It was a classic infidelity case. She'd suspected her husband had been cheating on her for a while. All the usual signs were there: he had lost interest in sex, was working longer hours than usual, he was leaving the dinner table to take secret calls on his cell. She wanted to hire a PI—that would be me, by the way—to carry out surveillance work on the husband. Find out who the mistress was."

"Don't tell me . . ."

"Yep. My new client was Tommy's wife. I was the mistress."

"And you had no idea?"

"None whatsoever. Some private eye, huh?"

"What happened?"

"I told her I couldn't take the case. Her husband was NYPD and the agency had a good relationship with the local cops. Chances were, we'd have contacts who were buddies with the husband. I advised her to go elsewhere."

"And Tommy?"

"He broke my heart so I broke his nose."

"You're joking?"

Jessica looked at him, arched her eyebrows. "What do you think?"

Connor chuckled. "I think I got off lightly with a bruised jaw that time. So, the handcuffs are about Tommy? Why open, though?"

"Because I escaped just in the nick of time. What about you?" Jessica asked. "Any near misses? Was there ever one who got away?"

Connor didn't answer right away. He drained his tumbler dry and then gave her a look that was so intense she could almost physically feel the weight of it. "Yeah, there was." He reached out and wiped at her cheekbone, just under her eye. "Mascara tears."

"So much for waterproof. Sexy, huh?"

"Yeah, you are."

He leaned in and kissed her. Soft at first and then harder. A bourbon and beer-flavored kiss that took her right back to a night in Hollywood just over six months ago. She realized now just how much she'd wanted to feel his mouth on hers again, had done this whole time. The water was cold but her skin burned where he touched her. She was vaguely aware of the song changing on Connor's iPhone. "I'm on Fire" by Bruce Springsteen. Jessica figured it was pretty appropriate for the way she was feeling right now. The soundtrack also drowned out all the doubts and questions swirling in her mind. She pushed them aside and allowed herself to get lost in the moment, tried not to think about bad desires.

After what seemed like a long time, Connor pulled away. "We shouldn't be doing this," he murmured against her ear. "It's a bad idea."

"The worst," Jessica agreed.

Then he kissed her again.

18

MALLORY—18 MONTHS AGO

It had begun with a kiss, and quickly turned into a whole lot more, but Mallory was now regretting confiding in her sister about the affair.

"I can't believe what you're telling me, Mallory." Lucinda sounded appalled. "You're really cheating on Terence?"

Mallory pulled the kitchen phone cord as far as it would go and looked out the window. Young Terence and Wade were playing out in the yard. "I thought you hated him?" she hissed. "Why are you on his side all of a sudden?"

"It's not about taking sides," Lucinda said. "Yes, he's a lazy drunk who should treat you a whole lot better, but he doesn't deserve this. He loves you deep down in his own stupid way. We both know it."

"Do we?" Mallory shot back. "I'm not so sure anymore."

"This isn't like you, Mal. What do you even know about this guy? I mean, *really* know about him? Nothing, that's what."

Mallory bit her lip. She knew Lucinda was right but she was sick and tired of doing the right thing. So what if she didn't know a whole lot about Randal yet? That was the whole point of spending time together, wasn't it? To get to know each other better. And what she did know so far, she liked. A lot.

She'd met him for the first time two weeks ago. He'd shown up on her doorstep to return the wallet she hadn't even realized she'd dropped outside the grocery store. He told Mallory he'd shouted after her and, when she didn't hear him and got into her car, he'd jumped into his truck and followed her all the way home to hand it back.

As they stood there, chatting on the doorstep, Randal had recognized her as the woman who made the knitted dolls, told her she'd sold him one for his niece at a local craft fair about a month back.

Mallory couldn't figure out why she didn't remember him from the fair. He was absolutely gorgeous. Tall, fair hair, and the most amazing blue eyes. And what a body! It was a cold day and he was wearing jeans and a sweater and a padded jacket but she could tell just by looking at him that he worked out. Then he'd stamped his feet and blown warm air into his hands and Mallory had remembered her manners, asked if he wanted to come inside for a hot drink.

He'd told her his name was Randal and he'd wound up drinking a couple of Terence's chilled beers after the coffee. The conversation had flowed easily between them and Mallory felt like she was being listened to for the first time in years. So much so, she'd completely lost track of time and was almost late picking up the boys from school.

She'd walked Randal to the front door and thanked him again for returning the wallet. Started to say something about him saving her a load of hassle cancelling her cards when he leaned down and kissed her. He pulled away immediately and apologized profusely. Said she was beautiful and kind and funny but he should respect the fact that she was married. Then they'd locked eyes and the next thing Mallory knew they were kissing passionately right there in her hallway. It was like something out of a movie. Mallory had never felt so alive.

The rest of the evening had passed by in a kind of dizzy blur. She could think of nothing other than the kiss with the beautiful stranger. She'd even managed to burn the dinner and had to order a pizza for Terence and the boys. Mallory had also somehow convinced Terence that he must've drunk the two beers himself he claimed were missing from the refrigerator.

The next day, Randal was back at her front door. Told her he couldn't stop thinking about her either. This time, she took him straight to bed. They made love twice that afternoon surrounded by her dolls. By the time he left, Mallory was pretty sure she was a little bit in love with him.

Now he wanted to spend some more time with her, someplace where they could have a drink and relax and enjoy each other without fear of being disturbed or discovered.

"Will you cover for me or not?" Mallory asked Lucinda.

"You know I'm a terrible liar."

"Please."

A sigh. "I'll do my best. What's the story?"

"I told Terence I'm going to a candle party at Debbie's house and not to wait up. He thinks you're going to be at the party too."

"Who's Debbie?"

"You know, Debbie from slimming class. The redhead. Just back me up if Terence starts asking any questions, okay?"

"Are you going to leave him for this guy?"

Mallory paused. "You know me and Terence haven't been getting along for a while. The drinking is getting worse and—"

"What about the boys? What about Young Terence and Wade? You'd seriously walk out on your family for someone you've only just met?"

Mallory heard the front door slam shut. "Look, I've got to go," she whispered. "Terence is home."

She replaced the receiver on the wall phone quietly. Flashed back to the cuts and bruises on Terence's knuckles on those nights he'd gotten himself into brawls at the Howlin' Wolf. He'd never once raised a hand to her in all the years they'd been together but if he ever found out what she'd done—what she was planning on doing—Terence would kill her.

Mallory knew it as sure as she knew night followed day.

19

CONNOR

Connor had fucked up big time.

Knew it as soon as he'd opened his eyes this morning; had known it the moment he'd kissed Jessica the night before.

It was the reason why, when he walked her back to her room last night, he didn't ask to go inside with her—even though he'd wanted nothing more in the world than to carry her over to the bed and peel off her wet panties and make love to her. It's not like he hadn't been thinking of exactly that scenario for the last six months.

And there he was, just walking away.

He'd told her they'd both better get some sleep. She'd smiled up at him, under the glow of the green neon strip lighting, clutching her clothes to her chest, and had said something along the lines of there being more interesting things to do than sleep. And he'd responded lamely about how they should get on the road early the next morning and get back to LA.

A look had passed across her face that he couldn't quite figure out. The tiniest frown. Maybe hurt or confusion. Then she'd nodded and told him he was right and said good night and closed the door behind her without another word. She probably thought his reluctance to take her to bed was down to them working together now.

If only it was that simple.

Connor threw off the bedsheets, showered, and dressed in some fresh clothes. Popped a couple of Advil in the hope of alleviating a dull ache behind his eyes. He'd found even a couple drinks after hitting forty meant a hangover the next day. Or maybe the headache was down to the stress of the conversation he knew he'd have to have with Jessica soon.

He went to the motel lobby and grabbed two coffees to go and piled some donuts onto a paper plate and knocked on Jessica's door. When there was no answer, he tried again, but louder this time.

"Yeah, yeah. Give me a minute, would you?"

She must have looked through the spy hole and knew it was Connor banging on the door because, when she opened it, all she was wearing were the black panties and a damp t-shirt from the night before. He'd clearly woken her. Her blonde hair was a mess, her makeup was smudged under her eyes, and one side of her face had pillow creases.

Connor thought she was beautiful.

He wanted to tell her what he was thinking. Wanted to tell her that he wanted her. That he'd wanted her last night. That he'd wanted her from the first second he'd laid eyes on her.

What he said was, "We should probably get going soon."

"Sure," she said, squinting against the harsh morning sun. "I just need to get ready and get my things together."

"I got you coffee and some breakfast."

"Thanks." She took the to-go cup and a donut. "Give me twenty minutes. I'll meet you by the truck."

Then she closed the door.

Connor couldn't decide if she was pissed at him or just tired and a little hungover. Maybe she was relieved things hadn't gone further. After all, he was technically her boss. Sure, she'd kissed him on two separate occasions now but maybe she wasn't all that into him. Both times, he'd made the first move.

Maybe everything would be fine.

Connor returned to his own room. He drank his coffee and ate his breakfast, then packed his belongings neatly into an overnight bag. His cell phone vibrated on the dresser. He glanced at the screen and sighed. Rejected the call. His eyes fell on the bottle of bourbon and two tumblers on the desk. He consulted his watch. It was just gone 9 a.m. Fuck it, he thought.

He crossed the room and picked up a tumbler. It had the faintest hint of pink lip gloss on the rim and a tiny pool of honey-colored liquid in the bottom of the glass. He unscrewed the lid from the bottle and poured himself a measure and threw it back in one go.

"Damn," he muttered, breathing fire.

Connor replaced the lid and threw the bottle into the duffel along with the rest of his stuff.

Outside, Jessica was standing by the truck smoking a cigarette. She was wearing denim cut-offs, a faded old Johnny Cash tee, and Converse high tops. Her hair was still wet from the shower. Sunglasses hid her eyes but he knew she was watching him, could feel the weight of her gaze. He walked over to the truck.

"Hey," he said.

"Hey yourself," she said.

They were on the Twentynine Palms Highway within seconds of dropping off their room keys at the motel's office.

"Are you planning on speaking to Zachary Dunne today?" Jessica asked.

"I thought it might be better if you did."

"Why?"

"I didn't get much out of him last time. He might respond better to someone else."

"Not both of us?"

"No. I think he'd feel like we were ganging up on him. Better you on your own. If you're happy to speak to him, that is?"

"Sure, no problem."

The conversation pretty much dried up from there. Jessica cranked up the volume on the radio. It was mostly the same country songs over and over again on a loop. Connor gazed out of the window. The landscape was more barren now that they'd left Twentynine Palms behind. He found himself wondering what had drawn Laurie, Amanda and Mallory out to a place of such lonely emptiness. He thought of Jessica's words, how the desert sky out here might have been the last thing those women ever saw. Connor shuddered. He really hoped that wasn't the case, hoped there was a simple reason why all three had disappeared out here in the high desert.

Connor's cell phone vibrated in his hand, startling him. He rejected the call. Could see Jessica looking at him from the corner of his eye, before returning her gaze to the open road stretching out before them. The phone pinged with a voicemail a few seconds later. Connor switched the device off without retrieving the voice message.

◆ ◆ ◆

A little under three hours later, Jessica parked outside the detective agency.

Neither one of them had mentioned what happened last night. Connor knew the conversation was inevitable, knew there was no way of avoiding it. He should have told Jessica the truth right from the get-go.

They left the truck and made their way to the agency. Connor moved to insert the key in the lock and froze. The door was already unlocked. The office lights were on. He was almost certain he had locked up and turned off the lights before making the trip to Twentynine Palms.

"Everything okay?" Jessica asked from behind him. She sounded worried.

Not half as worried as he felt.

He didn't answer. Pushed the door open slowly.

A blonde woman was sitting at the conference table. Steam rising from Jessica's new mug in front of her. The room smelled like caramel latte and Dior perfume. Connor knew the fragrance was Dior because he'd bought it for the woman.

Fuck.

"Where the hell have you been, Matt?" the blonde demanded. "I've been trying to get hold of you for two days."

"I've been working. I wasn't expecting you."

"Clearly."

Jessica stepped into the room and Connor noticed her discreetly slipping her gun back into her shoulder bag.

Fuck.

"Who the hell is she?" the blonde asked.

"I was just about to ask the same thing," Jessica said.

"Jessica, this is Rae-Lynn," Connor said. "Rae-Lynn, meet Jessica. She's a PI. She works here now."

Rae-Lynn narrowed her eyes. "Since when?"

"Since two days ago."

"Uh-huh. Is that so?"

"Are you a client?" Jessica asked.

"No, I'm not a client."

"You look kind of familiar."

Rae-Lynn's scowl was quickly replaced by her "knock 'em dead" smile. Connor had seen it a lot. "I'm an actress." She beamed. "Maybe you saw me in something."

"Maybe," Jessica said, doubtfully.

Connor sighed. "Rae-Lynn is a dancer at the Tahiti Club."

"Matt!" Rae-Lynn protested. "You know the dancing is temporary. Acting is my real job."

The Tahiti Club was a strip joint in Hollywood that Jessica and Connor had visited last year as part of a case. They had kissed for the first time in the alleyway outside.

"Sure, I remember you now," Jessica said. "The clothes threw me for a moment. You have a beautiful body, Rae-Lynn."

Rae-Lynn frowned, like she wasn't sure if she'd been insulted or complimented. "It's lunchtime, baby," she said to Connor. "Why don't you take me somewhere nice?"

Jessica stared hard at Connor, and he knew she was wondering what a dancer from a strip bar was doing with a key to his office. Why she was calling him baby and demanding to be taken out to lunch.

"Rae-Lynn is my fiancée," he said.

He wasn't sure what kind of reaction he expected. Yelling, shouting, another punch to the jaw. Jessica eyed Rae-Lynn, with her crop top and cute little skirt and sparkly sandals, and then turned to Connor and nodded like she finally understood. The disappointment in her eyes broke his heart, cut through him like a scalpel slicing soft flesh. That look was a million times worse than being hit, a far bigger blow than being struck on the face.

"Okay, I'm outta here." Jessica turned to leave.

"Jessica, please. Wait. Where are you going?"

"To do my job. Enjoy your goddamn lunch."

20

BURDEN

The slip of paper he'd found between the pages of Cara's battered old copy of *The Catcher in the Rye* told Burden several things.

He knew she'd pawned a ruby and diamond ring for five hundred bucks and she was now into the fourteen days' grace period during which she had to repay the loan or default on the pawned item. The danger zone, as he liked to think of it. Knowing a fair bit about her financial situation, Burden figured Cara would be unlikely to find the cash in time to pay off the pawn and prevent the ring being made available for public sale in-store.

What he didn't know was how important the piece of jewelry was to Cara, how desperate she was to find the green in time to prevent the ring ending up in the hands of a stranger.

The pawn slip was for a store in West Hollywood. Sonny's Pawn Shop was huge, more of an emporium than a shop, at least double the size of the other stores in the strip mall. Both the "S"s in the name were neon dollar signs. The words *"Casa de Empeño"* glowed red in a smaller neon sign under the main one. Other neon signage in the front window screamed: "We Buy Gold," "We Pay More," and "Pawn, Sell, Buy." There was a lot of neon going on. Moth-to-the flame beacons for those, like Cara, who need cash in their hand within minutes, with no credit check, and no obligation to repay the loan provided they were happy to lose their pawned collateral.

Inside, Fender electric guitars in every color you could think of hung from the ceiling like a scene from a Jimi Hendrix-wannabe's wet dream. One shelf was filled with ghetto-blasters that were so old they must be cool again. Another held DSLR cameras, and pancake lenses, and telephoto lenses, and every other size of lens in between.

A sign warned: "Never mind the dog, beware of the owner!"

Burden wandered over to a glass cabinet where the jewelry was on display. He bent down on his haunches for a closer look, pretending to be interested in the gold, silver, platinum and precious jewels glittering under strategically placed spotlights.

"Can I help you there, bud?"

Burden stood and turned toward the voice. Saw immediately that the humorous warning sign wasn't entirely a joke. The counter assistant was six-five and two hundred-fifty pounds of muscle, most of which was covered in tattoos, including his neck. He had significantly more hair on his chin than his shaved head. The guy looked more like strip club security than pawn shop server. He spoke through a serving window in thick glass that could probably stop a 9mm bullet and which separated the rest of the store from the secure section holding the money and all the good stuff. Despite appearances, the smile he offered Burden was friendly enough.

"I sure hope so," Burden said. "Bit of a long shot, though."

"Try me. We got all sorts here at Sonny's."

"My folks are celebrating their fortieth wedding anniversary soon and my dad wants to buy my mom a ruby and diamond ring as a surprise gift. Apparently, rubies symbolize forty years." Burden smiled. "I guess he's an old romantic."

The pawn guy chuckled. "Sounds like it. We have a few ruby and diamond rings. Let me show you."

He tapped a code into a control panel and there was a loud buzz as a secure door swung open and he entered the main area of the store.

Burden already knew the ring described on Cara's pawn slip wasn't in the display cabinet but he played along anyway. The guy talked him through the three rings in stock that fit what he thought Burden was looking for, droning on about carat sizes and clarity of stone and other boring stuff.

When the guy had finally finished his spiel, Burden said, "They're great but the stones are a little too big. My mom has really small hands and favors quite subtle jewelry. Plus, I'm guessing those three will be slightly out of my dad's price range."

The store guy told him the price of all three rings and Burden nodded. "Yeah, as feared, too expensive. My dad's not cheap, he's taking her on a luxury cruise too, but he really wanted to surprise her with a ring while onboard. Like I said, it was probably a long shot. Thanks, anyway."

Burden could almost see the cogs whirring in the pawn guy's brain. "When would you need this ring by?"

"They leave for the cruise in three weeks."

"I might have just the thing you're looking for."

The guy returned to the secure section of the store behind the bullet-proof glass, searched through various cartons on the shelves, then beckoned Burden over to the window. He opened a small black velvet box revealing a yellow gold and ruby and diamond ring inside. It was very old and the stones were tiny and its value would likely be more sentimental than financial. It was an exact match for the ring described on Cara's pawn slip.

"It's perfect," Burden said. "How much?"

The guy told him.

"I'll take it."

Burden already knew he wouldn't be leaving the store with the ring.

The guy shook his head. "No can do, bud. At least not yet. It's in the grace period. Nine more days and it could be yours."

Burden attempted a crestfallen expression. "Yeah, but surely it depends on how keen the person who pawned it is to retain ownership of it." He aimed for hopeful now. "Unless he or she told you they had no intention of paying back the loan. Would you even remember something like that?"

"You'd be surprised," the guy said. "A lot of folks in here are regulars. You get to know their stories. The woman who pawned the ring has made use of our services a few times in the past and has never repaid a loan so far."

"Sounds promising."

"She did seem real upset this time, though. Said it was her grandmother's ring and her family would be devastated if they found out she'd pawned it. Once she had the cash, she asked to see some of our DSLR cameras but left without buying one. I'd say chances of her defaulting on the loan are fifty-fifty."

"Okay, not so good," Burden said, while thinking what the pawn guy had just told him was exactly what he wanted to hear.

"I could take your name and cell phone number and call you if the ring's still here when the grace period is up?" the pawn guy offered. "If so, I'd be willing to hold it for you for a short time."

"I'd appreciate it, man. My dad will be thrilled if he's able to buy the ring."

Burden gave the guy a name and recited the digits of a cell phone he didn't own. He was tempted to purchase the ring himself, keep it as a little Cara trophy, but figured it would be too risky by then.

Burden waited until he was outside before allowing himself a satisfied smile. He had played the pawn store guy like one of his Fender Stratocasters.

And now he was going to make Cara Zelenka an offer he knew she couldn't refuse.

21

MALLORY—18 MONTHS AGO

It was an offer Mallory couldn't refuse.

A secluded motel in the arms of her lover. Just the two of them, drinking fine wine, and making love. Getting to know each other better. Forgetting about the rest of the world for a few hours.

Mallory had bought some sexy new underwear for the first time in years. Black lace with pink ribbon trim. Terence never touched her these days so the set would be wasted in the marital bedroom, but she was looking forward to seeing Randal's reaction this evening. Mallory had also made an effort with her hair and makeup and her outfit but Terence barely even glanced in her direction when she said goodbye and told him not to wait up. Just kept his eyes glued to his stupid TV show and hollered at her not to spend too much money on those "goddamn smelly candles."

When Mallory arrived at the motel, she headed straight for room 25. Nerves fluttered in her belly. When Randal opened the door, he told her she looked amazing and kissed her hard right there in the doorway. Then he pulled her inside the room, and onto the bed, where they made out again.

When they stopped to catch their breath, Randal groaned. "Shit, I forgot to pick up the booze."

"It doesn't matter. I'm not a big drinker anyway and let's just say I'm already in the mood."

She leaned in to kiss him again but he sat up and swung his legs over the bed and put his head in his hands. "No, it does matter, Mallory. I wanted it to be like a proper date. I wanted it to be special. Instead, I messed up."

Mallory crawled over next to him and put her arm around his shoulder and nuzzled his neck. "Oh, baby. It is special."

Randal looked at her. "Would you mind driving over to the gas station and picking up the wine? That way, I can have a shower and get all fresh and clean for you." He was still wearing his overalls from his landscape gardening job.

"I prefer you dirty," she giggled. "But sure, I'll go to the gas station if it'll make you feel better." Her hair was all mussed up and her lipstick smeared around her mouth. "I should probably tidy myself up first though. Make myself a little more presentable."

As she reached for her purse, Randal stopped her. "No point reapplying the lipstick. It'll just come off again as soon as you get back."

"True," she giggled again. "I'll just go grab a tissue from the bathroom."

Mallory wiped her face with some toilet paper and smoothed down her hair and peed quickly and quietly, hoping Randal wouldn't hear in the next room. When she emerged from the bathroom, he was holding his wallet and his expression was sheepish.

"What's wrong?" she asked.

"I'm so embarrassed. I was going to give you some cash but I'm all out. Must've used it all on the room. Would you be able to pay for the beer and wine for now and I'll hit an ATM and return the money before you go home?"

"Of course, no problem." Mallory knew she had around thirty dollars in her wallet. "I'll be back soon."

As she passed the motel office, Mallory had a thought. She stopped the car and went inside and assessed the contents of the vending machines. They held only candy and soda.

"I don't suppose you sell beer or wine?" she asked the man behind the desk.

"Does this look like a bar, lady?"

"Where's the nearest gas station?"

"Turn west onto the highway. About a mile down the road."

The gas station was lit up like Las Vegas against the black night sky.

Mallory picked out two nice bottles of red—or about as nice as you'd find at a gas station at least—and a beer four-pack. Grabbed some candy and chips too. She was always hungry after sex although she'd almost forgotten what it felt like to have any action in the bedroom until Randal had come on the scene. Excitement fizzed inside her like a bath bomb dropped in hot water. She must've had a big smile on her face because the kid behind the counter gave her a funny look as he rang up the purchases.

Then she saw there was no cash in her wallet after all and the fizzy excitement dropped a notch. She'd have to use her credit card. It would be fine, she assured herself. Randal had promised to pay her back and, if Terence questioned the gas station purchase on the statement, she'd tell him it was wine for the candle party.

Mallory drove a little too fast back to the motel, eager to return to Randal. Again, he met her at the door with a kiss. His hair was shower-wet and he smelled like soap and musky cologne. They opened a bottle of wine and drank it between more kisses while lounging on the bed. A radio played soul classics with the volume down low. Before long, they'd both shed their clothing. Randal was so hot in a pair of tight jockey shorts that Mallory felt suddenly self-conscious in the new underwear. Then he told her how sexy she looked and she believed him. Started to *feel* sexy.

"How about we spice things up a little bit?" he said.

"Oh?"

Randal opened the drawer next to the bed and pulled out two sets of handcuffs. Held them up and wiggled his eyebrows. "What do you think?"

Mallory wasn't sure, had never been into kinky stuff. Didn't even enjoy those "Fifty Shades" movies. But then Randal put his mouth on hers and gently pushed her back onto the bed and she let him cuff each wrist to the bed post. He straddled her and she expected him to pull down her black lace and pink ribbon trim knickers and make love to her but he reached for the dresser drawer again.

Of course, she thought. Condoms. Randal had been carrying protection in his wallet when they'd had sex at her house. But it wasn't a small foil square this time. When she saw what he was holding, panic exploded inside Mallory's brain. She tried to get off the bed but couldn't move. Her wrists strained painfully against the cold metal of the cuffs.

"No, Randal, please don't," she whimpered.

Mallory tried to kick out but he was too strong, had her legs pinned beneath his own body. He loomed over her, big and menacing. No longer the sweet, sexy man who had made love to her. Mallory opened her mouth to scream but he clamped a hand over it and shook his head.

"Shush," he whispered.

Mallory closed her eyes and felt the cool metal pierce her flushed skin.

22

JESSICA

Jessica slammed the door of MAC Investigations hard enough behind her to rattle the doorframe and tried counting to ten in an attempt to clear the red mist which was rapidly descending.

It didn't work. She was still furious with Connor for lying about Rae-Lynn.

She let out a frustrated roar and kicked the front tire of the Silverado, startling a passerby.

She counted to ten again. Reached fifty and was still pissed.

Jessica climbed inside the truck, started the engine, and tuned the radio to a hard rock and metal station. Cranked the volume up so loud the reverberations from the speakers rattled her bones. With a shaking hand, she tapped in the address she was headed for into the GPS system. Took a deep breath and pulled into the traffic, banged the steering wheel hard in time with the music. She knew she was angrier at herself than she was at Connor, for being stupid and naive enough to fall for his lies again.

After what happened with Tommy, Jessica swore she'd never be duped so easily by a guy ever again. Tommy had changed everything. How the hell was she supposed to believe in happy ever after when someone she'd loved—and who had claimed to love her back—could hurt her so badly? Was able to lie to her so easily? She knew she had commitment issues, that she'd find it hard to trust anyone again, but she'd figured being on her own was way better than the risk of deception and betrayal and hurt. That she'd finally chosen to let her guard down with someone like Connor, who had form when it came to lying and messing with her heart, made everything a million times worse. It wasn't even about the kiss; it was the fact that she'd opened up to him about her past, about Tommy, that really pissed her off.

Jessica joined the 10 heading east and her heartbeat began to slow to a regular beat again as she picked up speed on the freeway. She lit a cigarette. By the time she'd arrived in Downtown LA an hour later, the rage had dropped from red alert to amber. She found a space in the parking lot of a King Taco where she used her cell phone to search Google for a telephone number. She hit the call icon.

"Haywood, Dunne & Smith."

The woman's voice was deep and husky and sexy. More suited to talking dirty on premium-rate chat lines than answering calls at a legal firm.

"I'd like to speak to Zachary Dunne," Jessica said.

"Can I ask who's calling?"

"My name is Jessica Shaw. I'm a private investigator looking into the disappearance of Amanda Meyers."

There was a pause, then the woman said, "Oh, are you a friend of Matt's?"

Connor's contact from the bar. Apparently as attractive in the flesh as she sounded on the phone. Jessica wondered if he'd kissed her too after a few drinks.

"No, we're not friends. We work together."

"Mr. Dunne is out at lunch right now."

"I don't suppose you know where?"

"Yes, I do."

"Where?"

Another pause. Then the woman said, "You didn't hear it from me, right?"

"Right."

She gave Jessica the name and address of a diner not far from Dunne's office building. Jessica thanked the receptionist and was about to end the call when the woman spoke again.

"Miss Shaw?"

"Yeah?"

"Tell Matt that Vanessa said hi."

Jessica killed the connection. She started the truck and headed for the address provided by the receptionist.

The diner was old-school style, with a mix of red vinyl and white Formica booths and high stools in front of a counter. A slightly overweight bald man with glasses sat on one of the stools eating a sloppy sandwich. A paper napkin was tucked into his shirt collar like a baby's bib but she could see a Marvin the Martian necktie poking out below. His shiny dress shoes were on a footrest and the hems of his pants had ridden up enough to show off his Daffy Duck socks.

Jessica recognized the man from Connor's description.

Zachary Dunne.

She climbed onto the stool next to him. He was reading the sports section of the *Los Angeles Times*, and she noticed he had a fat dollop of mustard on the napkin. A waitress came over and asked Jessica if she'd like some coffee.

"Please."

The waitresses placed a mug in front of her and filled it from a steaming pot. "Are you eating too, hon?"

Jessica smiled. "I sure am."

The waitress handed over a slim, leather-bound menu. Jessica didn't bother opening it. "What do you recommend, Zachary?" she said.

The lawyer looked up from his paper, startled. "Sorry. Do I know you?"

"You don't but I know quite a lot about you, Zachary. Or do you prefer Zach?"

"What the hell is going on?" demanded Dunne.

The waitress appeared to be amused by the exchange and reluctantly dragged herself away from the conversation to attend to another customer. "Holler when you're ready to order."

Jessica watched her go, then said, "We're going to have a little chat about your affair with Amanda Meyers."

"You're crazy." Dunne dropped his half-eaten sandwich onto the plate and folded the paper. Started to get up from the stool.

"Sit back down, Zachary," Jessica said. "And don't make a scene. Not unless you want me to make a call to Detective Valdez over in San Bernardino County and his colleagues at the LAPD. Tell them how you withheld some interesting information from them."

Dunne sat back down.

"Now, what do you recommend I order?" Jessica asked. "I don't like mustard, by the way."

"You're seriously asking me about a fucking sandwich?"

"Yes. I'm starving."

Dunne shook his head in disbelief. "The spicy pulled pork with BBQ sauce," he said through gritted teeth.

Jessica caught the waitress's eye and placed the order.

"Who are you?" Dunne asked. "What do you want from me?"

"I want you to tell me about the night Amanda disappeared."

Dunne's eyes narrowed. "You got something to do with that PI who showed at my office?"

Jessica didn't answer, just stared at him expectantly.

"I'll tell you what I told him. I don't know what happened the night Amanda disappeared."

"You were supposed to meet her at the motel."

"I don't know where you're getting your information from but you're dead wrong. I had no plans to meet Amanda that weekend."

"But you *were* having an affair."

Dunne twisted a gold pinky ring nervously. Didn't answer her. He didn't have to. The look on his face was confirmation enough.

"Amanda called you that night, didn't she?" Jessica asked.

"No, she didn't."

"Don't lie to me, Zachary."

"I'm not lying. I never spoke to her."

"I didn't say you spoke to her. I know she left you a voice message. Seemed to think you'd stood her up."

Dunne's eyes widened. He'd make a terrible poker player.

Jessica went on, "I don't think it would be too difficult for Valdez to pull the call records from the motel's payphone. And if he did, he'd find your number, wouldn't he?"

Dunne pulled the napkin from his collar, balled it, and tossed it onto the counter. He appeared to have lost his appetite. "Yes, Amanda left a voice message that night. Like you said, she seemed to think I'd let her down. But, I swear, I had no plans to meet her. I'd never even heard of that motel until after . . . what happened."

"Where were you that night?"

"I was having dinner with my wife and another couple at a restaurant in Beverlywood."

"Kind of hard to prove it now, after all this time."

"Not really. I paid for the meal and I always pay by card. I'll have the statement in my files at home."

Jessica nodded. "I guess the statement would prove *someone* used your card to pay for the meal."

Dunne twisted the ring again, tapped his fingers nervously on the counter. "I'm not quite sure what you're getting at. Yes, I was sleeping with Amanda. No, I wasn't with her at the motel."

Jessica noticed the pinky ring bore three symbols. Greek letters? "Is that a college fraternity ring?"

"Yes, it is."

"Where'd you go to school?"

Dunne held her gaze. "California Southern Law School."

Jessica's sandwich arrived, and she took a bite, and made an appreciative noise. "This is amazing. Good call, Zachary." She swallowed and took a sip of coffee. "So, you went straight to law school from high school? That's where the fraternity ring is from?"

He paused for a long moment. "No, I was also a student at The Palms University."

"Which is where?"

"It doesn't exist anymore. It closed permanently several years back."

"Where *was* it located?"

There was an even longer pause this time, followed by a sigh. "Twentynine Palms."

There it was—a solid connection between Dunne and Twentynine Palms. Jessica felt the familiar bubble of excitement that always accompanied a breakthrough in an investigation, no matter how small. She kept on playing it cool with Dunne even though she felt anything but cool. She knew she was on the right track.

"Here's the thing about being a private eye," Jessica said, licking BBQ sauce from her finger.

"What?" Dunne asked.

"You quickly learn there's no such thing as coincidences."

Jessica dropped the sandwich onto the plate and picked up her cell phone from where she'd placed it on the counter. She opened the camera function and snapped the ring on Dunne's pinky finger.

"What the hell do you think you're doing?" Little red spots of indignation popped out on each cheek.

Jessica ignored him, signaled for the waitress again. "Can I have the rest of the sandwich to go and the check, please?"

Back in the truck, she tapped out a text to Connor asking which college Terence Wilcox had attended as a star baseball player.

He answered almost immediately: I don't know the name but their motto was "Go Hawks!" and the sports teams' colors were blue and gold.

She sent another message: What about his tattoo? Do you remember which fraternity he belonged to?

Connor responded with three Greek words that meant nothing to her. She told him it was the symbols she was after.

Thirty seconds passed and then her cell phone pinged with another message. It was a photo of a paper napkin with a biro sketch of three Greek letters. He was probably in the "somewhere nice" Rae-Lynn had demanded he take her for lunch.

Jessica swiped from Connor's photo to the one she'd taken of Dunne's pinky ring.

The symbols were an exact match.

23

AMANDA—TWO YEARS AGO

Amanda pulled up in front of the Tranquility Motel and assumed there had been some kind of mistake.

This couldn't be right.

The place was a total dump. Well, not a dump exactly, but definitely not what she was expecting. It was a basic motel, exactly like a million other motels, in a million other towns. Why make the trip all the way out here for something so . . . basic? There was no hint of luxury whatsoever.

She checked the address Zach had sent her.

Twentynine Palms Highway.

It was the right place.

Amanda thought about turning back. But she'd just driven for three hours, and it was dark now, and a weekend away from Victor Heights, and the prying eyes of Mrs. DuBois, was, admittedly, more appealing than a TV boxset and bottle of wine on her own. At least the motel had a pool, according to the sign, and she'd packed a bottle of Veuve Clicquot in a cooler so it wasn't a complete disaster. She'd insist Zach take her someplace nice for dinner tomorrow night, assuming there were any decent restaurants nearby.

She swapped her driving sneakers for the Louboutins sitting on the passenger seat and went into the office to pick up the room key from a fat guy who was eating a bucket of fried chicken and watching TV. Amanda wondered again what the hell Zach was thinking suggesting this dump. The Tranquility was hardly the fucking Waldorf Astoria. Maybe it had looked a lot nicer on the website but still.

Amanda got back into the Maserati and found the private parking behind room 25. Zach was being really paranoid if he seriously thought anyone would recognize either of their cars way out here in the middle of nowhere. She climbed out of the sports car onto the dirt and felt another stab of irritation. If her shoes got ruined, Zach had better buy her a new pair. She opened the trunk and pulled out her overnight bag and the cooler and made her way to the room.

It was unimpressive to say the least. Twin queen beds with old-fashioned floral covers and crap art on the wall, if you could even call it art. It was already after nine. Zach should be here any minute. After hanging up her clothes, and placing her toiletries in the bathroom, Amanda popped open the champagne. Wrinkled her nose at the thought of pouring it into a motel tumbler instead of a proper flute.

She sat on one of the beds and sipped the fizz and waited. Twenty minutes passed. There was a loud clunk from right outside the room where the Maserati was parked.

Zach.

Finally.

Amanda opened the door, champagne in hand. "Zach, is that you?" There was no response. She tottered to the end of the building, the shoes pinching at her feet. Leaned on the wall for support and peeked around the corner. "Zach?"

All she could see was the sleek silhouette of the Maserati in the darkness. No sign of Zach's BMW. Amanda had the weird feeling she wasn't alone. She shivered and went back inside. By 10 p.m., she was onto her second glass of champagne and had decided to phone Zach to find out where the hell he was.

No cell signal.

Great.

Amanda kicked off the designer heels and slipped on her driving sneakers, stormed past the other twenty-four rooms and the motel office, all the way to the side of the highway to see if she could pick up a signal there. She held up the cell phone and waved it around but those little signal bars refused to appear on the screen. Headlights rushed in her direction and she watched the traffic, hoping for sight of Zach's car, expecting him to be full of apologies for being so late. Forget simple apologies; he'd really need to make it up to her now.

Back in room 25, Amanda finished the champagne. At ten forty-five, she'd had enough. It was now blatantly obvious what had happened. Zach had blown her off for Stephanie after his wife had insisted they do something this weekend. And Zach had given in, as usual, despite his so-called business trip. He had stood Amanda up. Left her out here, on her own in a dive of a motel in the middle of the desert, like a fucking idiot.

Amanda no longer gave a damn about their rule about not using Zach's cell phone outside of work hours. She was pissed, and a little drunk, and she was finished with Zachary Dunne. After using the office payphone to leave a furious voicemail, Amanda angrily dumped her stuff into her overnight bag and got into the car. She wasn't really sober enough to drive, and it'd be around 2 a.m. before she made it home, but she couldn't face another minute at the Tranquility Motel.

The Maserati hadn't even reached the highway when it became apparent something was wrong. There was a weird noise coming from the car and the ride was nowhere near as smooth as it should be. Once on the highway, she picked up speed and the noise got louder and she could feel a strange juddering sensation beneath her.

Shit.

Lights flashed in her rearview and she panicked. A DUI would be a disaster for her career prospects. But it wasn't a cop. A young guy behind the wheel of a dark pick-up was gesturing for her to pull over. Amanda did so and the truck did likewise. The man got out and made his way toward her. She buzzed down the window and leaned out. He was gorgeous. Fair hair and blue eyes and a great body. A wedding ring too, unfortunately. Too bad.

"Looks like your rear wheel is loose," he told her. "I was worried it was going to come off completely and you'd end up badly hurt."

"Shit," she said. "I hadn't realized. It was fine earlier."

"Do you have a manufacturer's torque wrench in your trunk? I could try to fix it for you."

"I don't think so. I'm not sure I even know what that is."

"Short lug wrench?"

Amanda gave him an apologetic smile. "Sorry, I don't think I have any sort of toolkit."

"There's a twenty-four-hour auto repair shop about a mile and a half from here. I'll give them a call." He produced his cell phone from his jacket pocket. "Ah, shoot. No signal. You?"

Amanda checked her own phone. "Nope."

"I could stop by the auto shop myself and ask them to send someone out. But it could take a while and I don't feel too good about leaving you out here on your own, so late at night, with no cell phone signal."

"I'm sure I'll be fine. I'll keep the car doors locked."

"I don't know . . ." He ran his hand through his hair. "I don't want to scare you but it's a beautiful car and there have been some instances of armed car-jacking out here recently."

Amanda's eyebrows shot up. "Really? Shit."

"I'm afraid so. Why don't I drop you at the auto shop and you can ride back to your car with the mechanic once they have one available? Would that work?"

"I wouldn't want to cause you any inconvenience."

"Will take me two minutes to move the baby seat from the passenger seat to the flatbed and then we're good to go. I was heading in that direction anyway."

Amanda didn't have any better options. She was lucky this Good Samaritan, this gorgeous husband and dad, had stopped to help her out. "Only if you're sure?"

"I'm sure. It'll make me feel a whole lot better knowing you're safe. A pretty woman out in the desert on her own . . ." The man shook his head, didn't finish the sentence. He didn't have to. Amanda got the picture.

She stepped out of the Maserati and stood by the side of the highway in her dress and driving sneakers. There was a sliver of moonlight and a lot of stars but the night still felt ominously dark. A firm wind had gotten up and lashed at her hair and exposed flesh. Dirt got in her mouth. She rubbed her arms, and silently cursed Zach yet again, as the Good Samaritan moved the baby seat from the cab to the back of the truck.

He held open the passenger door. "All yours."

Amanda got in, fastened the seatbelt, and held her cold fingers in front of the heater vents. "How far did you say the auto repair shop was from here?" She wanted nothing more than to snuggle under the covers of her own bed in Victor Heights.

The man pressed a button and the door locks snapped into place with a loud click. The sound seemed amplified in the enclosed space. "We're not going to the auto shop, Amanda. We're going someplace else."

Amanda's head whipped round and her heart punched her ribcage. "How'd you know my name? I didn't tell you my name."

Then she noticed he was holding something. The metal glinted in the pale moonlight shining through the windscreen, illuminating the truck's cab.

The man said, "It'll be better for us both if you don't struggle."

24

DEA—1990

Two Fridays had passed since the incident in the parking lot and there'd been no sign of the cute guy back in the bar.

Thankfully, Merv hadn't had the front to show his face at the Desert Heart either. Didn't mean Dea wasn't nervous each night she finished a shift, though. The first couple times, she'd made some sort of excuse for Diltz to walk her to her car.

By the third weekend, Dea had begun to relax, felt sure Merv had found someplace else to get lit and aggressive on a Friday night. But she'd also all but given up hope of seeing her knight in tan chinos and red shining sports jacket again. Was surprised by just how disappointed she was by the thought.

She crouched down to stack the shelf below the counter with clean glassware, while Diltz served another customer at the other end of the bar. When she stood up, Cute Guy was right in front of her, a big grin on his face.

"Hey there," he said.

"Oh, hi," she said, trying to come off all casual and not break into a smile of her own.

"How're you doing?"

"I'm good, thanks."

He lowered his voice. "Any more trouble?"

Dea hadn't told Diltz what happened with Merv, didn't want her boss thinking she wasn't capable of being left in the bar on her own. She appreciated Cute Guy's discretion, figured it was real thoughtful of him.

"No, none at all," she said. "Thanks again."

"Any time. Although, hopefully there won't be a next time."

Dea smiled. "I think Merv got the message loud and clear. Pabst?"

"You got it. Can I order some food too? Same as before."

"You want the regular portion?"

"No, the larger one."

"Even though it beat you last time?"

He laughed. "I'm willing to give it another go. What's an extra dollar, right?"

She poured his beer—not too much frothy foam—and placed it on the counter. "I'd give you the drink on the house as a thank you but"—she inclined her head towards Diltz—"the boss is in tonight and I don't think he'd be too pleased about me handing out freebies."

"Your smile is reward enough." He shook his head, embarrassed. "Sorry, I can't believe I just said that. Talk about the corniest line ever."

"I like corny. I'll bring your food over when it's ready."

Later, Dea noticed he'd left almost half the meal once again while clearing away the plate. "Beat again?"

"Looks like it. I hope it doesn't lower your opinion of me."

Dea took the plate out back, made sure there was no sign of Diltz, then finished off the leftovers. The Desert Heart sure did some good-ass food. When she headed back out front, the cute guy was waiting at the bar again.

"Another beer?" she asked.

"Please." He hesitated. "And I wanted to ask you something."

"Sounds intriguing," she said, working the beer tap.

"I don't suppose you're free next Saturday night?"

Heat rushed to Dea's face and she overfilled the beer schooner. Was he asking her out on a date? She wiped down the schooner and placed it on the rubber drinks mat in front of him.

"Um, I don't know. Why?"

Cute Guy lowered his voice again, like he'd done before. "I can pay you five hundred bucks for the whole night."

Dea blinked, stunned. "*What?*" she hissed. "I'm not a fucking hooker. Now take your beer and get away from me or you'll end up wearing it."

The cute guy's face turned as red as his sports jacket. "Shit, no! That's not what I meant at all. Fuck. That came out all wrong. I was offering a shift payment to serve drinks at a party."

He looked over at the other end of the bar and Dea followed his gaze. Diltz was watching the conversation with interest. Cute Guy said, "Can we talk about this someplace more private?"

"I don't think that's such a good idea." Dea still wasn't convinced by his explanation.

"I swear I wasn't offering to pay you for sex. Just hear me out. Please."

"My break isn't for another half hour."

"I'll wait."

Dea sighed. "Okay. Just don't make me regret it."

Thirty minutes later, she caught the cute guy's eye, and gave a slight nod toward the exit. He got up from his stool at the beer barrel, his usual spot under the number plates, and grabbed a matchbook from a bowl on the bar and made his way outside.

Dea waited a full minute then told Diltz she was taking her break. "I'm going to step outside for a breath of fresh air, if that's okay?"

Diltz threw a pointed look at the door, where Cute Guy had walked through. "Everything okay, Dea? Seemed like you were having kind of an intense conversation earlier."

Diltz was all long hair and tattoos and bandanas but he was as harmless as a puppy. He was about two decades older than Dea and, even though she wasn't a kid, he knew a bit about her home situation, seemed to feel some sort of obligation to look out for her. A kind of father figure trying to make up for the absence of her real dad.

"Everything's fine, Freddy. Really. He's a nice guy." Dea felt the blush start at her cheeks and creep all the way down her neck to her chest.

"A nice guy, huh? Well, he'd better be. And he'd better be a fast talker too, because you only got ten minutes. Place is filling up now."

Outside, Cute Guy was staring out at the highway, watching the traffic going by, smoking a cigarette. He turned as she approached. "You came out. I wasn't sure you would."

"I don't have long."

"D'you smoke?"

"Only when someone else is supplying the cigarettes. It's an expensive habit."

He held out the pack and Dea took one. She placed it between her lips. He snapped a match from the matchbook, struck it, and she leaned in toward his cupped hand as he lit the cigarette. Dea thought he smelled good. Expensive cologne and soap. Nice and fresh. Not like old Merv.

"Tell me about this party," she said.

"It's in a big house, not far from here."

"So, a house party?"

"Yes, kind of."

"Do you live in the house?"

"I do, along with some other folks."

"And it's going to be an all-night party?"

"It'll definitely be a late one. Or early one, depending on how you look at it. There'll be a poker game going on. I thought it'd be cool if you served the drinks."

"Why me?"

"You're good at serving drinks. And you look amazing while you're doing it."

Dea was glad it was dark so he couldn't see her cheeks flush, just as they had done when Diltz had teased her about Cute Guy. "I don't know . . ."

"It's easy money. All you have to do is wear a nice dress and keep everyone's glasses topped off at the poker table. Simple."

"I don't own any nice dresses."

"Let me buy you one. Size two, right? How about red? You like red? I know you suit it. I remember the red satin blouse you wore one night."

"You don't have to buy me a dress." Dea sounded a little more defensive than she meant to.

"I know I don't but I want to. I want you to have nice things, Dea."

"You know my name?" she asked, surprised.

"Sure I do. Dea, pronounced like the letter that comes after C in the alphabet. I can pay you half tonight and the rest at the party when I get more cash from my housemates."

Dea finished the cigarette, crushed the butt into the dirt beneath the sole of her sandal. "I'd need to think about it. I don't even know your name."

"You have a pen?"

Dea patted her jeans pockets. Came up with a lipstick and an eyeliner pencil. Gave him the eyeliner. He opened the matchbook and scribbled on the plain cardboard inside. Handed the matchbook to her and closed her hands around it. Her skin tingled at his touch.

"My name and the number you can reach me on. Think it over and give me a call."

Then he flicked the cigarette butt away in a burst of tiny orange sparks and walked off toward the highway.

25

JESSICA

Zachary Dunne was right. The Palms University had closed permanently fifteen years ago due to falling enrolment numbers.

Even so, Jessica was able to confirm the school's motto had been "*Go Hawks!*" on account of their mascot, Hal the Hawk, which Jessica thought was possibly one of the worst mascot names she'd ever heard. The sports teams' colors were blue and gold, just as Connor had said.

Jessica began a new text, this time to Renee Simmonds, asking her to send over a contact number for her husband.

Renee: Jessica, great to hear from you! Any news about Laurie?

Jessica: I'm following up some leads. Nothing definite yet. Would be good to speak to Trey . . .

Renee: Of course. Trey will be at the office. Attaching his direct line and cell phone number.

Jessica waited for the attachment to drop, then clicked on the office number and waited for the call to connect.

"This is Trey Simmonds." He sounded wary, probably unused to unknown callers having access to his direct line.

"Mr. Simmonds, it's Jessica Shaw. I met you at the party at your house."

"The private investigator. I remember. What can I do for you, Miss Shaw? Have you tracked down my daughter?"

Jessica felt bad about raising his hopes. "I'm afraid we still don't know Laurie's whereabouts. But I do have some more questions for you, if that's okay?"

"Yep, shoot. What do you want to know?"

"Where did you attend college or university? And were you ever a member of a fraternity?"

"Huh? I'm sorry, I don't understand. What does my educational background have to do with finding my daughter?"

"I appreciate these questions may seem a little strange but your answers could help to establish a further connection between Laurie and the other two missing women."

Simmonds sounded angry now. "I already told you, there *is* no connection between Laurie and those other women. I don't know why they vanished and, to be perfectly honest, I don't really care. They have nothing to do with my daughter."

Jessica pressed on, undeterred. "Amanda Meyers' lover and Mallory Wilcox's husband were both members of the same fraternity at The Palms University. Do you know either of those men? Their names are Zachary Dunne and Terence Wilcox."

"I've never heard of them."

"Did you attend The Palms University? Were you a member of the school's fraternity?"

"This is ridiculous. I said from the get-go I was against hiring strangers to snoop into my daughter's business. I warned Renee it was a mistake—and I was right. You people are nothing but leeches, preying on grieving families, taking their money."

"Mr. Simmonds, I was just—"

"Consider your contract terminated with immediate effect."

"With all due respect, Mr. Simmonds, our contract is with your wife. Not you."

"With all due respect, Miss Shaw, I'm the one paying for this farce of an investigation. I'll deal with Renee. But, right now, I'm ordering you to drop your interest in me and my daughter."

Simmonds ended the call.

Jessica stared at the phone, taken aback by what had just happened. She opened the web browser and found his biography on his company's website.

She didn't know if he'd ever been a member of a fraternity.

But right there, on the tiny screen, was confirmation that Trey Simmonds had majored in Business, and minored in Economics, at The Palms University.

Jessica stood at the end of Venice Pier, drinking a beer and watching a fireball sun slide into the Pacific Ocean. The perfect moment was ruined by the sound of Connor's voice behind her.

"You do know you're not allowed to drink alcohol on the pier?"

Jessica didn't turn to face him. "What're you going to do? Fine me?"

"No, but the cops might."

Jessica shrugged, took a defiant swallow of Bud Light. It wasn't her first bottle of the evening and it wouldn't be her last.

Connor leaned on the pier railing next to her. "I could've done with some Dutch courage myself before coming out here to speak to you."

"How'd you find me?"

"It's what I do."

"Yeah, tracking me down when I don't want you to is becoming a bad habit of yours. What do you want?"

"I owe you an explanation. About Rae-Lynn."

"Save it. I'm not interested. You're a liar, Connor. That's all I need to know."

"It's not that simple, Jessica. Believe me, I never set out to hurt you."

Jessica spun around to face him. "Is that so? You know what? Maybe I *am* interested in what you've got to say for yourself. Please, feel free to explain why it's so goddamn hard for you to be straight with me."

"Jessica . . ."

"Why didn't you tell me you were engaged? Why the hell did you kiss me knowing you were with someone else?"

"I was going to tell you about Rae-Lynn. I guess I was waiting for the right moment. As for the kiss . . . I don't know . . ." He shrugged helplessly.

"You don't know?"

"Okay, I wanted to kiss you. I've been wanting to kiss you since you first showed up at Larry's bar a few nights ago. Yes, I knew it was wrong. But you wanted the truth. Now you have it."

Jessica shook her head. "How long have you and Rae-Lynn been together?"

"Almost six months."

"I'm assuming you picked her up at the Tahiti Club? The place where we . . ." Jessica couldn't bring herself to finish the sentence. Just the fact that "their place" was a back alley behind a strip club said it all about how fucked up Jessica and Connor's relationship really was.

"I met her in the Tahiti Club, yes. You had left town. Or so I thought. I didn't think I'd ever see you again."

"Oh, so it's my fault? I forced you into the arms of a stripper?" She was shouting now.

"Jessica, please. Can you keep your voice down?" Connor glanced around the pier and Jessica followed his gaze. A young couple, holding hands, were pretending not to eavesdrop. A grungy guy, with long greasy blond hair and a hipster beard, stood nearby fishing.

"She sounded Southern."

"Yes, Texas."

"Stripper name?"

A sigh. "Miss Lone-Star."

"Oh, how appropriately cute."

"Whatever you think of me, Rae-Lynn is a good person. She's not at fault here."

Jessica's cheeks burned. He was right. Hating on the woman was wrong. Jessica had no problem with exotic dancers and certainly didn't judge their choice of career. Plus, he'd lied to his fiancée too. It was Connor she was mad at, not Rae-Lynn.

"How long have you been engaged?"

"A few months."

"Wow, so you were sending drunken texts to me not long after popping the question to someone else? Real classy, Connor."

"I didn't pop the question. We were in Vegas. We'd both been drinking. I got a big win in the poker room at the Bellagio. I told Rae-Lynn I wanted to buy her something special in the Tiffany store. I meant a bracelet or a necklace. I guess she misunderstood and picked out a diamond ring. I just kind of went with it."

Jessica laughed bitterly. "Well, at least you didn't wake up with a hangover and a bunch of photos from a Little White Chapel wedding with Elvis conducting the ceremony."

Connor didn't laugh. "I don't love her, Jessica."

"I don't want to hear it," Jessica snapped. "You keep that shit to yourself, do you hear me? It's no business of mine."

"You're wrong. It is."

Jessica shook her head. She finished the beer, walked over to a trash receptacle and dropped the empty bottle inside with a clatter. Connor followed her.

"Trey Simmonds fired us," she said. "Zachary Dunne and Terence Wilcox were members of the same fraternity and both attended the same college—which just happened to be right next to Twentynine Palms. A definite connection, by association, between Amanda and Mallory. Simmonds didn't take too kindly to me asking if he fit the pattern too. Spoiler alert—he does."

"So, he fired us?" Connor asked incredulously. "Why? I mean, this is great work, Jessica. Our first real breakthrough in the case. Further evidence of a connection between the missing women other than their last known whereabouts. It makes no sense that Simmonds would want us off the case now."

"I guess he doesn't like private eyes who, you know, do their jobs and ask questions."

"Shit." Connor ran his fingers through his hair in frustration and sighed. "I guess that's that, then."

"What does that mean?" Jessica asked sharply.

"It means, if we're off the payroll, there's not a whole lot we can do about it."

"What happened to finding out the truth no matter what? We're supposed to just forget about Laurie and Amanda and Mallory?"

"Jessica, we're not a pro bono agency. We can't afford to be. There are other cases to work on, other clients who are paying for our services."

She fixed him with a hard stare. "So, we *are* still working together? You've not fired me too?"

"Of course not. If you're happy for us to continue working together, I'm cool with it."

"I'll work with you, but I'll never trust you again."

He reached out a hand to touch her arm. "You can trust me, Jessica."

Jessica shrugged him off. "You're about as trustworthy as a TV evangelist. And you don't get to touch me ever again."

"I'm really sorry you feel like that."

"Well, I do. I'll see you tomorrow."

"Where are you going?"

"I'm going to get drunk. You're not invited."

As Jessica began the long walk along the pier, the beach and restaurants and hotels ahead of her in the distance began to blur. She quickened her pace, tried to get as far away from Connor as she could, before the tears began to fall.

26

BURDEN

Students swarmed noisily out of the photography class in groups of two and three and four. Burden waited patiently until he spotted Cara before making his move.

When she eventually appeared, she was trailing behind the others on her own, engrossed in her class notes. She wore jeans and a tight brown tee with "'U2" in a retro yellow and orange print. Maybe she wanted her classmates to believe she was younger than she actually was.

Burden approached her. Anticipation made his skin tingle.

"Excuse me, is this the photography class?"

She looked up from the pages and brushed her bangs out of her eyes. "Um, yeah, it is." She seemed distracted, probably still trying to process what she'd just learned in class. He admired her dedication.

Burden felt like he knew Cara Zelenka intimately by now but it was the first time he'd actually spoken to her, the closest he'd ever gotten to her. Mixed in with her perfume was her own intoxicating scent that he'd noticed while inside her apartment. He felt like electricity was charging through his veins.

"Cool," he said, more calmly than he felt. "I'm in the creative writing class." He jutted a thumb behind him vaguely in the direction of some nearby classrooms. Gave her a friendly smile. "I was hoping someone from your class might be able to help me out."

"Okay . . ." Cara had a wary look about her now, like she thought he might be trying to hit on her.

Burden had washed his hair for the first time in days, and shaved off the hipster beard, and lost the middle-aged spread padding. He was dressed casually, but fashionably, in blue jeans and a t-shirt and designer trainers. His skin was lightly tanned and his teeth were white. A couple of the women from Cara's class were whispering and giggling and glancing over their shoulders at him in an indiscreet way. He knew he was attractive. He also knew he wasn't Cara's type. Seduction wasn't going to work this time. He moved quickly to put her at ease.

"I need to hire a photographer urgently for a photo shoot. It's a cash in hand job seeing as it's such short notice. I was hoping one of you guys could help me out."

She stuffed her notes into her bag. "I might be able to help." Now he had her full attention. "What kind of shoot is it?"

He indicated for them to move to a quieter spot further down the hallway, away from the noisy throng.

"It's an engagement shoot," he said. "I know, I know. They're kind of corny but my fiancée, Summer, has her heart set on one. Anyway, I booked us a photographer—someone recommended by a coworker—and I've just found out the guy can't do it anymore. I don't want to tell Summer he's cancelled at the last minute. She's already stressing big time about the wedding planning as it is and she'll freak out if she finds out the shoot is off."

"Yeah, I can imagine," Cara said, with a sympathetic smile.

He pulled his cell phone from his jeans pocket and swiped through some photos. Held up one, a stock photo of a woman on a beach that he'd found on Google Images. "This is Summer. Gorgeous, isn't she?" He laughed. "I think so anyway but I'm totally biased, of course."

Cara smiled, started to relax. The first rule of putting people at ease, Burden had discovered, was to convince them you were normal, that you were just like them. Pretty fiancée, popular with coworkers, nice to look at. Most people had ridiculous preconceptions about what dangerous folk were supposed to be like—and it didn't include any of the above.

He said, "The thing is, I need a replacement photographer—and I need one fast. It's a pretty simple job. Just take some shots of the happy couple looking, well, happy in a pretty setting."

"I'm not a professional," Cara said. "You know this is a class for beginners, right? But I'm sure I could manage what you're asking for. You want to see some of my work?"

"Sure, I'd love to."

She produced her own cell phone from her bag and tapped on the Instagram app. Handed the phone to Burden. "You can scroll through the feed for a mix of portraiture, both posed and candid, as well as landscape shots in and around LA."

Burden dutifully swiped through the Instagram feed, as though he hadn't already seen every one of those photos a million times. They weren't great but he nodded appreciatively as he pretended to study them. Handed the phone back.

"Those are great," he said. "You interested in the gig, then?"

"You mentioned cash in hand. How much?"

Direct and to the point. No messing around. He was beginning to like her even more.

"I can pay you five hundred bucks. One-fifty now and the rest after the shoot." He laughed. "You know, just to make sure you show up. Does that sound fair?"

Cara pretended to think about. He knew there was zero chance of her refusing the job if it meant getting her grandmother's ring back. "Yeah, I think that's doable. Depends when you'd need me though."

Burden pretended to hesitate. "That's the thing. It's tomorrow afternoon."

"I can do tomorrow. Where's the shoot taking place?"

"That's the other thing. It's a bit of a distance away. But I can give you the cash for gas right now, and I'll also throw in lunch too."

"Sounds good to me."

Burden smiled gratefully, as though she'd just agreed to do him the biggest favor. "Fantastic. Summer really loves the idea of a shoot in the desert."

"Whereabouts in the desert?"

"Joshua Tree National Park. Out by the Twentynine Palms Highway."

27

JESSICA

She was dreaming of a vast desert, and a bright white moon, and so many stars it would take a lifetime to count them all.

He was there with her, his arms around her. It felt good and it felt right. Even as it was happening, Jessica was aware, on some level, that she was dreaming. Real life was never this perfect.

Click.

She told herself the noise was part of the dream. Tried desperately to stay in the desert with the moon and the stars and him. She didn't want to wake up just yet. Somewhere deep in her subconscious, she knew the hangover was already starting to kick in. Her mouth was as dry as the desert sand and the familiar throbbing was starting behind her eyes. She didn't want to face reality just yet.

A faint breeze tickled her face. Just part of the dream, she told herself.

Click.

This time reality smashed into the dream like a wrecking ball.

She wasn't out in the desert.

She was in a motel room in Venice.

And someone was in the room with her.

She could feel their presence. Hear them breathing. She didn't want to open her eyes.

You're imagining things, Jessica. You had too much to drink, is all. You're alone. You're safe. There's no one else here.

Jessica opened her eyes. The room was washed in red and blue from the neon sign outside her window. She must have forgotten to pull the curtains closed when she'd returned to the motel. She could hear the buzz of the neon light and the faint fizz of the soda in the can on the dresser. And she could still hear the slow, steady breathing of someone else.

Slowly, she turned from her side onto her back.

A figure in black stood at the end of the bed. He wore a ski mask and gloves and he was holding a gun.

"Don't scream," he said quietly.

Her mouth was even drier now. Her throat constricted so tight with fear, she almost couldn't breathe. Jessica couldn't have screamed even if she wanted to. Instinctively, her hand reached for the dresser where she kept the Glock. She knocked over the soda can. The gun wasn't there.

"You left your gun in your bag," the man said. "Same as you left the curtains open and the security chain unlatched. Very sloppy. You need to be sharp, Jessica, not sloppy."

Jessica.

He knew her name.

What did he want with her?

Was he going to rob her?

Rape her?

Shoot her?

Jessica was suddenly aware that all she was wearing was a thin t-shirt and underwear. She pulled her knees up to her chest and the bedsheet up to her chin. Pressed herself against the headboard and tried to put as much distance as possible between herself and the intruder.

"What do you want?" Her voice was thick with fear and last night's booze. "What are you going to do to me?"

Her fists gripped the bedsheet tighter.

"I'm not going to touch you," he said calmly. "I'm not one of those men. But I will shoot you if I have to. If you don't do as I tell you."

Jessica's heart raced like she'd just sunk ten energy drinks, pounded so hard against her chest she was sure the figure in black must be able to hear it. Her head swam. Sweat dampened her brow and lay slick on her upper lip. She felt like she was going to pass out.

"Breathe," the man said.

She did as she was told. Drank in big lungfuls of air until her head began to clear and her heart rate dropped to a less critical level. Her brain began to register some details. Pale eyes visible through the slits in the ski mask. Tall. Muscular. A young voice she didn't recognize. She guessed the man was in his thirties or forties.

"What do you want?" she repeated.

"I want to give you something."

"Huh? What do you want to give me?"

"Close your eyes and hold out your hand."

She stared at him. "What? Are you serious?"

"Just do as I say."

Jessica closed her eyes and held out her right hand. She felt him place a small object onto her open palm and close it into a fist. It was cool and smooth with sharp corners that dug into her skin.

"Keep your eyes closed. Count to one hundred slowly. Don't open your eyes until you're done or I'll put a bullet in your head. And remember what I said—you need to be sharp, not sloppy."

She began to count in her head.

"Out loud."

"One. Two. Three. Four. Five."

Jessica kept on counting. She could hear the spilled soda dripping onto the wooden floor. When she reached twenty, she felt the cool night breeze on her flushed cheeks, followed by a soft click. She shivered. She thought—*hoped*—he was gone but didn't dare look in case he was still there, at the foot of the bed, testing her, gloved finger on the trigger.

She kept on counting, her hand still outstretched, her fingers growing damp around the small object in her grasp.

"Ninety-eight. Ninety-nine. One hundred."

Jessica opened her eyes and blinked.

The red and blue neon outside the window was all that illuminated the gloomy surroundings. She looked around warily, terrified the man in black would still be there, hidden in a dark corner of the room.

She was alone.

Slowly, she opened her hand, like a flower in bloom opening its petals. Her fingers trembled. She studied the item the intruder had given her and frowned in confusion. "What the hell?"

It made no sense at all.

28

LAURIE—TWO MONTHS AGO

They called Indio the "City of Festivals"—and Randal had just given Laurie a VIP pass for one of the biggest and best. For two whole days.

She rushed back to her apartment on Speedway to pack for the surprise weekend away after the unexpected meeting with Randal on the beach. She wheeled the smallest suitcase from the luggage trio—all three of which hardly ever got used—out of the closet by the front door into the living room and unzipped it. Then she set about grabbing all the things she'd need. Some toiletries from the bathroom, perfume from the dresser, an armful of clothes.

As she folded the dress and skirt and tank tops into the suitcase, Laurie had a sudden, crushing, moment of doubt.

She'd never been to the festival before but knew it was almost as famous for its fashion as it was for the line-up of bands and singers. Instagram would be flooded with pouting, picture-perfect selfies of young women whose stylish outfits would be accessorized by flat bellies and big lips and hair extensions and designer handbags. Her own clothes would seem cheap and tacky in comparison. What if she embarrassed Randal in front of his important New York art contacts? What if they were expecting one of those Instagram girls?

Laurie shook her head. "Just chill, would you?" she said out loud.

She'd met Randal twice now. He knew exactly how she dressed and wouldn't have invited her if he thought she wasn't cool enough. Anyway, she had a pretty cool accessory herself—the VIP wristband.

She carried the case downstairs and laid it flat in the back of her orange-and-white camper van. Went back upstairs to the apartment and into her studio. Randal had told her to bring her two best paintings and Laurie knew exactly which ones to choose. Like most of the others, they were Venice beach scenes depicted in vibrant slashes of color. But they'd both been the outcome of an unforgettable weekend of insomnia where she had been consumed by an almost feverish passion to spill her emotions onto the canvas after a particularly upsetting fight with her parents over money.

To Laurie, both pieces stood out from the others as a result of their sheer intensity and she was sure Randal and his associates would be able to appreciate how much she had poured her heart and soul into them. They were also larger works, five grand apiece, and the thought of making $10,000 gave her goosebumps. She carefully wrapped them in brown paper and made two further trips to the van with the paintings.

As she climbed in behind the wheel, Laurie briefly considered telling Elizabeth the truth about her plans. She'd messaged her earlier to say she had stuff to do and wouldn't be around in the afternoon, which was technically not a lie but not exactly the whole truth either. But she knew Randal was right when he'd suggested keeping quiet about the festival. He only had one spare pass and Elizabeth would be pissed if she knew she was being left to look after the shop alone while Laurie was off someplace enjoying herself. Especially after her friend's reaction to Randal's interest in Laurie at the art fair.

Laurie also decided against telling her folks about her plans. There had been more arguments than usual lately about her mom still treating her like a little kid when she'd be twenty-four soon. Laurie fired off a text saying she was super-busy with work and would call her mom tomorrow. Then she downloaded some songs by artists who would be playing the main stage onto her iPhone to get her in the mood, lit the remainder of the joint from earlier, and set off for the high desert.

She'd arranged to meet Randal at a motel out by Twentynine Palms Highway, where he had booked a bunch of rooms for Laurie, himself and his contacts. Everyone wanted to have a good time at the festival, Randal had told her, but they were less enthusiastic about spending two nights at a campsite.

"Remember, we're all old compared to you," he'd said with a self-deprecating smile. "I'm sure the guys will be up for a few beers and some pot too—wink, wink—but all-night parties might be pushing it. Don't worry, you won't have to drive until you head home on Sunday. I've arranged for a car to shuttle us between the motel and the festival both days."

Laurie was secretly glad she'd be sleeping in a comfy bed and would have access to a hot shower each morning. She'd never been a fan of camping.

The plan was to showcase her paintings to the potential buyers at the motel, hopefully conclude some business, and then head on over to Indio to catch the early evening acts and celebrate a successful transaction.

Laurie felt a tingle of excitement as she took the exit for the Tranquility Motel. She drove to the end of the block of rooms, as instructed by Randal. There would be a dirt lot around the back of the building with more than enough space for her van. She was surprised to find him standing by his truck in the lot waiting for her, rather than in his room. Laurie got out of the van and Randal gave her a quick, unexpected hug. She guessed he was starting to think of them as friends now.

"I saw your van coming along the highway from my room window," he explained. "Thought I'd better head on out and help you with your luggage and paintings."

"This is a fantastic motel," she said, sliding open the side door of the camper. "So much character."

"It's great, isn't it. I just knew you'd love it."

"The paintings are pretty big," she said. "I'll climb in back and pass them out to you one at a time, okay?"

Laurie turned around when Randal didn't answer. He was standing right behind her now, far too close. His smile was gone. He was holding something in his hand.

He plunged it into her flesh before she could scream for help.

29

JESSICA

Jessica was still shaken by the night-time intrusion when she arrived at the detective agency the next morning.

Connor was at his desk, tapping away noisily on his computer keyboard. "Morning, Jessica," he said a little too brightly, clearly trying to pretend yesterday's clash on the pier hadn't happened.

"Good morning," Jessica mumbled as she sat down at her work area at the conference table and fired up her laptop. She could feel him watching her.

"Heavy night? How's the head?"

"What?" she snapped.

Connor held up his hands in defense. "I was just going to offer you some painkillers if you have a headache. That's all."

Jessica realized he thought the dark circles under her eyes, and the lack of color in her cheeks, and the tremble in her hands were all down to a bad hangover.

"I'm fine."

She'd already decided not to tell Connor about the intruder. It would feel like she was confiding in him, confessing to her vulnerability, opening herself up to smothering concern that she could really do without.

"You sure? You don't look too good."

"Gee, thanks."

"Sorry, that's not what I meant."

"My head is absolutely fine," she lied. The truth was, she felt like Ringo Starr and Chad Smith were having a drum-off inside her skull. "In fact, my head is clearer now than it has been in months, now that I know exactly where I stand. How's Rae-Lynn, by the way?"

Connor didn't answer. He pulled two files from the stack on his in-tray and walked over to the conference table. Dropped the files in front of Jessica. "These cases just came in. Take your pick."

"What are they?"

"Surveillance and background check or infidelity investigation."

"Infidelity investigation? Really?" She raised an eyebrow.

"Yes."

"I want to keep working the Laurie Simmonds case."

If she'd been reluctant to drop the case before, the motel intruder—and the purpose of his visit—meant it was now out of the question. She thought about the item he'd placed in her hand. An old matchbook from a bar in Twentynine Palms. Jessica needed to understand the significance of that matchbook and why he'd given it to her.

Connor slipped into the seat facing her. "Jessica, we spoke about this already. It's not happening. Renee has been in touch. She's officially terminated the contract. Trey has pulled the plug on the funding."

"I can't just give up on those women. Not when I feel like I'm getting somewhere with the investigation."

"I'm not running a charity, Jessica. I have bills to pay." He tapped the two files on the desk. "We have other, paying, clients to think of."

"Let me work the Simmonds case in my own time."

"No."

"Why not?"

"I don't think Trey Simmonds would be too pleased to find out you're still snooping around in his and Laurie's affairs."

"He doesn't have to know."

"I don't know, Jessica . . . I don't like it."

"Do you care about what happened to those women or not?"

"Of course I do."

"So, let me work it. If the shit does hit the fan, I'll take full responsibility, say you knew nothing about it."

Connor sighed, resigned. "Okay. But you give priority to our paying clients. Deal?"

"Deal."

"Which case do you want?" he asked, indicating the two files still sitting unopened on the desk in front of Jessica.

"Background check and surveillance," she said. "Seems to me spotting lying, cheating douchebags isn't my forte."

Connor stood, picked up the infidelity investigation folder, and returned to his desk.

"Oh, and Connor?"

"Yes, Jessica?"

"I'll need your notes on the Simmonds case."

"Right."

He went over to a filing cabinet, unlocked it, and opened the middle drawer. Thumbed through the files and pulled out a folder. Crossed the room and handed it to her. She made a point of setting it to one side and opening the background check and surveillance case file.

"You want a coffee?" he asked.

"Please." Jessica opened the folder. "And a couple of Advil."

Connor started to speak. Jessica held up her hand. "Don't say a word, okay?" She heard him chuckling as he made his way to the kitchenette. "Asshole," she muttered. Figured she was right about what the "A" in MAC Investigations stood for after all.

Jessica read through the details of her new case. The client was a woman called Marcia Pressman. Marcia was fifty, divorced, and apparently had plenty of assets extending beyond the double-D breasts and expensive facelift on show in the attached photo. Next to her was her boyfriend, Caleb J. Dolan. If you could call a man of sixty a boyfriend and still keep a straight face. Marcia had met Caleb J. on a dating app and, having been a victim of catfishing in the past, wanted to make sure her latest beau was legit before deciding to get serious about him.

Jessica sighed. She couldn't escape potentially untrustworthy men, whether at work or in her personal life, no matter how hard she tried. Her headache worsened.

Connor placed her mug and two pills next to her without a word.

"Thank you," she said.

"You're welcome. Hope you feel better soon." He grabbed his car keys from his desk. "I'm heading out for a while."

"Where are you going?"

"To make a start on the infidelity investigation. Catch you later."

Jessica waited until the door had closed behind him and she heard his Ford pick-up start up outside. Then she swapped Marcia Pressman's file for the notes Connor had given her on the Simmonds case. She scanned the pages quickly. A lot of it she already knew from their discussion over drinks at the Fine Line bar. She felt a weird pang thinking back to the evening they'd spent together in Twentynine Palms. The thrill of the kiss in the pool, the feeling of rejection as she'd stood dripping water onto the concrete outside her motel room door, the churning feeling in her gut the next morning when Connor had acted like nothing had happened between them.

The subsequent discovery that he was engaged to a pole dancer almost half his age.

Jessica washed down the painkillers with a mouthful of coffee and massaged her temples gently. Tried not to think about Connor or Rae-Lynn or her own bruised ego. Focused on the words on the page in front of her instead.

Connor was detailed with his note-taking, she'd give him that. His conversation with a Mrs. DuBois, the Neighborhood Watch block captain on Amanda Meyers' street, interested her most. Specifically, the reference to a "mystery vehicle" she'd spotted parked outside Amanda's building on several occasions leading up to the night of her disappearance. Connor had noted his attempt at finding out the owner of the vehicle through a contact at the DMV and had concluded the plates were fakes and the truck was most likely stolen.

Jessica didn't know if Connor had contacts within the LAPD—she assumed he did—and whether he'd followed up on the Dodge Dakota with a cop source. Jessica definitely had a contact within the LAPD she knew she could trust. She picked up her cell phone.

"Pryce? It's Jessica."

"Hey, Jessica. How's things?"

"Not too bad."

"Things working out okay with Connor?"

"I'd rather not talk about Connor."

"Ah. It's all gone south already?"

"Please don't say 'I told you so.'"

"Wouldn't dream of it. What's up?"

"I have a favor to ask."

She heard him chuckle. "Of course, you do. Is this favor going to get me into trouble?"

"Nope. It's just a stolen-vehicles check. Very simple."

"What kind of vehicles?"

"I need a list of all gray Dodge Dakotas reported stolen in the Los Angeles area. I'm especially interested in models from the last ten years."

"How far back do you want to search?" Pryce asked.

But Jessica wasn't listening. As she'd said the words out loud, her mind had flashed back to yesterday morning when she'd left her motel room. She'd passed by a truck parked outside the office. The driver had been reading a newspaper and drinking coffee, and she'd realized she didn't have time to grab a coffee of her own. Just hours before an intruder had broken into Jessica's room and pointed a gun at her.

The pick-up had been gray. There had been some minor rusting, so not brand-new. Had the truck been a Dodge Dakota? Jessica couldn't say for sure. She was no expert on car makes and models. A cold feeling washed over her. It was like she'd told Dunne: she didn't believe in coincidences.

"Jessica? Are you still there?"

"I'm still here. What did you say?"

"I asked how far back you want the search to go?"

Jessica considered for a moment. "Let's try within the last five years and take it from there."

"I'll be in touch as soon as I have anything," Pryce said. "Oh, and Angie wants to know when you're free for dinner."

"Dinner would be great. Any night is fine by me so just whatever suits Angie. Thanks, Pryce."

The thought of food made Jessica's belly rumble loudly and she decided to take a break for lunch. She needed some fresh air and wanted to check out the trattoria a couple of blocks away. She found herself scanning the streets and alleyways for any sign of a gray Dodge Dakota but was fairly sure she wasn't being followed by the time she arrived at the restaurant.

Once inside, she asked for a table for one and set up her laptop. Ordered a tuna melt sandwich and washed it down with two domestic beers that helped ease her hangover. While she ate and drank the beer, Jessica began working on the catfishing case, quickly establishing Caleb J. didn't have a criminal record or any restraining orders out against him. He also appeared to be exactly who he said he was. By the time she'd paid the check, Jessica was satisfied Marcia Pressman was not the victim of catfishing on this occasion. Maybe Marcia had lucked out this time. Maybe romance wasn't dead after all.

When Jessica returned to the office, it was empty. Connor was still out. Maybe he was also sitting in a restaurant, working on his laptop. Enjoying the change of scenery and a break from Jessica's foul mood. She felt an unexpected pang of guilt. He'd given her a job, and she'd worked for him for less than a week, and already she'd driven him out of his own office.

She dumped her stuff on the conference table, and was about to make her way to the kitchenette for another coffee, when she heard the jangle of her cell phone from inside her bag. She fished it out just before it rang off. It was Pryce.

"You have something for me already?"

"Yep, my guy ran the search." There was concern in Pryce's voice. "You mind me asking what this is for, Jessica? You still working the MP?"

"Yes. Although, technically, I'm looking into three missing persons now, trying to establish if there's a connection between them all. Why, what's up?"

"The search threw up a few hits. One, in particular, stood out from the others."

"Sounds interesting. What's so special about it?"

195

Pryce said, "Gray Dodge Dakota, 2015 model. Registered to a Cade Porterfield. Most likely stolen from outside Mr. Porterfield's property in Culver City a little under three years ago."

"'Most likely'? What does that mean? Surely this Cade Porterfield knows exactly where his truck was stolen from?"

"That's the reason why this hit stood out. Porterfield is dead. He was murdered, Jessica. Executed in his own home. The Dodge Dakota was probably stolen at the time of the murder by the person who killed him."

30

DEA—1990

The highway stretched out deserted and lonely. The white center lines flashing by in the Chevette's high-beams were almost hypnotic.

On these long journeys home from the bar, Dea's mind often wandered. Mostly, she'd fantasize about living in a big house, with plenty of money in the bank, like her old Brodie High School classmate, Kristy Jensen. Just like Kristy, she'd have a huge kitchen to cook in and a fridge-freezer stuffed full of the best food, rather than what was on offer at the store just before the use-by date was up.

Buddy would have a proper kid's bedroom, with a car-bed, and Spider-Man curtains, and a chest stuffed full of toys and games. He wouldn't want for anything but he'd appreciate everything. Her Buddy was a good boy, would never turn out to be a spoilt brat like the kids who lived in the McMansions she cleaned most weekdays.

Tonight, though, her thoughts were occupied by the cute guy from the bar.

Cade.

She knew his name now, no longer had to make up silly nicknames for him.

"Cade."

Dea said the name out loud, liked the feel of the word on her tongue.

"Cade."

Liked the sound of it in the enclosed space of the car, just hanging there suspended in the air.

It was Friday night and he hadn't shown at the Desert Heart. Dea guessed it was because the party was tomorrow night and she'd never called him. As much as the extra cash would have been welcome—and she wanted to spend more time with him away from the bar and the watchful eye of Diltz—she'd decided she couldn't leave Buddy on his own for so long. Returning home from her shifts at the bar around 1 a.m. was bad enough. The way Cade had been talking, the house party would just be getting into full swing at that time. It'd likely be almost dawn by the time Dea returned home to Yucca Valley. What if Buddy had a nightmare? Or got up to use the bathroom in the middle of the night and panicked because Dea wasn't there? No, it wasn't worth it.

She assumed Cade was mad at her and wondered if she'd ever see him again and have the chance to explain. She had his number now, of course, but, so far, hadn't been able to bring herself to pick up the phone. Tell him no, she didn't want to serve drinks at his party. But, yes, she did want to spend some time with him.

Dea's reverie was interrupted by a loud double whoop that made her jump. She checked the rearview mirror and her eyes were blinded by flashing blue lights.

Oh, shit.

Dea flicked the blinker and pulled over onto the dirt shoulder, where it was safe to stop. She shut off the engine and Joe Elliott was cut off mid-chorus. She'd forgotten the cassette tape had even been playing until the car was filled with sudden silence. The only sound now was her pulse thrumming in her ears.

The patrol car pulled in behind her, about twenty yards away. The light bar kept whirling but the cop hadn't blasted the siren again. Dea knew she hadn't been speeding. She pressed a hand to her belly, a physical attempt to stem the rising panic, but her brain jumped straight to the worst-case scenario. The stealing. That had to be it. The fancy hand cream, the designer lipstick, the bookmark for Buddy. Dea thought they wouldn't be missed. She'd been wrong.

She kept her eyes on the rearview as the driver's side door of the patrol car opened and the cop stepped out. He was wearing khaki-green pants and a short-sleeved silver-tan shirt bearing the logo of the San Bernardino County Sheriff's Department. The flashing blue lights continued to spin on the patrol car's roof, making Dea feel dizzy. The cop patted his belt, where his firearm was holstered, and began walking slowly toward her car.

Please God, this can't be happening.

Who had ratted her out? Kristy Jensen? Dea bet it was Kristy. Dea had only helped herself to the anti-anxiety pills twice—okay, three times—but Kristy must have noticed they were missing. Maybe she'd mentioned it to Derek over dinner, and Derek had suspected the hired help, and had called the cops. Told them what kind of car she drove.

The cop was ten yards away now. Taking his time, his walk almost a swagger, taunting her. Dea's underarms were damp. Part of her knew she was being irrational but the more dominant part of her brain couldn't stop catastrophizing. Stealing drugs. She could go to jail. They'd take Buddy away from her. They might not even let him visit her in prison.

The cop was right outside her door now. He made a lazy circular motion with his hand, indicating she should wind down the car window. She did as she was told.

"Something wrong, officer?" Dea tried to sound nonchalant, like an innocent person would. The words came out high-pitched and shaky. Like a guilty person, who was hiding a body in the trunk.

Or someone who had been stealing drugs from the people who had employed her, had trusted her, had welcomed her into their homes.

The cop was old, close to retirement age. He bent down and leaned on the sill of the open window. Dea thought he had kind eyes but that was probably just wishful thinking on her part. He didn't smile.

"Do you know why I pulled you over?"

"No, sir. I do not." Dea realized she was gripping the steering wheel now. She dropped her hands to her lap.

"Your taillight on the right side is out. Were you aware it was broken, Miss?"

Dea almost laughed with relief. That damn busted taillight. She'd noticed it two weeks ago, in the Desert Heart's parking lot. The broken glass on the dirt had shimmered under the neon lights and she'd put it down to a customer backing into her car by accident after too much liquor. Someone who didn't want to own up to the bump for fear of being barred. Or maybe old Merv had come back and kicked out the light as an act of petty revenge. Truth be told, she'd forgotten all about the busted taillight until now. Didn't have the cash to get it repaired in any case. Dea was so relieved, she decided to be straight with the cop.

"I'm sorry, officer. I meant to get it fixed. It's just that money has been tight recently and . . . well, I'm sorry."

His eyes—Dea still thought they were kind eyes—took in the interior of the car. The rips in the upholstery, the scuffs on the dashboard's faux leather. All the imperfections highlighted by the blue lights on top of his patrol car.

"What's a young woman like yourself doing out on the highway so late at night on her own anyways?"

"I work at the Desert Heart bar. I just finished a shift."

The cop nodded. "I know the place. It's a good bar. Decent selection of Scotch and the food isn't half bad, either. You know I should write you up a ticket, don't you?"

Dea closed her eyes. More money. It was the last thing she needed. "Yes, I know."

"But I'll let it go this time."

She opened her eyes and let out a deep breath. "Really? Thank you, officer."

He held out a business card. She took it from him. It was for Don's Auto Repairs in Yucca Valley. Dea knew the place. The cop said, "Don is a buddy of mine. Tell him Mitch sent you and he'll do a good deal for you."

Dea just nodded.

"Make the call," he said. "The next cop who pulls you over might not be so understanding."

"I'll get it fixed, I promise."

"You do that." He slapped a hand against the roof of her car. "Safe home now."

Dea started the engine. Def Leppard burst into life, making her jump. She switched the tape deck off and pulled back onto the highway. The card for Don's Auto Repairs on the dashboard kept catching her eye. Even with a few bucks knocked off the price, Dea would still need to find the cash—and fast.

She could think of only one way to make that happen.

◆ ◆ ◆

Saturday morning.

Dea hadn't made a decision so much as reached an inevitable conclusion.

"Honey, can you go to your room and play with your toys awhile?"

Buddy was still in his dressing gown, sitting cross-legged in front of the black-and-white portable television, giggling along to some silly cartoon. The volume was up loud and the picture was fuzzy but clear enough to show Tom being hit over the head with a mallet by Jerry. Buddy laughed again.

"Buddy," she said, louder and firmer this time.

"Yes, Mommy?" he replied, not taking his eyes off the flickering screen.

"Can you go to your room while Mommy makes a phone call, please?"

"But, Mommy! It's my favorite." He dragged the word "favorite" out to emphasize the point.

"I just need five minutes. If you're a good boy, I might take you for ice cream tomorrow."

That got his attention. Buddy turned to look at her. "With sprinkles on top too?"

"Definitely sprinkles on top."

"Cool!" Buddy got up and dumped his empty cereal bowl in the sink and padded off to his room in his slippers. Dea waited until she heard the door closing behind him. She turned the cartoons off. Went over to where her purse was sitting on the dinette table and found the matchbook. Turned it over and over in her hands. Noticed, as she did so, how dry and red and rough the skin was. The ugly hands of an old woman. Why would anyone want to pay her money to serve drinks at a fancy party?

Dea set the matchbook down next to the telephone. Went into the bathroom and removed the lid from the jar of hand cream on the sink, the one she'd taken from Mrs. Abbott's home. Scooped out a dollop and massaged it into her hands as she made her way back into the living area. Dea picked up the matchbook and opened it. Cade had written his name and telephone number in black kohl.

Just Cade. No surname.

She liked that. A little bit of mystery, the promise of more to discover. And Dea was very keen to find out more about Cade No-Surname. She thought—and hoped—he felt the same way about her.

Dea picked up the telephone receiver and dialed the digits Cade had written down for her. With each whir of the rotary dial, her nerves cranked up another notch. She took a deep breath to steady her nerves. There was a click and then the sound of harsh ringing at the other end.

"Hello?" It was a man's voice. Not Cade's. Too old. His father? No, he'd mentioned house-mates, rather than living with his family.

"May I speak with Cade, please?"

"Sure, who's calling?"

"Tell him it's Dea."

"Hold on a minute."

There was a dull thud as the receiver was dropped onto a hard surface. The same voice yelled, "Cade! There's a girl on the phone for you." She heard some whooping and catcalls and kissy kissy noises, followed by the sound of footsteps hurrying toward the phone.

The older man said, "Some broad by the name of Dea."

"Thanks, Jonny."

Then Cade's familiar voice, louder now. "Hello? Dea?"

The way he said her name made her insides melt like a candy bar left out in the sun.

"Hi, Cade."

"Hey. I didn't think you were going to call."

"I wasn't." There was an awkward silence, then Dea blurted out, "I missed you in the bar last night."

"I had to help the guys with the prep for the party."

"Oh. I thought it was maybe because I hadn't called you."

"No, not at all. If you don't want to come to the party, that's okay. No pressure."

"I do want to come to the party. If it's not too late to say yes?"

She could almost hear his smile through the phone. "It's not too late! You sure you're okay with it?"

"Yeah, I'm sure." Even though she wasn't.

"Fantastic! Remember I mentioned buying you a dress? I have one on hold at the store, just in case."

"You really picked out a dress for me?"

"Well, I had a little assistance," he said sheepishly. "My buddy's girlfriend helped out. She found some matching shoes too but I didn't know what size you were."

"Seven and a half," Dea said, without thinking.

"Great, I'll pick those up too."

Dea was embarrassed now. "Really, you don't have to buy me a dress and shoes."

"I already told you, I want to. You can repay me by having dinner with me one night."

Dea was glad Cade couldn't see the huge grin on her face.

"But only if you want to," he added hastily.

"I want to."

"Then it's a date."

Dea wrote down the address and directions for where the party was taking place. Told Cade she'd see him tonight and replaced the receiver in the cradle.

A date.

She'd only been on a date once before, a long time ago, and it had been a very bad experience. But she wouldn't allow herself to think about that night. This time it would be different. She felt a flutter in her belly, like a thousand butterflies had been unleashed.

Nerves.

And excitement.

Dea liked a boy. And he liked her.

The "Girl Most Likely to Succeed" might just have finally lucked out.

31

BURDEN

Burden heard the now familiar *put-put-put* of the VW Bug's engine before he saw the little yellow car turn into the parking lot.

He was sitting at a window table at the J-Tree Cafe, perusing the menu, while keeping an eye on the main highway. He felt the muscles in his neck and shoulders relax. If Cara had decided not to show, his plan would have been shot to shit. Now it was good to go.

Cara was expecting to meet both Burden and Summer for lunch, to discuss ideas for the shoot, before all three drove out together to Joshua Tree National Park for the photos.

Of course, the fictional Summer wouldn't be joining them for lunch today.

Cara pulled into a space in front of the window and he watched over the top of the menu as she got out of the car and bent down to check her hair and makeup in the wing mirror. He smiled. He guessed she was keen on making a positive impression on Summer, probably thought there could be an even more lucrative gig as wedding photographer up for grabs if she impressed the bride-to-be.

Burden waved to Cara to catch her attention as she entered the restaurant. It was busy with tourists and truckers and most of the tables were occupied. Just as well he'd phoned ahead to make the reservation.

The place had a laid-back vibe, very chilled and relaxed. Decor that likely hadn't been updated since the '90s. Low ceiling with wooden beams, off-white cinderblock walls and high-backed metal chairs. He'd been a few times before and knew the food was good and the staff were friendly but not too friendly. The best thing about the J-Tree Cafe was they had just two security cameras—one outside the front door covering the lot and one inside covering the till area. On this occasion, Burden had worn a baller cap and shades when he'd first arrived and made sure his back was to the indoor camera when seated. The table was big enough for four but there were only two menus and two sets of cutlery and paper napkins.

Cara pulled out the chair facing him and dumped her purse on the vacant one next to her.

"Hi, Cara."

"Hi, Randal." A confused frown lined her pretty face when she saw the table was set for two and she realized Summer wasn't in the bathroom or grabbing something she'd forgotten from the car. Only two of them would be eating. "Where's Summer? She is coming, right?"

"Summer had some kind of emergency at work this morning that, apparently, only she could deal with. Can you believe it? She's not going to make lunch, unfortunately. She'll meet us at the park later."

"But she'll definitely be at the shoot, won't she? This work emergency isn't going to be an all-day thing?"

Cara was worried now. He could almost read what she was thinking, like a cartoon thought bubble above her head. What if the fiancée couldn't make the shoot? What if Cara didn't receive the rest of the payment as promised?

Burden smiled reassuringly. "Summer will be there. Don't worry. She phoned earlier, she's already on the road as we speak."

"Okay, that's good if she's already on her way."

"Trust me, there is no way in the world Summer is going to miss this shoot. She's spoken about nothing else for weeks." He tapped a plastic folder on the table in front of him. "And she's sent me here armed with many, *many* examples of the kind of thing she's after."

He handed Cara one of the menus. "Why don't we order? Then we can discuss some ideas." He laughed. "Or rather, *Summer's* ideas."

Cara seemed happier now, no longer worried she'd made the journey all the way out to the desert for nothing. She ordered the chicken club sandwich with a side of chili cheese fries and a large diet Pepsi and Burden opted for the tuna salad sandwich with no side. He was starting to feel nervous about what lay ahead.

While they waited for the food, Burden popped open the fastener on the plastic folder and pulled out a couple dozen sheets of paper. He'd spent hours online last night trawling through hundreds of images of other people's engagement shoots. Some of them even had their own dedicated websites. He wasn't sure who, other than the couple themselves, would want to visit it. But those websites were perfect for Burden. He'd printed off a whole bunch of shots, especially those taken against a desert backdrop. He spread them on the table between himself and Cara now.

"These will give you an idea of the kind of thing Summer wants." There was the forehead kiss, the loving gaze into each other's eyes, the close-up of the ring. "She's not really into the jokey, goofy ones."

Cara studied the printouts. "Yeah, she clearly prefers ones that really capture the romance of the couple. She has good taste. I can do something similar, no problem at all."

"Great, I knew you'd be just perfect for the job."

The food arrived and they ate and discussed poses and backdrops some more and picked out a handful of images that captured Randal and Summer's vision for their own shoot. Burden had already told Cara he'd pay for lunch and, when the check arrived, she made no offer to go fifty-fifty, just picked up a couple of the printouts again. He took some bills from his wallet and tucked them into the check presenter, along with a tip for the waitress. All cash. No electronic trail back to Burden.

The original plan, at least as far as Cara was concerned, had been for all three of them to travel to the park together and Burden suggested they both still take his pick-up. He pointed out the truck would be better suited to the rougher terrain than Cara's VW Bug, plus she would save on gas. He'd drop her off at the cafe's lot after the shoot. Burden fastened the baller hat onto his head and slipped on the shades as they made their way outside.

Cara opened the trunk of her car and Burden lifted out her photography kit and carried it over to his own wheels. Carefully loaded the bulky camera bag and tripod onto the flatbed. He could tell by the expression on Cara's face that she wasn't expecting him to drive a five-year-old pick-up with hubcaps that were beginning to rust. The trendy clothes, and the cash for the photography job, and the offer to pay for gas and lunch all gave the impression of a man with a few bucks in the bank. The truck didn't fit with his slightly flashy image.

"My dad's truck," he explained. "My Audi is less than six months old and I didn't want it getting all mussed up by the sand and dirt out here." He smiled sheepishly. "I guess that makes me sound pretty lame."

It was partly the truth. Burden *had* bought an Audi A5 Cabriolet less than six months ago but he was more concerned about DNA from missing women being found inside it than he was about some dirt on the bodywork on the outside.

Cara returned the smile. "Not lame at all. It's like you said, a truck is better suited to the rough terrain. In fact, I used to drive a pick-up myself. I only traded it in for the Bug when I moved to LA."

"Oh, you're not from LA originally?"

"No, I grew up in Indio. Not too far from here, as it happens. I'm planning on spending the night at my brother's place and driving back to Hollywood in the morning."

"Sounds like a good idea," Burden said, thinking Cara wouldn't be seeing her brother, or anyone else, tonight. He held open the passenger-side door for her. "Hop on in."

She did as she was told.

He walked around the truck to the driver's side and glanced around. The cafe was right in the heart of downtown Joshua Tree. One of several eateries in the immediate vicinity. There was also a liquor store, and a vintage clothing boutique, and a real estate agency, and a shop selling rocks, gems, and minerals. Burden had considered whether arranging the meet with Cara in such a bustling setting was a bad idea, if it would be too risky. Then he'd decided it was ideal. With so many other folks about, who would pay any attention to a young couple out having lunch? There was also the added bonus of the yellow VW Bug being nice and prominent and easily spotted from the highway.

Burden wondered what would happen first—the pissed owners of the J-Tree Cafe reporting an abandoned car taking up space in their lot. Or Cara's brother filing a missing person's report when she didn't show this evening.

Once on the road, Cara continued to sift through the photos he'd printed off, while droning on and on about things like composition and lighting and bokeh effects. She really was taking it all very seriously.

Soon, the bars and restaurants and stores of downtown Joshua Tree were far behind them, no longer visible in the rearview mirror. In front of them lay only flat, empty blacktop and desert. Burden drifted onto dirt packed at the side of the road like small snowdrifts and stopped the truck.

Cara looked up from a photo showing a groom-to-be on his knee re-enacting the proposal for his delighted fiancée.

"Is there a problem, Randal?" There was the tiniest bit of alarm in her eyes.

"My cell phone is vibrating in my back pocket. It'll be Summer calling, making sure we're on our way. Give me two minutes to speak to her, find out where she is."

"Sure, go for it." Cara went back to the picture. Swapped it for another one. This time the loving gaze.

Burden unbuckled his seatbelt and shifted his weight so he could reach into the back pocket of his jeans. But it wasn't a cell phone he pulled out. He uncapped the syringe and leaned toward Cara quickly before her brain had a chance to react to what was happening.

"I'm so sorry, Cara."

Then he injected her with the needle.

32

JESSICA

Connor didn't return to the office for the rest of the afternoon, all but confirming Jessica's suspicions that he was avoiding her. She seriously doubted he'd spent half the day birddogging a wayward husband. Not unless the guy was banging his secretary during work hours and had an impressive amount of stamina.

At 5 p.m., she packed up her laptop, notepad, pens, and case files, turned off the lights, and locked up behind her. She had no plans to return to her motel room tonight—and not just because she no longer felt safe there. Jessica was planning on visiting a bar. But, this time, it wasn't to get lit. It was to get some answers.

She purchased a sandwich and a bottle of water and a takeout coffee from the deli next door to the agency. Once inside the truck, she tuned the radio to a station playing classic rock songs, lit a cigarette, and settled in for a long journey.

When she arrived in Twentynine Palms three hours later, it was almost full dark. She passed the motel where she'd spent the night with Connor but had slept in different rooms and the bar where they had shared a few drinks that led to the moment between the two of them in the pool. Jessica kept on going. It was a different bar she was headed to. One right on the edge of town. She spotted the blue and red of the neon sign bright against the black sky.

The Desert Heart.

She found the matchbook the motel intruder had given to her. It was very old and tattered, as though it had been handled a lot. On the front flap was the bar's name and a row of palm trees and a heart-shaped moon against a black sky. The address and phone number and "The coldest beer in town" claim were printed on the back flap. Inside, there was a black smudge, where something had once been written but was now illegible. Two matches were missing, having been ripped out and used, judging by the scuffs on the rough strip.

You need to be smart, Jessica, not sloppy.

There was no doubt in Jessica's mind that the motel intruder—and this bar—were connected to the disappearances of Laurie, Mallory, and Amanda. But how?

As Jessica got out of the truck, something by the roadside glinted in the glow of the bar's neon signs, catching her eye. She walked over and bent down to inspect it. It was a license plate. Slightly dented, from Texas. She picked it up and went inside the bar.

The Desert Heart was a spit-and-sawdust establishment, with the kind of clientele that seemed to be older and male, whereas the nearby Fine Line had attracted a mix of ages and offered a range of entertainment. There didn't seem to be a whole lot to do in the Desert Heart other than drink.

The bartender could best be described as a rock chick. She had long, dyed red hair and more tattoos and piercings than Jessica and wore a lot more leather. Jessica approached, holding up the battered number plate.

"Texas. Great. Another one for the collection." The bartender pointed behind Jessica, to where old beer barrels were acting as tables. Above the beer barrels, nailed to the wall, were dozens of similarly damaged plates of every kind—vanity plates, regular plates, different colors and designs, and near on every state in the country represented.

"Quite a collection," Jessica said.

"There's a bump on the blacktop right outside the bar. Cars tend to drive a little too fast out here, hit the bump, and off comes the plate. The bar staff have been collecting them for years."

"Speaking of collectibles . . ." Jessica showed the bartender the matchbook.

"Very cool." The woman turned it over in her hands. "I've never seen one of these from the Heart before. Then again, can't smoke in bars now so why would we still have them? Don't even have a cigarette machine these days." She handed it back to Jessica. "Even so, maybe I should bring the matchbooks back as retro, gimmicky advertising. People love that stuff. How'd you come across it?"

Jessica avoided answering the question. "I'm a private detective investigating the disappearances of three women from the area over the last couple years. I think the matchbook might be a lead."

She removed photos of Laurie, Mallory, and Amanda from her bag and placed them on the bar top. The bartender leaned on her elbows and studied them. She shook her head. "Sorry, I don't recognize them, other than the one with the birthday cake. I think she's the girl on that huge billboard just outside town."

"How long have you worked at the Desert Heart?"

"I've owned the place about six years."

"Any idea who the owner would've been when matchbooks were still being printed up for the customers? This would probably have been before '98."

Jessica had already discovered that the state of California had adopted a smoking ban in bars, casinos, and gaming clubs in 1998.

The bartender was about forty, so likely not old enough to have been serving drinks for a living back then.

"I bought the bar from a guy by the name of Freddy Diltz. He'd been owner of the Desert Heart for forever and would most likely be the guy you want to speak to."

"How're you spelling the surname?" Jessica asked.

"D-I-L-T-Z," the bartender told her.

"Is this Freddy Diltz still living?"

"Oh sure, still comes in here every now and then. Practically need to throw him out at closing time. I guess he still likes the beer and the company. He's not in tonight though."

Jessica took in the room. It was empty save for herself and two old men. "Any idea where I can find him?"

"In town, for sure, but I don't know the address off the top of my head. Sorry."

Jessica thanked the woman for her time, ordered a beer, and perched on a stool next to the beer barrel under the license plates collection. She checked her cell phone and saw she had a text from Connor.

Everything okay today? Sorry, got held up with the new client. See you tomorrow.

Jessica didn't respond. She did a search for a Freddy Diltz in Twentynine Palms and quickly found a listing for the man. She drank her beer and noticed the time on a big wall clock and decided it wasn't too late to pay a house visit to a guy who apparently enjoyed late-night drinking and chatting.

Twentynine Palms had a bunch of streets named after various times of the day, such as Sunrise and Morning and Sunset and Starlight. Freddy Diltz resided on Twilight Avenue, where most of the houses were single story and neutral-toned and had front yards filled with rocks and boulders and big fat palm trees. Diltz's home was no different. A dusty cream and fake-wood-panel station wagon was parked in the drive. The curtains were drawn but there was a lamp on in the living room. A good sign.

As she approached the front door, Jessica could hear music playing. She felt confident the former bar owner was still awake and hadn't turned in for the night. The screen door opened with a creak and she knocked loudly so as to be heard over the music. A silhouette appeared in the hallway through a pebbled window and the door opened to reveal an elderly man with a confused expression on his face.

Freddy Diltz was about seventy, maybe a shade older. He had short silver hair and a neatly trimmed goatee that shone like moonlight under the lantern lamp above the door. He wore a faded t-shirt and jeans and bare feet and his back was as straight as a poker. Jessica could now tell the music he was listening to was vinyl on a scratchy old record player.

"Can I help you, Miss?"

"Mr. Diltz? I apologize for calling so late. My name is Jessica Shaw and I'm a private investigator from Los Angeles. I wondered if it would be possible to have ten minutes of your time?"

"A private investigator? What's this all about?"

"Honestly? I'm not entirely sure myself but I think it has something to do with this." She held up the matchbook from the Desert Heart.

"This is about the bar? You'd better come on in."

Jessica followed him into a cozy living room. "I hope I'm not disturbing you. I wasn't sure if you'd be in bed already."

Diltz smiled. "No, I'm a night owl. Always have been. Been trying to get to grips with that thing all evening." He gestured to a coffee table with a huge jigsaw puzzle on top. Or at least, the outside edges of the puzzle. The box was on the floor and had a picture of a barren landscape with a smattering of shrub and cacti under a blazing sunset. The puzzle was called "Desert Dream" and had a thousand pieces. "It's a tough one. I keep telling myself all the pieces are there. It's just a case of being patient and resolute and I'll get the full picture eventually."

"Sounds a little like being a private detective," Jessica said.

"I gotta say, I'm intrigued as to why you're here. But I'm forgetting my manners. Would you like a drink? Tea, coffee, beer, soda?"

"Coffee would be good, thanks. Black, no sugar." It had been a long day after a rough night.

Diltz told Jessica to take a seat on the couch, while he went into the kitchen to prepare the drinks. He returned a few minutes later with two mugs and handed her one and she noticed he had faded old "LOVE" and "HATE" tattoos across his knuckles. He walked over to the turntable. "I'll turn this off so we can talk."

Jessica said, "'Sweet Dreams' by Patsy Cline. It's a great song."

"One of my favorites. I always liked it much more than her better-known ones, like 'Crazy' or 'Walkin' After Midnight.' More emotional or something. And it's always better on vinyl."

Jessica nodded. "My dad had an old turntable too. We used to listen to Johnny Cash and drink beer together. These days, I travel around a lot so it's mostly whatever's on the radio."

"Johnny Cash, huh? Takes me back. When I was much younger, I played guitar and sang a bit and, sometimes, I'd put on an impromptu show for the regulars at the Desert Heart. Johnny Cash was a big favorite. Those sure were the days. Back when you could enjoy a smoke with your whiskey." He chuckled. "My wife always said I loved that bar more than I loved her and I guess she was right. I had the bar way longer than I had a wife in any case."

"Must have been hard giving it up," Jessica said. "It seems like a cool place. I bet it was even better back then."

"I'm not going to lie, it was a wrench letting it go, but I'm an old man now. All I got to look forward to is special offers on cremations through the mail. On a good day, I might receive a flier for a retirement home instead. It was the right time to hand over the baton to someone younger and Jeannie is doing a fantastic job."

"I spoke with her earlier but I figured she wouldn't have been behind the bar when there were still matchbooks so she probably wouldn't be much help. That's why I tracked you down."

"May I see it?" Diltz asked. Jessica fished the matchbook from her pocket and handed it over. Diltz came over all wistful. "Man, I haven't seen one of those in years. Probably stopped ordering them in the mid-nineties sometime. They were starting to go out of fashion by then and then the smoking ban came in. How'd you come by it?"

Jessica didn't want to go into details about an intruder breaking into her motel room with a gun. She said, "It was given to me anonymously. I think it has something to do with the case I'm working on."

"What case?"

"A missing person. An artist from Venice Beach by the name of Laurie Simmonds. She vanished two months ago." Jessica found a photo of Laurie in her bag and gave it to Diltz.

He nodded. "Yep, I know who you mean. Very sad."

"You know her? Did you see her before she disappeared?"

"No, I never saw the girl in the flesh but I've seen the billboard out by Joshua Tree plenty of times. Her photo's been on it for weeks. Usually it's ads for real estate and hamburgers."

"Of course, the billboard," Jessica said, deflated. She showed him photos of Mallory Wilcox and Amanda Meyers. "What about these women? Do you recognize either of them?"

Diltz shook his head. "Can't say that I do. Are they missing too?"

"Yes, they are. The last known whereabouts of all three was on, or close by, State Route 62."

"And they all visited my old bar?"

"No, not as far as I know. I have no idea what connects the women to the Desert Heart, other than its address. I was hoping you might be able to help me figure it out."

Diltz's brow furrowed. "How long have they been missing?"

"Amanda was the first to disappear—that was two years ago. Mallory vanished eighteen months ago and Laurie has been missing for two months."

"Only one missing person I can think of who was connected to the Desert Heart."

"Really," Jessica asked. "Who?"

Was there someone else Renee hadn't come across while doing her Google searches? Someone who'd also slipped under the cops' radar?

Diltz's shoulders slumped, his expression forlorn. "Her name was Dea Morgan. She worked for me as a bartender. But I can't see how she'd have anything to do with your case."

"Why not?"

"Those women all vanished recently. Dea was last seen on a late summer's night thirty years ago."

33

JESSICA

"Tell me about Dea."

There were tears in Diltz's eyes now. He cradled his coffee mug and stared off into the distance and Jessica knew he was no longer in his living room in the here and now; he was in the Desert Heart three decades ago.

"She was a good kid." He smiled sadly. "I should really say young woman, shouldn't I? After all, she wasn't a kid. Must've been, what, twenty-three or twenty-four. Real smart. I never could figure out how she wound up working in a bar. And that's not being disrespectful to bar staff, I worked in bars myself my whole life. But when I say smart, I mean really smart. She had this amazing knowledge, she just *knew* stuff. I always thought that girl should have been a doctor or a lawyer or one of those university academics. She was a hard worker and friendly too, but there was always a real sadness about her."

He placed the coffee mug on the carpet by his feet and got up from his chair. "I should have a photo of her someplace." Diltz went out into the hallway and Jessica heard a closet door open and the sound of rummaging and a box being slid out. He returned with a dusty photo album in his hand and settled back into his seat. Blew the dust off the maroon leatherette cover and began flicking through the pages. From where she was sitting, Jessica could see the book was filled with shots of the bar she'd been in earlier. A photographic account of the many years Diltz had owned the place.

"There she is." He carefully pulled back the clear cover and peeled two photographs from the page's sticky back and handed them to Jessica. Like the others in the album, both had been taken in the Desert Heart. The bar didn't look a whole lot different back then to what it did now, except for the thick haze of cigarette smoke.

Dea Morgan had long black hair and hazel eyes and pale skin. She was very slim and dressed simply in jeans and a halter top. She was smiling but Diltz was right, there was a sadness about her, like she was carrying the weight of the world on her shoulders.

In one of the photographs, a much younger Diltz was standing next to her. Back then, he had a Motörhead hairstyle and a full beard and might've been intimidating if it weren't for the big grin. A guy who was clearly having the time of his life and wanted everyone else to have a good time too. The second photo showed Dea on her own. She was behind the bar, one hand resting on the beer tap. It was a close-up shot and showed the dark circles under her eyes. Jessica thought the woman was attractive but she looked exhausted.

"Dea was very pretty," she said, handing the photos back. "How long before she disappeared were these taken?"

"Probably around six months earlier. She didn't work at the Desert Heart all that long. I never did find out her whole story but I know she was estranged from her parents and had been for a long time. I always felt protective of her, like I should be looking out for her. I guess I didn't do such a good job."

"Tell me about her disappearance. Did you see her on that last day?"

"That I did not." Diltz returned the photographs to the album, smoothed down the clear cover, making sure there were no air bubbles. "We worked a shift together the night before. Friday night as usual. She was last seen the following evening—Saturday—by both her little boy and a neighbor."

"She had a kid?" Jessica asked.

"Yep, I think he was about six or seven. Dea was a single mom, never mentioned the father. I'm not sure what happened to the kid. Probably taken into care. He told the cops his mom had left their home on Saturday evening after putting him to bed, said she was going to work. The next day, he fed himself with cereal and peanut butter and jelly sandwiches. When Dea still hadn't returned home by Monday morning to take him to school, he called the cops."

"Poor little guy. How sad. What about the neighbor?"

"The guy lived in the same mobile home park in Yucca Valley. He was returning home after a few drinks at the local bar when he spotted Dea getting into her car. She also told him she was heading to work. He didn't think she was telling the truth."

"Why did he think she was lying?"

"It was late for starters. Already dark. She had an overnight bag with her. He said she seemed edgy and was keen to shut down the conversation."

"And was she supposed to be working that night?"

Diltz shook his head. "Not in my bar anyways. She never worked Saturdays. She had another job, cleaning houses during the day, so that didn't fit either. I had no choice but to tell the cops the truth."

"Why wouldn't you tell them the truth?"

"Dea had lied to her kid and she had lied to the neighbor. She wasn't working that Saturday night. Then there was the over-night bag the neighbor claimed he saw her with. It was pretty clear what conclusion the cops were leaning toward—and it wasn't one I agreed with or liked. Not one bit."

"What was the cops' theory?"

"That Dea had just upped and left. Had had enough of struggling for money and working two jobs and the responsibility of being a single mom. Had decided to just abandon her kid. I think they thought she'd run off with a Marine for a better, easier life someplace."

"A Marine? Why would they think that?"

"You know there's a Marine base nearby town?"

"Sure, but it's a bit of a leap, is it not? A woman goes missing and there's a Marine base not too far away so there must be a connection? Can't say I'd link the two without good reason."

If Diltz had been sad before, now he appeared downright distressed.

"What is it, Freddy?" Jessica asked gently. "What aren't you telling me?"

"I need a drink." He got up from the chair again and, this time, walked over to a sideboard, slid open the front of the plywood unit and pulled out a bottle of whiskey. "You want one?"

"No thanks." Jessica had already decided to stay overnight in Twentynine Palms, but the memory of this morning's hangover was still fresh in her mind. As were the words of the intruder in her motel room.

You need to be sharp, Jessica, not sloppy.

Diltz produced a single crystal tumbler from the sideboard too and poured himself a generous amount and gulped it down, then refilled the glass and took it back to his chair. He said, "Not long before Dea disappeared, there was a young guy hanging around the bar most weekends. Young, good-looking, very short dark hair, muscular, like he worked out a lot or played some sports. I guess you'd say he looked like a soldier or a jock. I figured he was either from the Marine base or the university."

The university.

Jessica felt the hairs on the back of her neck stand on end, like a cold finger was tracing an icy trail down her spine. "Go on."

"I could tell the kid had a crush on Dea. He couldn't take his eyes off her most of the time. And he was always in the bar on his own, never with friends. I figured he was biding his time, before making a move. Then I got to thinking something was going on between them. You know, hushed conversations, smoke breaks outside together. That kind of thing. I never saw the guy in the bar again after Dea vanished."

"You know the guy's name?"

"I never asked. Didn't think it was any of my business."

"But you told the cops about him?"

Diltz swallowed some whiskey and nodded. "I had to. If anything had happened to Dea, my money was on this guy being involved. I didn't think they'd turn it around on her, though, insinuate she'd run off with him."

"Could she have?" Jessica asked.

Diltz shook his head firmly. "And leave her kid behind? No way. That's not the Dea I knew. I tried to tell the cops but they weren't interested." He drank some more liquor. "There was something I didn't tell the cops."

"What?"

"A couple months later, one of my old regulars appeared in the bar. Guy by the name of Merv Nelson. I hadn't seen him in weeks. I actually thought he'd passed on or been ill in hospital. Anyways, he told me he'd been keeping his distance for a while after being warned to stay away from the bar by this very same guy. Said he'd simply been chatting to Dea in the parking lot one night and the kid beat him up in a jealous rage."

"Why not tell the cops?"

"I felt as though I'd done enough damage already. Like maybe the reason they weren't looking for Dea properly was down to me. If I'd only kept my mouth shut about that damn Marine . . . Then I spent a long time thinking maybe the Marine had hurt Dea. If he was the jealous type, and had a temper and was quick with his fists like Merv said he was, maybe he used his fists on Dea one night and it went too far." Diltz emptied the glass and rubbed his eyes. "Thinking about shit like that will keep you awake at night, believe me."

"I don't think you can blame yourself, Freddy. Sounds to me like the statements from Dea's little boy and the neighbor were enough to convince the police Dea had simply left town. I don't think any of this is on you."

"Yeah, maybe." Diltz didn't sound convinced.

"I'm just sorry I brought a lot of bad memories back to the surface for you. I'm assuming Dea was never found?"

Diltz met Jessica's gaze with such profound sadness, it made her heart ache for the old man. "That's where you're wrong. They did find Dea. Eventually. You know that stretch of highway out past the sign on the edge of town warning there's no services for a hundred miles?"

Jessica shook her head. Dread clutched at her belly. "No, I don't know it."

"As you'd expect, it's real desolate. Nothing but highway and desert and the occasional trailer. About as lonely as it gets."

"Okay . . ." Jessica wished she'd accepted his offer of a whiskey now, to ready herself for the words she knew he was going to say.

"Out there is where they found Dea's body."

34

DEA—1990

After his bath and helping him into fresh pajamas, Dea tucked Buddy into bed with his favorite stuffed toy. She smoothed back his hair and kissed his forehead.

"Mommy has to work tonight, honey," she told him.

Buddy's brow furrowed. "But it's Saturday. You don't work on Saturday nights."

"I know, but it's a special favor for a friend. You okay being my big brave boy for an extra night?"

"I guess so."

"I might be a little later than usual getting home so don't be afraid if you wake up and I'm not here, okay?"

"What if I have a bad dream?"

"Remember what I told you, the monsters in your dreams aren't real. They can't hurt you. Plus, Duke here will protect you from any scary monsters." She leaned down toward the stuffed dinosaur. "Isn't that right, Duke?" She pretended to listen to the toy's response, then said, "Duke says you're safe with him."

Buddy giggled.

"You remember the number to call if there *is* a problem?"

"Yep. Nine-one-one."

"Good boy." She ruffled his hair and kissed him again. "Night, honey. Love you."

"Love you too."

Dea switched off the overhead light, leaving only the faint glow of the nightlight on. She closed the bedroom door behind her.

Started thinking about what she'd need for the party.

Dea went into the bathroom and tossed her toothbrush, toothpaste, deodorant and hairspray into a cosmetics bag. Added the fancy hand cream too. It would smooth out her rough skin and smell nice in the absence of expensive perfume. She returned to the living area and pulled an overnight bag from the closet.

She'd need it for the new dress and shoes that Cade was buying for her. She assumed Cade would let her keep the new stuff but didn't want to drive home at dawn wearing a fancy dress and heels. What would the neighbors think if they saw her? She dropped the cosmetics bag into the overnight bag. Grabbed her robe from the closet too. She could wear it while applying her makeup before putting on the dress. She wondered what the dress would be like and if she'd let Cade kiss her if he made a move on her.

Dea went to the bedroom to check on Buddy. He was fast asleep. She could hear his soft snores in the near-darkness. She collected her purse and overnight bag and made her way outside, careful not to bang the door shut. Was almost at her car when she spotted a figure staggering toward her. Her heart sank.

It was Norm Shuffler. He lived in the mobile home two down from her own and shared a carport space with Dea. A regular at the bar where Dea used to work, he was clearly on his way home from there now having had several drinks.

"Shit," she muttered under her breath. She glanced behind her at the bedroom window where Buddy's nightlight glowed softly through the thin curtains. She didn't want her neighbors knowing she was leaving her son home alone for the night.

"Evening, Dea."

"Hi, Norm."

He eyed the overnight bag. "Off someplace nice?"

"Um no, just work."

Norm Shuffler frowned. "At this time of night?"

Dea opened the trunk, threw the overnight bag inside, and made her way quickly to the driver's door. "Sorry, Norm, I'm running late. Gotta go." She slipped inside and slammed the door shut before he could say another word.

◆ ◆ ◆

Once she arrived in Twentynine Palms, Dea pulled over in the Desert Heart's lot to consult the directions Cade had given her.

He'd assured her the place was easy to find from the bar. She wasn't a native of the town, didn't recognize the street names, but the route from here on out didn't seem too complicated. She made the first couple of turns, which took her onto a long stretch of road. A sign for The Palms University whizzed past and she kept on driving. Found the next turnoff and spotted a sign confirming she was on the right street. Cade had told her it was the last house on the block, at the far end. As she approached the property, Dea's heart sank when she spotted the three huge Greek symbols on the building's frontage.

The party was taking place at a fraternity house.

Dea had never made it to college. She wasn't a part of that world, wouldn't feel comfortable in that kind of environment, surrounded by kids enjoying the kind of life she'd been denied herself. She knew, right then, agreeing to the party had been a bad idea.

A bunch of cars were parked haphazardly in front of the grand three-story house. Disco lights flashed blue and red and green and yellow behind darkened windows. Dea slowed the car to a stop in the middle of the street. Turned off the engine. Her hands gripped the steering wheel just as they had done the night before when she'd been pulled over by the cop. The card for Don's Auto Repairs was still on the dash.

She needed the money, true. But did she need it this much? She could leave right now, turn the car around, and forget all about the dumb party. Explain to Cade later. Just as Dea was about to leave, the front door opened and Cade bounded across the lawn toward her. The smile on his face was so bright it could have powered the whole town.

Dea sighed. Rolled down the car window.

"Dea! You found it, okay!" Cade hesitated just for a second, then leaned in the open window and kissed her on the cheek. She could smell beer on his breath and the clean soap smell on his skin. "Nowhere to park, huh? Head on round the back and you'll find a spot right next to Zee's old Cutlass."

"Zee?"

"One of my buddies." He grinned. "I can't wait for you to meet them. You're going to get on like a house on fire."

35

JESSICA

Jessica spent the night in the same motel where she'd stayed with Connor. Not for any sentimental reasons. It was reasonably priced, centrally located in the town, and she knew exactly what she was getting for her money as a return visitor. She made a point of avoiding the pool area this time though.

The lack of sleep the night before, the lingering effects of the hangover, and the long drive and a late finish, all meant Jessica was exhausted by the time she crawled into bed. Even so, it took a long time for her to fall asleep. She tossed and turned and thought about what Diltz had told her about Dea Morgan. How her decomposed body had been out there in a shallow grave in the desert, in the most remote stretch of highway, undiscovered all those years. How she'd been missing, and presumed to have run away and left her life behind of her own accord, until the truth was discovered, along with her body, just three years ago.

It was the very same assumptions being made now about Amanda Meyers, Mallory Wilcox and Laurie Simmonds three decades later. All four women connected by 150 miles of highway.

Jessica awoke early the next morning to a glorious day, the blue skies and nodding palm trees outside her window instantly brightening her mood. She no longer felt tired; she felt reinvigorated by the investigation. She was onto something, could feel it in her bones. The murder of Dea Morgan was connected somehow to Amanda and Mallory and Laurie. Jessica just had to figure out how. There was no way she was returning to Venice this morning.

She fired off a text to Connor, letting him know she would be unlikely to make it into the office, saying she was planning on spending the day doing surveillance work on the Pressman catfishing case. Almost immediately, Jessica's cell phone began to vibrate in her hand with an incoming call. It was Connor.

"Shit," Jessica muttered. She thought about rejecting the call but knew, if she did, he'd just keep on trying. She swiped to answer. "Connor. What's up?"

"Just checking in and wondering where you're at?"

"Didn't you read my text? I'm out working the Pressman case."

"I meant where you really are, Jessica." She started to protest but Connor cut her off. "I swung by your motel late last night. You know, after you didn't respond to my text? There was no sign of your truck outside and the curtains in your room window were wide open. Same story first thing this morning."

"You're checking up on me now?" Jessica demanded.

Connor ignored the question. "You're in Twentynine Palms, aren't you? Still working the Laurie Simmonds case full-time."

Jessica didn't say anything.

Connor went on, "It's okay, Jessica. You don't have to lie to me. I've had time to think on it and you were right and I was wrong. We can't just give up on those missing women."

"Really?" Jessica couldn't hide the disbelief from her voice.

"Yes, really. I think you're onto something with the college connection."

"So, what're you saying?"

"I'm saying, keep working the case—and let me know if I can do anything to help from here."

Jessica didn't know if Connor's concern for the missing women was genuine or if his change of heart was an attempt to ingratiate himself with her after the Rae-Lynn business, but it didn't matter right now. What mattered was finding out what happened to Laurie and Amanda and Mallory.

"Okay, sure," she said.

"Do you have a lead you're working in Twentynine Palms?"

Jessica thought about the matchbook and last night's visit with Freddy Diltz and what she'd discovered about Dea Morgan.

"Maybe," she said. "I want to do some more digging. See what I can find out about the college angle."

"Okay," Connor said. "And, remember, I'm here to help if you need me to."

Jessica ended the call and made her way outside to the truck. She drove to a nearby Denny's for a huge breakfast of pancakes, sausage, eggs and hash browns, washed down with orange juice and lots of coffee. Her next stop was the public library.

Freddy Diltz had assumed the guy Dea had been getting friendly with at the Desert Heart was a Marine and it was easy to see why, considering the close proximity of the Marine base to the bar and Diltz's description of a young, muscular man with very short hair.

But Jessica didn't think he was a Marine; she was almost certain he was a student at The Palms University. And, her gut was telling her, he'd also been a member of the school's fraternity, a "brother" along with Terence Wilcox and Zachary Dunne.

Jessica got settled in one of the reading rooms and spent the next couple of hours checking out books on the local area and old newspapers, as well as conducting searches on her laptop to find out as much as possible about the fraternity.

Like a lot of Greek letter organizations, it had a reputation for only recruiting those who were good-looking, rich, and who liked to party. Most of the parties took place on Frat Row, close to the campus, which wasn't really a fraternity row so much as one large house accommodating twenty-five brothers. There were a few reports in the local newspaper of hazing incidents going too far but nothing serious enough to result in convictions or to seriously damage the reputation of the school or the fraternity or to get the frat house shut down. It did finally close its doors for good fifteen years ago when The Palms University also closed permanently.

As well as the hazing incidents, there were some good news stories in the local press, including several articles on Terence Wilcox who, as he'd told Connor, had been hailed as the state's next big baseball star. The stories, and accompanying photos, were all from 1989, his freshman year. Jessica thought he was kind of cute and seemed a little full of himself. He'd earned his place at the school through scholarships as a result of his sporting prowess, didn't come from a particularly privileged background like the majority of the other students, who seemed to be rich kids with rich parents.

Even so, Jessica could see how Wilcox fit the bill for the fraternity thanks to his looks and sporting success. She didn't find any articles mentioning Zachary Dunne or Trey Simmonds, the latter of whom was a few years older than the others.

One name that did keep cropping up was that of Jonathan "Jonny" Bateman, who had a long association with the fraternity, first as a brother and then as house director, a role he performed for over three decades. Jessica discovered a house director—or "house mom" or "house dad" as they were sometimes known—was the person who upheld house rules, while acting as a mentor and looking after the wellbeing of fraternity brothers and sorority sisters.

In Jonny Bateman's case, he'd lived in-house for part of his tenure. It seemed to Jessica that, if anyone knew about previous brothers and what really went down at that fraternity, it'd be Jonny Bateman. She just hoped the man was still alive and not now a guest at that big frat party in the sky. She mentally crossed her fingers while she did a search and came up with a potential hit—and thankfully not at the local cemetery. A Jonathan Bateman was a resident of a care home in Palm Springs, around an hour's drive from Twentynine Palms.

Jessica hopped back onto the highway and passed the smiling face of Laurie Simmonds on the huge billboard. Did commuters even pay attention to these ads? Ever wonder what had become of the missing girl? The journey took her through Yucca Valley, where Dea Morgan had lived with her young son, into the Morongo Valley, where the road was more twisty and the bends were tighter. The terrain here was almost claustrophobic, with pockmarked hills and mounds looming over the traffic on either side of the highway. As she crossed into Riverside County, the landscape flattened out again heading into Desert Hot Springs.

There was nothing ahead of Jessica, other than desert flora and fauna and a never-ending azure sky as far as the eye could see. She drove for miles at a time without even seeing another vehicle. The starkness made Hundred Acres, the sleepy desert town where she'd spent the last six months, seem like Times Square. Jessica thought a person could go mad if they spent too much time surrounded by so much nothingness. The complete and utter desolation sparked a sudden yearning in her for the noise and bustle and people of New York. Then she remembered she'd feel just as lonely among a crowd of thousands as she did out here in the desert wilderness now that Tony was gone.

After mile upon mile of wind turbines, their blades slicing through the cloudless sky, Jessica was relieved to finally witness signs of life again as she entered Palm Springs.

Jonny Bateman's retirement home was large and powder-pink with pillars and stone balconies and lush bursts of summer blooms dotted around the manicured lawns. It was more like a Hollywood star's holiday home than a seniors' care facility and Jessica double-checked she had the correct address. She did. She made her way inside.

She was greeted by a plump nurse in a dark-blue top and matching pants and white sneakers. The woman had a big mouth and a wide smile but also an air of brisk efficiency that suggested she didn't take any shit from residents or their visitors.

"Can I help you?" the nurse asked.

"I'm here to see Jonathan Bateman."

"Sure. Are you a family member?"

Jessica had no idea what kind of state Jonny Bateman was in. If he was a frail old guy with a fragile mind or easily upset, the nurse might not take too kindly to him speaking to a private eye.

"No, not family," Jessica said. "My father knew Jonathan when he was at school in Twentynine Palms. Mr. Bateman was my father's house director when he was a fraternity brother."

The nurse's smile widened further. "Jonny is going to be thrilled to see you. There's nothing he likes more than talking about his days at college and keeping all those young men in check."

She pushed a book toward Jessica to sign and then led her into an activity room where a half dozen old people were scattered around watching television or reading or playing card games. An old boy in a wheelchair, with a shock of white hair and matching moustache and a deep tan, was loudly accusing someone else of cheating at whatever game they were playing. The nurse headed for the loud guy and crouched down next to him.

Jonny Bateman.

"Jonny, you have a visitor. Young lady here to see you. Her father was an old friend of yours."

Jonny glanced over to where Jessica stood on the threshold and she gave a nod of acknowledgment. He threw down his cards and told the other player to find someone else to cheat, winked, and shouted, "Looks like it's my lucky day!" Then he pushed himself over toward Jessica a hell of a lot faster than she would've thought possible with his skinny arms. "Let's go back to my place." He threw a wicked grin over his shoulder at his buddies. "We can sip drinks out on my private deck. Let's go, Toots."

He whooshed past Jessica in the chair and she had to hurry to catch up with him as he wheeled down to the end of a hallway to a smart studio apartment. It was clean and tidy and, sure enough, had patio doors thrown wide open revealing a little sun trap.

Jonny scooted over to a small refrigerator and opened it. "I got Dr. Pepper or Dr. Pepper," he called out.

"Dr. Pepper it is." Jessica stepped out onto the deck. It had a great view of the gardens and the sun was beating down and there were even some butterflies fluttering about. The grass smelled freshly cut. Jonny joined her, two chilled cans of soda on his lap, and offered her one. She thanked him and took a seat on the only chair.

He popped open the tab on his soda and said, "So, your daddy was an old buddy of mine?"

Jessica hesitated. "I wasn't entirely honest with the nurse earlier. My dad never met you as far as I know. I'm a private investigator."

Jonny sipped his soda and eyed her over the top of the can. Jessica waited for him to speak. Eventually, he said, "Are you investigating me?"

"Investigating you? In what way?"

"Found some illegitimate kid someplace or someone who says I owe them money?"

Jessica laughed. "No, nothing like that."

"Just as well because I ain't got no money for long-lost offspring or old debts. All my cash goes toward paying for my bachelor pad here."

"I wanted to ask you about a case I'm working on. See if you knew some of the folks involved. It's a missing person investigation. Say, you're not going to throw me out of your bachelor pad for lying to the nurse, are you?"

"Throw you out? Are you kidding me? A visit from a lady PI is the most exciting thing to happen to me since my last bed bath. Ask away."

Jessica told him how she'd been hired by the parents of a young woman who had been missing for two months. The investigation had then led Jessica to two other missing women.

"Uh-huh. And what do these missing broads have to do with me?"

"At the time of their disappearances, the other two women were both in relationships with men who were once students at The Palms University and members of the fraternity. These men probably resided at the frat house when you were house director."

"What're their names?"

"Terence Wilcox and Zachary Dunne."

Jonny scrunched up his face like he was thinking real hard and Jessica was worried the fog surrounding his memories may be too thick for a man of his advanced years to remember names from so far back in the past.

"I remember them," he said. "Junior and Zee."

"Junior and Zee?"

"Yep." He laughed. "Most of the kids went by nicknames back then. Zee is pretty self-explanatory—short for Zachary. Junior on account of being given the same name as his old man."

"What do you remember about Zee and Junior?"

"Zee was smart, like top of the class smart. I always thought his brains would take him far, even if the personality was lacking somewhat. Junior was the opposite. Struggled academically but really set the sport field alight. I never saw a college kid strike a ball as good as he did. I always thought it was a helluva shame when he dropped out completely in his sophomore year. Can't say I ever kept in touch with either one, though."

"Wilcox lives in Whitewater," Jessica said. "Doesn't have a job but does seem to have a daytime drinking habit. Dunne is partner in a legal firm in LA."

"Doesn't surprise me one bit."

"What else can you tell me about them?"

"Freshman year, they were both part of a real tight group. Liked to call themselves the Four Amigos. I'll show you. Be a doll and have a look in the big drawer under the TV. You should find a shoebox full of old college photos."

Jessica did as she was told. Jonny searched through the contents of the shoebox, a lot of which seemed to be group shots of young men in either preppy attire or matching fraternity symbol sweaters. He pulled out two photos. "Freshman year group shot of '89 and graduation celebration photo four years later. Only two of the Four Amigos graduated—Zee and Nick." He passed the freshman photo to Jessica. "That's Zee second from left and Junior right next to him holding the baseball."

Junior was already familiar to her from the newspaper articles she'd read in the library. She also recognized Dunne. He looked weird with hair, and was in better shape when the photo was taken, but there was no mistaking him as the man she'd spoken to in the diner.

"And the other two Amigos?"

"Far right is Nick and next to him is Cade."

Jessica's head snapped up. "Cade? Cade who?" She already knew what the answer would be.

"Cade Porterfield," Jonny confirmed. He finished his Dr. Pepper, belched softly, and crushed the can. "I guess those two didn't care too much for nicknames. He didn't graduate either. Dropped out sophomore year, same as Junior."

Cade Porterfield.

The murdered owner of a gray Dodge Dakota. Just like the one seen stalking Amanda Meyers, according to Mrs. DuBois, the Victor Heights Neighborhood Watch block captain. Pryce had told Jessica that Porterfield had been an addict for many years who'd had several spells in expensive rehab facilities at the expense of his parents. The homicide was still unsolved but cops had been working on the theory he had crossed the wrong dealer, who had subsequently stolen the truck as collateral for an unpaid drugs debt after putting a bullet in Porterfield's head.

She took a closer look at the young man Jonny had pointed out as Porterfield in the photograph. Tall, muscular, cropped dark hair. A real winning smile. The kind of guy who would have had his pick of the girls at college. But did he have his head turned by an older woman who worked in the local bar instead? Jessica thought Porterfield certainly matched Freddy Diltz's description of the young man he'd spotted with Dea at the Desert Heart.

"Does the name Dea Morgan mean anything to you?" she asked Jonny.

"Can't say that it does. But, then again, I didn't have much to do with the sorority girls. And I never could keep track of all my boys' lady friends."

"She wasn't a student at The Palms University," Jessica clarified. "She worked at the Desert Heart bar. Went missing back in 1990."

Jonny shook his head. "I've never been a big drinker. Hardly ever ventured to the bars in town unless one of the guys was having a birthday celebration or whatnot."

"How about Trey Simmonds? Did you know him? Was he one of your frat guys?"

Jessica already knew Simmonds had been a Palms University student but not whether he'd also been a fraternity brother.

Jonny's wrinkled face twisted into a horrible sneer and the old man practically spat the name out. "Trey Simmonds? Oh, I knew him all right. Yes, he was a member of the fraternity but that asshole had no idea what it meant to be a brother. Had no damn respect for the values of the fraternity. Simmonds was a selfish bully who only cared about number one."

Jessica was taken aback by the ferocity in the old man's voice. "Simmonds is older than the Four Amigos, right?" Laurie's father wasn't in either of the photos Jessica held in her hand.

Jonny nodded, went back to the box, and pulled another photo from the stack. "Here you go. Simmonds is right smack bang in the middle." It was a different group of young men, definitely much more of an '80s vibe going on with the hair and fashion. She would have picked out the young Trey Simmonds, with his blond hair and blue eyes and almost-handsome face, even if Jonny hadn't pointed him out.

Older than the others. Part of a different crowd completely. Jessica wasn't seeing the connection.

What did Trey Simmonds have to do with the Four Amigos?

36

DEA—1990

Dea drove round the back of the frat house like Cade told her to. There was only one other car parked there, a mud-brown Oldsmobile. She guided the Chevette up onto the dirt next to the Cutlass.

The back yard was crazy paved, with two long wooden tables with benches on either side, and a brick BBQ pit, and a basketball hoop. A door opened and Cade motioned her inside. He took her overnight bag and led her through an industrial-sized kitchen into a dusky hallway with dark wood ceiling beams and dusty old framed photos on the wall. Dea could hear music and chatting and laughter coming from elsewhere in the house, could feel the bassline beat of a recent chart hit pulsating through the house's old foundations.

Her stomach knotted again. Why on earth had she thought it was a good idea going to a party with all these cool students when she didn't even know anyone? When she didn't even really know Cade? She wanted to run through the kitchen and out the back door into the safety of her car. Instead, she followed Cade to a staircase leading down to a closed door.

"The basement," he explained. "It leads to the secret chapter room. It's where the poker party is taking place. Strictly speaking, you shouldn't even know it exists, let alone be allowed inside it, but what the hell? The other guys are okay with it. Which reminds me." He plunged his hand into his jeans pocket and came up with a roll of dollar bills. "The rest of your shift payment."

"Thanks." Dea stuffed the cash into her own pocket. The thick roll immediately made her feel a whole lot better about the party. Maybe it wouldn't be so bad after all.

They descended the stairs and Cade produced a key and unlocked the door. The basement was in near darkness, just a couple of spotlights lighting the way. Dea heard soft moaning and sucking noises and spotted two people in a very heated embrace on a sofa in the corner.

"Guys," Cade said loudly. "You know you're not supposed to be down here. The party is upstairs."

The guy and the girl jumped apart. The girl smoothed down her electric-blue leather mini-skirt, which had been up almost around her armpits. She was blonde and gorgeous in a cheerleading captain kind of way and Dea felt like a total frump in comparison in her jeans and t-shirt and no makeup.

"Sorry, dude," the guy said as he passed Cade and Dea, hot-pink lipstick smeared around his mouth, the girl in tow behind him. The amorous couple closed the door behind them in a fit of giggles and headed back upstairs, their footsteps pounding noisily on the old wooden steps.

Cade shook his head and smiled. "To be fair, it *is* a great make-out spot down here." Then he fixed Dea with a look that made her forget all about the hot girl and her own plain clothing. Cade pushed a lock of black hair away from her face and bent down and kissed her. His lips were cool and soft, his tongue gently probing at first. Then the kiss was deeper and more urgent, one hand tangled in her hair and the other resting lightly on the small of her back. Dea literally felt her knees go weak, like her legs might give way. She hadn't kissed many guys before but this one went straight to the top of the list. When they finally stopped, they were both slightly out of breath.

"Wow, that was intense," Cade whispered, twirling the lock of hair between his fingers. "I've been wanting to do that for weeks."

"Me too," she whispered back, her arms still draped around his neck. Dea didn't want to let him go. The warmth of his body felt good against her own.

"How about next week for that dinner date?" he asked.

"Sure, as long as it's not chicken wings and fries at the Desert Heart," she teased.

"Deal."

They shared another kiss, shorter this time but still every bit as good, and then Cade took her hand.

"Follow me."

He unlocked another door, led her down a short corridor, turned the corner and there was another heavy wooden door. Dea could hear muffled voices and music coming from inside. Cade rapped his knuckles hard five times on the door in what seemed to be a specific rhythm.

Knock-pause-knock-knock-pause-knock-knock.

"Secret code," he told her.

Dea heard a deadbolt being scraped aside from inside the room and then the door opened to reveal a guy with curly hair and a nice smile. He was tall, like Cade, but slimmer.

"Nick, my man," The two young men exchanged a one-armed "bro hug" complete with double backslap. Then Cade said, "This is Dea."

"Hey, Nick."

"Pleasure to meet you, Dea." Nick made a big show of kissing the back of her hand. He already seemed a little drunk.

"Don't worry," Cade said good-naturedly. "I already warned these reprobates to behave themselves tonight. Come and meet the others."

The chapter room was about the size of Dea's entire trailer. A long oak table dominated the middle of the room and held some drinks and a deck of cards spread out on it. There were a couple of sofas and another table shoved up against a wall stacked full of booze. On the wall were posters of topless women with baby-oiled bodies and large breasts, as well as both this year's and last year's Pirelli Calendars starring similarly scantily clad models.

"Oh shit, I forgot about the posters," Cade groaned. "I'm so sorry."

"It's fine," she laughed.

Dea was introduced to two other frat brothers called Zee and Junior. Everyone seemed friendly enough and she felt herself begin to relax. Cade opened a can of beer and poured it into a paper cup for her. Then he walked over to a door, opened it and placed her overnight bag inside. "This is the bathroom," he said. "You can get changed in here. Take your time, there's no rush."

Dea went into the bathroom and closed the door behind her. There, on a hook on the back of the door, was the dress Cade had bought for her. It was red, one-shouldered, with a chiffon ruffle down the front. Dea touched the fabric. It was beautiful. On the tiled floor were a pair of white stilettos with red polka dots nestled in tissue paper in a shoebox. On the sink was a single red rose and the card attached to the cream ribbon tied around its stem read "For D. From C. x"

She lifted the rose and inhaled its fragrance and felt tears prick her eyes. No one had ever made her feel this special before; no one had ever bothered to make such an effort just for her. She placed the flower inside her overnight bag.

Dea changed into the robe she'd brought with her, brushed her teeth and splashed cold water on her face. She set out her drug-store eyeshadow, eyeliner and mascara on the sink, along with the fancy lipstick and hand cream she'd pilfered from Mrs. Abbott. She stared at her reflection. Her black hair hung in thick waves to her shoulders and Dea thought her hazel eyes had a sparkle about them for the first time in a long time. She touched a finger to her lips, thinking about the kiss earlier.

After applying her makeup, Dea slipped the robe off and stepped into the dress and shoes. Assessed herself in the mirror again. It was as though a completely different person was staring back at her. She picked up the paper cup with the beer and drank it down fast. Immediately felt a buzz from the booze. Then she took a deep breath and opened the bathroom door and walked out into the chapter room.

The chatter stopped and the four college guys gaped at her. Dea panicked, thinking the makeup and the dress and the shoes were too much. She met Cade's eyes, seeking reassurance that she hadn't made a fool of herself and him, and he smiled and walked over to her and kissed her on the cheek.

"You look absolutely stunning. Like Julia Roberts in *Pretty Woman*—but even prettier." He lowered his voice. "Now, the quicker you can get these guys drunk so they lose all their money, the sooner we can go upstairs and enjoy the rest of the party."

Dea raised an eyebrow. "Sounds to me like you're looking for an unfair advantage."

"I don't know about that," he murmured. "I'm not sure I'm going to be able to concentrate on a card game now that I've seen you in that dress."

Over the next two hours, Dea made sure the poker players' drinks were topped off, first beer, then bourbon and Coke, and then tequila shots. She dealt the cards and had a couple more drinks herself and began to enjoy the night. She could hear the music from the party upstairs—Madonna and Prince and Tiffany—and she was looking forward to having a dance with Cade later on. Hoped for a slow number and another kiss before the long drive home.

It was clear Junior didn't have the same kind of cash to play with as the others and he was first to drop out of the game. He seemed happy to watch from the sidelines and knock back the free booze, while chatting to Dea. She discovered he was on a sports scholarship and was hoping to make the major leagues after graduating if he could impress the scouts who often checked out the Hawks' games.

His girlfriend, Mallory, who Dea had discovered was the one who'd picked out the dress and shoes, was upstairs with her friends, who were all sorority sisters. Mallory sounded sweet and Dea hoped she might meet some new girlfriends tonight as well as finding a potential boyfriend in Cade.

The thought gave her pause. Did she want a boyfriend? She knew she had feelings for Cade but there was a lot to consider. What had happened in the past; what was best for Buddy; whether she was ready to get serious about someone.

Yes, Dea decided, she was ready. She knew in her gut Cade was a good guy, that he would understand why they had to take things slow.

"What're you smiling at?" he asked her as he passed her on his way to the bathroom.

"Just having fun."

"Good, I'm glad." He gave her hand a little squeeze.

Dea went over to the booze table and picked up the bourbon and a plastic bottle of Coke and filled everyone's cups. She was pouring a small one for herself when there was a loud banging on the door.

"Secret code, please?" Nick yelled.

"Are you fucking kidding me? Open up!" The voice on the other side of the door sounded slurred and aggressive.

"Shit, it's Dusty," Junior said. Dea thought he looked kind of panicked.

Then came the secret code.

Knock-pause-knock-knock-pause-knock-knock.

Nick got up from his chair and made his way over to the door.

"Don't open it," Junior hissed. "He's fucking smashed. Keep quiet and he might go away."

Nick hesitated, obviously torn.

"I gave you the code," the voice hollered. "And I can hear you dipshits talking in there. Now open the fucking door—or Dusty is gonna get real mad."

"Fuck," Junior said.

"What's wrong?" asked Dea.

"Dusty is a total prick. Hates my guts. Even tried to blackball me during rushing and pledging last year."

"Why?"

Junior shrugged. "For being poor."

"Open the door," said Zee, who, so far, had spoken the least out of the group.

"Yeah, we've got to let him in," Nick agreed. "He's still got sway with the frat leaders, remember? He could get us all thrown out if we piss him off."

Before Junior could protest any further, Nick slid back the deadbolt and opened the door. A tall blond guy stumbled into the room. He was clearly drunk or high or both.

"About time, you fucking douchebags. Now, where's the booze?"

Dea stood frozen to the spot. Her blood turned to ice.

Dusty's gaze landed on her. He swayed slightly and put a hand out to steady himself against the doorframe. "What the fuck is a chick doing in the chapter room?" Then his mouth twisted into an ugly smirk. "No way. You little shits got a hooker. Now this is my kind of party!"

A john flushed and the bathroom door opened and Cade reappeared. "Oh, great," he muttered. "Night's ruined, then."

Dea said to Dusty, "It's you."

Cade said, "Are you okay, Dea?"

Dusty's eyes narrowed and he squinted at her. "Do I know you?"

"Yes, you do." Dea's legs felt weak again but not in a good way this time.

Cade said, "What the hell is going on, Dea? How do you know Dusty?"

Beer and bourbon churned in Dea's gut. "His name isn't Dusty," she said.

37

DEA—1982

"What movie are you going to see, honey?"

Dea's mom was standing in the living room doorway when Dea came downstairs. She'd been hoping to make it out of the front door with only a quick "Bye!" to her parents. No such luck. She hated lying to them. Was convinced they could see the guilt written all over her face.

"The one with Richard Gere."

"Oh, I'd quite like to see that myself. He's so handsome in that white uniform."

"I am right here, you know," Dea's dad called from his chair in front of the television.

"You know I'd rather have you over Richard Gere any day of the week, Randy."

"Gross," Dea muttered under her breath.

"Is it a double-feature tonight?" her dad asked.

"Um, yes. It is."

Shit.

Dea prayed he wouldn't quiz her about the later showing. He'd totally freak out if he knew she was going to see a slasher movie.

"Okay, home by eleven, sweetheart."

Dea's curfew was usually ten-thirty but her dad allowed her an extra half hour once a month to go to the Brodie drive-in with Maxine because there was always a long line to exit the lot after the late movie had finished. But Dea wasn't going to the drive-in theatre with Maxine this evening. She was going on a date.

"I think I hear Maxine's car. Better go."

"Don't forget your cardigan." Dea's mom pulled the lemon knit from the hook by the door. "You'll be cold later in just that summer dress."

"Thanks, Mom."

Dea took the cardigan and opened the front door. Ran down the path and got into Maxine's car. Dea was hoping her dad would buy her wheels of her own for her eighteenth birthday in a few months. She'd certainly dropped enough hints since passing her driver's test last year.

"All set for the big date?" Maxine grinned, poking her in the ribs.

Dea groaned. "I'm so nervous. What was I even thinking saying yes?"

Maxine tilted her head and pretended to think about it. "Hmmm, let's see. One of the hottest guys in school asks you out on a date and wants to take you to see a totally romantic movie. Duh. Why *wouldn't* you say yes?"

"I guess."

"Hey, you think you'll go to second base tonight?"

"Maxine!"

"What? You've already been to first base and you haven't even been on a proper date yet."

Dea felt shame wash over her. It was true. They'd seen Trey Simmonds hanging around the diner a few times and Dea had spoken to him once or twice in advanced math class. He was good with numbers and, for some weird reason, that impressed her. Then, last Friday night, Trey had followed Dea and Maxine out into the diner's lot and asked if he could speak to Dea on her own. Maxine's eyes had bugged out and she'd hurried off to wait in the car. Once they were alone, Trey had asked Dea if she'd go see a movie with him and she'd been so shocked that no words came out and she'd only managed to nod like an idiot.

"Great," Trey had said. Then, without warning, he'd leaned down and kissed her. It wasn't a great kiss. In fact, it sucked big time. His tongue had poked in and out of her mouth so fast she'd almost gagged. When it was over, he told her he'd meet her back at the diner the following Friday.

Dea and Maxine slid into a window booth now so they could watch for Trey's car. Maxine ordered a cheeseburger and fries and a strawberry milkshake and the waitress asked if Dea wanted the same.

She shook her head. "Nothing for me."

"Suit yourself." The waitress dropped the notepad back into her apron pocket and returned to the counter.

"You should have something to eat," Maxine said.

"I'm not hungry." Dea fidgeted with a paper napkin from the dispenser.

"You'll be starving later," Maxine said, eyeing the shreds of tissue on the table.

"If I am, Trey can buy me a hotdog."

"You should at least have ordered a soda."

"I don't want to have to pee once the film starts, do I?"

"I suppose." Maxine's milkshake arrived and she took a noisy slurp. Once the waitress was out of earshot, she said, "So, are you gonna?"

"Gonna what?"

"Let Trey get to second base."

Dea shifted uncomfortably on the booth's vinyl seat. "I don't know. I don't think so. Maybe just another kiss."

Maxine took another slurp. "Hopefully it's better than the last one, for your sake."

"Maybe he was just nervous."

Maxine frowned, like she didn't think a guy like Trey Simmonds would ever be nervous around a girl. "Yeah, maybe. You know, this double-feature has second base written all over it, don't you think?"

"What do you mean?"

The waitress arrived with the food and Maxine took a bite of the burger, wiped tomato ketchup from her chin, and then leaned over the table toward Dea.

"Okay, this is how it works. Super-romantic movie to start off with, which will have you feeling all slushy and mushy. Sure, your date ain't exactly Richard Gere but he'll do. Then follows the horror movie where you'll be so scared, you'll be jumping into your date's big, protective arms at the really gory parts." Maxine popped a French fry into her mouth. "Next thing you know, Trey's hand is down the front of your dress and he's squeezing your boob."

"You seem to know a lot about this stuff."

"Well, I have watched *Grease* about a million times. We both have. Trust me, you're going for a ride in Trey Simmonds' sin wagon tonight."

"Yeah, if he ever shows up."

Dea watched out of the window for Trey's car while Maxine ate the rest of the cheeseburger and fries. She checked her watch again. "He's late. You think he's going to stand me up. He's going to stand me up, isn't he? Oh god, how humiliating."

"He's fifteen minutes late," Maxine pointed out. "You need to relax, Dea. Tonight is supposed to be fun, remember?"

Dea didn't say anything.

Thirty minutes later, Maxine was onto her second milkshake and Dea had lost all hope of Trey Simmonds showing for their date. "Okay, I'm done waiting. This is really embarrassing now. Could you drop me back home, please?"

"We could go see the movie together instead?" Maxine offered.

"No, I just want to go home."

"Okay." Maxine paid the check and they made their way outside just as a Mustang screeched to a stop in front of the diner's entrance. "Eye of the Tiger" blasted out from the car radio way too loud.

Trey Simmonds leaned out of the car's open window. "Evening, ladies. Am I getting two dates for the price of one?"

"I was just leaving," Maxine said. "And you're late."

"Yeah, sorry about that," Trey shouted over the music to Dea. He didn't offer any explanation. Just inclined his head toward the passenger side. "Go on, jump in."

Maxine gave Dea a kiss on the cheek. "Have fun. I'll give you a call tomorrow for all the details."

Dea got into the car and fastened the seatbelt. Trey turned down the volume on the radio and said, "You all set? I was thinking we could pick up some beers on the way to the movie theater." He smelled like he'd already been drinking.

"The movie will be almost finished by the time we get there."

Trey screwed up his face. "You mean that stupid romantic shit? Fuck watching that crap. Still plenty of time for the later showing. It's supposed to be real scary going by the early reviews."

"Great," Dea said.

Trey put the car into drive and gave her thigh a squeeze so hard, his fingers left little red dots on the flesh.

When they did finally arrive at the drive-in, the lot was jam-packed and they had to park right at the very back. Their view of the big screen wasn't great but Dea didn't want to get out and sit on the front hood for a better view like some other folks were doing. She was worried about being spotted by someone from her dad's congregation. Being on a date with a guy *and* watching a horror movie? She'd be grounded for at least a month. Probably two.

"I was thinking it'd be better if we watched the movie from inside the car," she said.

Trey smiled slowly, his eyes on her bare legs. "Sure thing. I hear ya."

He fiddled with the radio until it picked up the right frequency and the audio from the movie flooded through the speakers just as the opening credits began. Trey handed her a beer. Dea noticed he hadn't offered to buy her any snacks or soda once they'd arrived at the theater.

She thought about what Maxine had said at the diner. Her friend was right. The movie was scary and all the screaming as the body count rose quickly began to give Dea a headache. Maxine was wrong about wanting an excuse to snuggle into Trey's arms, though. Yes, he was good-looking, with his blond hair and blue eyes and deep summer tan, but he wasn't her type at all. He was kind of an asshole, truth be told. Dea had already decided she wouldn't go on another date with him if he asked.

"Not enjoying it?"

Dea assumed Trey meant the movie, rather than the date itself.

"Not really," she said, meaning both.

"Yeah, it sucks. I can think of something much more fun we could be doing."

He lowered his seat back as far as it would go and flipped a lever on the side of Dea's seat so it was almost flat too. Then he pushed her down a little too roughly and put his arms around her and pulled her in close to him.

This kiss was just as bad. That horrible little tongue, flicking in and out like a lizard's. A strong taste of beer and liquor. Once again,

Dea tried not to gag. Then Trey shifted position and suddenly he was on top of her. She twisted her face away from his and tried to push him off her but he was too heavy.

"Trey," she said. "Let me up."

The date was over as far as Dea was concerned. She wanted him to take her home right now.

"It's okay, no one can see us." His boozy breath was hot against her ear. His hand was on her boob now, just as Maxine had predicted but, thankfully, on the outside of her dress. It didn't stay that way for long. His hand crept lower, pushing up the skirt of the dress and then his fingers were pulling at her underpants, pushing them to one side.

Dea gasped in shock. "Trey, stop. I don't want to do this."

"Sure you do. Just relax."

She felt him fumbling at his jeans, heard the zipper being undone, and she tried to squirm out from under him but he had her pinned to the car seat.

"Trey. *No.* Please stop."

But he didn't stop.

Dea felt a burning pain, and then he was breathing harder and faster and moaning softly, and she blinked tears down her cheeks and closed her eyes.

The screaming was much louder now but she didn't know if it was coming from the movie or if it was inside her own head.

38

JESSICA

"Would Trey Simmonds have known the Four Amigos?" Jessica asked Jonny Bateman.

"Oh sure. Even when he graduated The Palms, I couldn't get rid of the bastard. Liked lording it over the younger brothers. Some looked up to him and wanted to be like him, others were plain scared of him. He would oftentimes show up at the house, acting like an asshole. In his sophomore year, I tried throwing him out after finding drugs in his room but he was back under my goddamn roof before the week was out."

"You let him back?"

"Nope, not my call." Jonny rubbed his thumb and forefinger together. "Money. And his folks had plenty of it. A nice big donation to the alumni association, who owned the house, and I had my orders—don't make any more trouble for the Simmonds kid. Part of me thinks that's why he still hung around even after he graduated—just to wind me up."

"Sounds like a real nice guy."

"You don't know the half of it."

"Oh?"

Jonny paused a beat, then shook his head. "I shouldn't say any more. Nothing was ever proved at the time."

"Tell me," Jessica prompted. "It stays between us two. Promise."

Jonny sighed. "It wasn't the first time his parents made a problem go away. His freshman year, there was an allegation made by another freshman, one of the sorority girls. I can still picture her now. Petite, kind of skinny, long red hair, pale skin and freckles. Very pretty. Her name was Brooke something. Anyway, there was a party at the sorority's halls of residence and, long story short, this Brooke girl claimed Simmonds followed her to her room and forced himself on her. He denied it, insisted the sex was consensual."

"Shit," Jessica said. "What happened?"

"The girl's life ended up in ruins is what happened. Simmonds' folks hired the best defense lawyer in town and it wasn't long before the brief had a list of Simmonds' buddies claiming the pair had been flirting and dancing and drinking all night at the party, and they had headed to her room hand in hand. Then the lawyer found a couple of ex-boyfriends willing to testify that Brooke wasn't as sweet and wholesome as she made herself out to be. Her reputation was dirt. She dropped the allegations and the case never went to trial. A month later, I heard she'd transferred to a school out east with a big pay-off."

"Trey Simmonds' folks paid Brooke to drop the charges?"

"It was certainly the rumor at the time. I believe that girl was telling the truth about what happened at that party but she knew she'd be ripped to shreds in the witness stand. So, she took the money and tried to rebuild her life someplace else. I don't blame her for wanting to put as much distance between herself and Dusty as possible. His favorite phrase back in those days was 'Frat bros and sorority hoes.' Pretty much sums up the guy's attitude to women."

"Whoa, back up a second. Dusty? Who's Dusty?"

"Trey Simmonds. It's what he was known as back then. I told you, those boys loved their nicknames."

"Why was he called Dusty?" Jessica asked. She felt sick listening to Jonny's story. The Dr. Pepper roiled in her belly.

"On account of his fondness of drugs, especially cocaine. You know, Charlie, snow, dust. Always shoveling that shit up his nose. I always thought that boy would wind up dead or in jail."

"Neither," Jessica said. "He's an accountant. President and co-founder of a large CPA firm in Los Angeles. Huge house on Mulholland."

Jonny whistled through his false teeth. "I guess he managed to sort himself out then."

"I guess so." It was pretty clear now why Simmonds was so angry about her digging into his past, specifically his college years, what with the rape allegation and the drugs habit. "You said the Four Amigos would have known Trey Simmonds. Would they have been friends?"

"I don't know if 'friend' is the right word. It's like I said, a lot of the younger guys were afraid of Dusty but they would have definitely hung out together—especially if there was a party happening. Dusty never missed a party."

"Simmonds told me he didn't know Zachary Dunne or Terence Wilcox."

"Maybe he didn't recognize their real names," Jonny said doubtfully.

"Or maybe he was lying," Jessica said.

"You told me you're looking for a missing girl. You think Dusty has something to do with her disappearance?"

"It's his daughter who's missing. Her name is Laurie Simmonds. Simmonds' wife hired me to find her."

"What does his daughter have to do with the Four Amigos?"

"That, Jonny, is what I'm trying to figure out."

Jessica studied the photos again and considered the key dates. Junior Wilcox and Cade Porterfield both dropped out early into their sophomore year, so around the fall of 1990. Dea Morgan vanished in September 1990, after "getting friendly" with a guy matching Porterfield's description. Her body was found three years ago. Porterfield was shot dead just weeks later. Then Zachary "Zee" Dunne's lover, Terence "Junior" Wilcox's wife and Trey "Dusty" Simmonds' daughter all disappeared in quick succession.

Which left the fourth Amigo.

"Tell me about Nick," Jessica said. "Any idea where I might find him?"

◆ ◆ ◆

On paper, Dr. Nick Zelenka seemed almost too good to be true.

He worked as a therapist out of his own private practice in Indio, where he was born and had spent most of his life, other than the years he'd spent at university garnering various psychology qualifications. He volunteered at a local rescue mission, where he provided pro bono counselling sessions to the poor, homeless and addicted one afternoon per week. "Dr. Nick"—as he was known in the area—also gave up his spare time to coach Little League on the weekend, even though Jessica could find nothing to suggest he had kids of his own. There was no mention of a Mrs. Zelenka either.

The photos Jessica found online showed a handsome man with curly brown hair streaked with gray, a healthy tan, good teeth, and a smile as warm as his brown eyes. Just like the photos, Jessica thought Nick Zelenka's life seemed too airbrushed, too perfect. It reminded her of those online dating profiles that sounded great on paper until you met IRL and your date was at least ten years older and twenty pounds heavier than he claimed to be and his idea of working out was walking to the refrigerator for another beer.

Maybe Jessica was just too cynical, had come across too many liars and cheats and bad people in her line of work to believe anyone could be this *good*. She wondered if Nick Zelenka's philanthropic spirit was really down to a genuine desire to help those less fortunate than himself. Or if he'd spent most of his adult life sacrificing his time and expertise for other people in an attempt to make amends for something that had happened in his past. Something involving his old college buddies.

Jessica called the therapy practice and asked for Dr. Zelenka.

"Dr. Zelenka has left for the day."

"Already?" It wasn't five yet. Not even close.

"Yes, already," the woman snapped. "Call back tomorrow between nine and nine-thirty and Dr. Zelenka should be in his office then." The receptionist hung up.

It took Jessica almost fifty minutes, bumper to bumper on the 10, to drive the twenty-five miles from Palm Springs to Indio. She found Nick Zelenka's house, an impressive Spanish-style villa with a burst of vibrant magenta bougainvillea in the front yard, on a quiet cul-de-sac. There were no cars in the drive and no answer to the doorbell chimes inside the house.

A neighbor across the street was working in his garden, hosing down lush rose bushes. He shut off the water stream as Jessica approached, her hand shading her eyes from the afternoon sun. "Hey there. I don't suppose you know where Dr. Zelenka might be? I tried his practice but he's already clocked out for the day."

"Have you tried the rescue mission over on Calhoun?"

"I thought he only volunteered there on Tuesday afternoons."

The neighbor nodded. "That's right. His therapy sessions at the mission are on Tuesdays but he helps out in the kitchen and serving meals other days too."

"Got it, thanks."

The Indio City Rescue Mission was a five-minute drive away. A black woman with colorful dreadlocks and overall shorts was pinning posters to a corkboard in the front lobby. Jessica could see a bunch of folk setting up tables and chairs beyond a set of open double doors.

"You okay, there?" the woman asked. "Can I help you?"

"I'm looking for Dr. Zelenka. I was told I might be able to find him here?"

"That's right. Dr. Nick is in the main hall helping to set up for the evening meal session. Who should I say is asking for him?"

"My name is Jessica Shaw."

"Is Dr. Nick expecting you, Jessica?"

"No, but it's important I speak to him right away."

"Of course. Say no more." The woman hurried into the main hall and Jessica realized she'd mistaken her for one of Dr. Nick's patients who needed an emergency appointment.

Jessica strolled over to the corkboard and read the posters while she waited. They were mostly appeals for volunteers and food and clothing donations. A charity yard sale was planned for later in the month. The flier listed Dr. Nick as head of the organizing committee.

"Jessica? Someone said you wanted to speak to me? It sounded kind of urgent."

Jessica turned to see Dr. Nick looking just like he did in the online photos. No airbrushing required after all. The only difference was he was taller and slimmer in real life than she'd expected him to be. He appeared concerned.

Jessica extended her hand and he shook it. His grasp was firm but not overly so. "Dr. Zelenka. My name is Jessica Shaw, I'm a private investigator."

His concern turned to confusion. "A private investigator?"

The woman with the dreadlocks returned with more fliers and Jessica said, "Maybe we should speak outside where it's a little more private."

"Sure." He gave his co-volunteer a reassuring smile as he held open the front door for Jessica, and she felt bad knowing she was likely about to ruin Dr. Nick's day. He followed her outside and they stood under a California fan palm tree, its big leaves shading them from the fierce rays.

"What's this all about?"

"Okay," Jessica said. "I'm just going to cut to the chase because someone could be in danger right now. Tell me about Dea Morgan."

Dr. Nick couldn't have been any more shocked if Jessica had slapped him. The summer tan drained from his face. His mouth dropped open. Then he seemed to regain some of his composure. "I have no idea who you're—"

Jessica cut him off. "Dea Morgan. Vanished in 1990 and her body was found buried out by Twentynine Palms Highway three years ago. You and your old college buddies are connected to her in some way. I need to know how."

"I'm sorry," Dr. Nick stuttered. "I really think you have the wrong person. I have no idea who this woman is."

Jessica gave him a hard look. "When I said someone could be in danger, I meant someone close to you."

"What?" Panic flashed in his eyes, quickly replaced by anger. "Look, I don't know who you are but I don't appreciate threats against my family and friends."

"Cade Porterfield is dead," Jessica said. "Trey Simmonds' daughter is missing. So is Terence Wilcox's wife. Ditto Zachary Dunne's lover. Those women were all last seen in the vicinity of the Twentynine Palms Highway. One of your loved ones could be next if we don't act fast."

Zelenka ran his hands down his face. The panic was back. His eyes had a wild look about them. "Oh, God. No. Please, not Cara."

"Who's Cara?" Jessica demanded.

"My younger sister. She was supposed to stay overnight last night after a photography job but she never showed. I've been trying her cell all day. I assumed she forgot or changed her mind."

"Where was the photography job?"

"Joshua Tree National Park."

"Out by Twentynine Palms Highway."

Zelenka just nodded.

"Listen to me carefully, Nick. This all links to Dea Morgan somehow. If I'm going to have any chance of finding Cara, I need to know what happened the night Dea disappeared. You know what happened, don't you?"

Zelenka nodded again. Swiped tears roughly from his cheeks. Took a deep, steadying breath.

Then he told Jessica everything.

39

NICK—1990

"His name isn't Dusty," the woman said. "His name is Trey. Trey Simmonds."

Everyone in the room was staring at her. Except Dusty, who wasn't so much staring as squinting at her through a booze haze. His expression a mixture of confusion and amusement.

What was her name again? Nick couldn't remember. It had sounded like a letter of the alphabet, he knew that much. Bea or Dea. Or Kay or Elle. Something like that, anyway.

Whatever it was, the woman was terrified.

All of them were a little scared of Dusty, if they were being totally honest with themselves. He'd been one of the fraternity's leaders before graduating and had made every single one of their lives hell last year during pledging and rushing, despite no longer even being a student here.

Hazing was supposed to be banned at The Palms University but that didn't stop it happening behind closed doors in the chapter room or out in the desert or anywhere else Jonny and the rest of the staff wouldn't know about it.

And the reason it still happened was guys like Dusty.

He didn't just encourage it; he led the way. Relished every moment of it. Thought it made him powerful and feared. He was right. It didn't make him popular, though. Most of the brothers hated him as far as Nick could tell. But fear was stronger than hate, which is why Dusty still called the shots.

The last person Nick and Junior and Cade and Zee wanted to see crashing their party was Trey "Dusty" Simmonds. They had known there was a better than average chance of him showing up tonight but they'd hoped he would stick with the main event upstairs where all the college girls were. They'd been wrong. Right now, you could cut the tension between them all with a knife. But the woman was something else altogether. She was shaking and her fear was coming off her in waves.

"I want to go." The words were directed at Cade but she didn't take her eyes off Dusty.

"How do you know Dusty?" Cade asked again.

"I don't know her," Dusty said. "I've never set eyes on her before." He took a step toward her. "Or have I?"

Another step.

The woman flinched.

The radio was playing an inappropriately upbeat tune.

"Wait a minute." Dusty was grinning now. It was a horrible, leering grin. "I do know you. Brodie drive-in, right?" His eyes traveled slowly from her face all the way down to her high heels.

A predator sizing up its prey before attacking, Nick thought.

Dusty said, "Hell, talk about a blast from the past. Can't say I remember too much about the movie we saw but I sure do remember those legs. You scrub up well."

Tears stained the woman's cheeks and her eye makeup was all smudged. "I'm leaving now." Her voice was a whole lot louder and more determined than Nick would've thought possible considering how upset she was.

"Let's go." Cade took her hand and eyeballed Dusty. "This party sucks all of a sudden."

Dusty laughed. "What? You two are an item? Didn't think you were one for sloppy seconds, Porterfield." He winked. "Little tip for you, bro. This one puts out on the first date. Don't let her tell you otherwise."

Cade lunged at Dusty and landed a decent right hook on his jaw. The woman screamed and Dusty staggered backward, and Zee and Junior both shot up out of their seats and held Cade back as he tried to throw another punch. Nick got up from his own chair and backed up against the wall. He'd never seen Cade so angry. He was usually the laid-back one in the group, never got wound up about anything. Even laughed when Dusty and the other frat guys paddled his bare ass during his own hazing.

No one was laughing now.

"He's not worth it," Junior said, trying to defuse the situation. He still had a fistful of Cade's sports jacket sleeve in his grip and Zee hadn't let go either. Dusty was tall but Cade had both height and strength and there was no telling the damage he could do if let loose on Dusty.

"Let me go." Cade's voice was low and furious as he tried to shake off his two brothers. "I'm done with him. I'm outta here. I'm taking Dea home."

Dea.

That was her name.

Cade reached for the woman's hand again and they made their way to the door that Dusty had left open when he'd first arrived, breaking one of the main rules for the chapter room. They crossed the threshold and then Dea said something about forgetting her overnight bag and she let go of Cade's hand and stepped back into the room.

What happened next seemed to take place in slow motion even though Nick knew Dusty had to have moved real fast when he slammed the door shut and snapped the deadbolt into place, locking Cade outside.

"Not so fast, sweetheart. The boys want to have a little fun."

Next thing Nick knew, Dusty had pushed the woman roughly onto the table, scattering cards and casino chips and dollar bills and paper cups everywhere. She was screaming and clawing at Dusty, and Cade was banging on the door and shouting and cussing, and the bassline beat from the music from the party upstairs kept on pulsating through the old house along with the *thud-thud-thud* of dancing feet.

Dusty was on top of the woman, holding her down on the big wooden table. One of her shoes fell off as she struggled to push him off. He had a wild, crazed look about him, as though he was no longer in control of his actions.

"Okay, which one of you boneheads wants to go first?"

No one moved. Nick felt sick. The beer and bourbon and tequila were churning up in his gut like the world's worst cocktail, like he might upchuck at any second. Junior and Zee looked like they might toss their cookies too.

The woman kept screaming.

Cade kept banging on the door.

The music kept playing upstairs, the partygoers oblivious to what was happening right below them in the secret room.

"You first, Junior," Dusty ordered, his voice loud and demanding above all the noise. "Get yourself some hot ass for a change instead of that fat bitch you've hooked up with."

Junior shook his head. "No fucking way. This is bad, man. Let her go."

"What? Are you chickenshit or something?"

"Forget it, Dusty. It's not happening."

"It is if you want a future as a brother."

"I'm not a pledge now," Junior said. "You don't get to tell me what to do anymore."

Nick flashed back to "Hell Night" last year. How Dusty had forced Junior to drink shot after shot of bourbon until he'd passed out, then left him handcuffed, naked and smeared with rotten food out in the desert for the rest of the night. Dusty would've gone further, wanted to make the hazing a lot more physically painful, but the other brothers weren't prepared to risk the school's best baseball hope in years winding up with a serious injury.

Dusty glared at Junior. "First thing tomorrow, you're out on your ass, Poorboy. Out of the brotherhood *and* out of this house." Then his wild eyes darted between Nick and Zee. "Who's up for some fun, huh? I can't be the only one, surely? Come on, she's not bad-looking."

Neither one of them moved.

Junior was right. This was a bad situation. The woman's screams had become hoarser, her throat raw from the exertion. She was sobbing quietly now.

"Do I really have to show you assholes how it's done? Seriously? Okay, one of you hold her down for me. Or this lame-ass fraternity is going to be needing some new pledges tomorrow."

To Nick's surprise, Zee drank his bourbon and Coke in one go and silently walked over to the table, pulled the woman's arms above her head, and gripped her wrists tight enough to leave bruises.

"Zee, no," Nick said.

"What the hell are you doing, Zee?" Junior said.

But neither one of them made any move to help her.

Nick felt like his sneakers were superglued to the floor.

Dusty let out a whoop and began unbuckling his belt. "Now that's what I'm talking about. Seems to me like my man Zee might fancy a go after all but you'll have to get in line now. Little Dusty is ready for action."

He ripped off her panties and tossed them aside. Pushed her thighs apart.

The woman began pleading with him. "Please, Trey. You don't have to do this. I have a little boy, he's only seven. Please don't hurt me. Think about my little boy. Think about Buddy."

Oh shit, Nick thought. *She's a mom. She has a little kid. This is so wrong.*

"Stop it, Dusty," he heard himself saying. "This has gone too far already."

But Dusty wasn't listening to Nick and he wasn't listening to the woman. He undid the top button of his jeans and unzipped them. He was breathing harder now as he climbed on top of her. Sweat beaded his forehead.

"Please, Trey. Think of my little boy. He's your son too."

Dusty heard that all right. Looked like he'd been slapped hard. He took a step back and called her a lying bitch. Zee was stunned too. He let her wrists go. She unleashed a roar and lashed out at Dusty with her bare foot, the heel catching him square on the nose. Blood exploded from his nostrils and he fell back against the wall.

The woman leaped off the table and threw herself at the door, scrabbling desperately at the deadbolt. Cade was shouting her name.

Dea.

Why did Nick keep forgetting her name? It didn't matter now. Dea was going to be okay. That's all that mattered. She started to slide back the deadbolt, and almost had it all the way back, when Dusty pushed himself off the floor and threw himself at her. He smashed her head against the door with a sickening crack and she crumpled to the floor like an unwanted ragdoll. Then his hands were on her throat, fingers pressing hard against the soft flesh, calling her a fucking liar over and over again.

The signals from Nick's brain finally connected with the rest of his body and he sprang into action, launching himself at Dusty. He tried to pull him off the woman, whose eyes were now closed and her lips had no color at all. But with all the booze and coke and rage surging through Dusty's veins, he was too strong.

In the end, it took three of them—Nick, Junior and Zee—to drag him off. Cade kept on asking if Dea was okay from the other side of the locked door. He sounded way more panicked now that there was silence, now that all the screaming had stopped.

But Dea wasn't okay.

Nick knew in that moment nothing would ever be okay again.

40

JESSICA

Dr. Nick Zelenka was crying openly now, trying to catch his breath between heaving sobs. The cheerful volunteer, the dedicated Little League coach, the concerned shrink, they were all gone. He'd aged a decade in the time he'd spent outside the rescue mission telling his story.

Jessica didn't know Dea Morgan, knew next to nothing about her, but a fist had been clenched tight around her heart as she'd listened to Zelenka's account of the woman's traumatic last minutes before the life was choked out of her. No one should ever have to go through what Dea Morgan had suffered in that fraternity chapter room thirty years ago.

The big palm tree's leaves flapped softly in the light wind and traffic whooshed past on the main road as life carried on as normal for everyone else around them. The sun was blazing hot but Jessica felt cold.

The volunteer with the dreadlocks stuck her head out of the front door. "Dr. Nick, they're asking for you inside." She noticed the tears and red-rimmed eyes. "Are you okay, Dr. Nick?"

"I'm fine, Lena. There's some stuff I have to deal with right now. I'll be there just shortly."

"Of course." She threw a glance in Jessica's direction, then went back inside.

"It's weird, isn't it?" Zelenka said. "I've spent my whole career encouraging patients to open up about their problems, share what's on their minds. I never followed my own advice until now. I guess, despite everything, I do feel better for offloading. Not cathartic, as such, but lighter somehow."

"Thirty years is a long time to carry the weight of such a dreadful secret," Jessica said. "What happened next?"

Zelenka said, "When we realized Dea was dead, we were worried Cade would kill Dusty if we opened the door. But we had no choice—we had to. He would've stood there all night otherwise. He didn't go for Dusty. Maybe it would've been better if he had because his reaction was much worse. He was just so . . . distraught. Sobbing and holding her body in his arms.

"Dusty was slumped in the corner, kind of shell-shocked. I guess we all were. I remember thinking it was like being in a bad movie, that it didn't feel real. But it was real. After a while, Cade stopped crying. He said we had to phone 911 and tell them what had happened, get the dispatcher to send an ambulance and cop car to the house."

"I'm guessing that didn't happen?" Jessica said.

"Dusty was back in control now, had switched into survival mode. He reminded us of the fraternity rules. Nobody else was allowed to know what happened inside the chapter room. Hell, no one was even supposed to know it existed other than the brothers."

Jessica was incredulous. "Even when someone had died?"

"Yes," Nick said quietly. "It wasn't the first time."

"What? Are you serious?"

"There had been stories about an 'incident' that happened before my own time at The Palms. We'd all heard some version or another. One year, during pledging and rushing, a pledge drank far too much liquor in the chapter room during hazing—we're talking a BAC over five times the legal limit—and ended up in a really bad way. He was left unconscious by the highway to be found by a passerby so there would be no blowback on the school or fraternity. You know, just a kid who'd had too much to drink one night. He died the next day in hospital."

"Why would anyone want to be a part of an organization where that kind of shit is seen as acceptable?"

"I don't know," Zelenka said helplessly. "I guess it's just that whole thing of being away from home for the first time, wanting to be accepted, to be a part of something, part of a family. We all thought the story about the drunk kid was an urban myth. That he really did just get loaded in a bar one night, that his death had nothing to do with the fraternity."

"But you did agree to help cover up Dea Morgan's murder?"

"Dusty convinced us It was an accident, that he didn't mean for her to die. Said the cops would never believe it."

"You all watched him strangle her. How could you believe it was an accident?"

"We were scared. I guess we all wanted to believe it was just a situation that'd gotten way out of hand. He was so full of booze and coke, maybe he didn't realize what he was doing until it was too late. He told us we'd all go to jail for murder and our lives would be over. Convinced us we had no option other than to . . . dispose of the body."

"And Cade went along with this plan too?"

"Not at first. He was the one who carried her upstairs but only because he wanted her out of that room. We took her into the kitchen."

"You took a dead woman into the kitchen at a party? Wouldn't it be full of people helping themselves to drinks?"

"No, it was a big industrial kitchen, not like the ones folks usually have at home. We had tables set out in the living room with ice boxes full of booze and paper plates with snacks and we had pizza delivered to the house. Looking back, we were lucky no one was in there making out or looking for extra food in the refrigerator. It's where we decided what to do about Dea."

He went on, "Most of us agreed with Dusty. No cops. We had to take care of the body ourselves. Cade was the only one who said no. He wanted Dusty to pay for what he'd done. We pleaded with him. Tried to make him see how we'd all have to pay for what happened, including Cade. He kept shaking his head, saying she was only at the party because of him, how it was all his fault. Someone—I don't remember who—pointed out that going to the cops wasn't going to bring her back. It wouldn't change anything, other than ruining our lives too. I guess we wore him down in the end.

"Cade never did tell the cops but he refused to help bury the body. Once he left, we found trash bags and a shovel and some flashlights. We carried her out to Zee's car and put her in the trunk and buried her someplace we thought no one would ever find her. It wasn't until we got back around dawn that someone remembered her overnight bag. That damn bag. It was the reason she'd walked back into the chapter room. We found car keys inside and realized the tan Chevy out back belonged to her. We burned the car and the bag out in the desert."

Jessica couldn't help but think about what might have been for Dea and Cade. Both dead long before their time. Maybe their romance would've crashed and burned in a few months. Maybe they would have gone the distance. Got married, had kids, a little brother or sister for Buddy. Either way, their lives would likely not have ended in such tragedy. Dea in a shallow grave in the desert for decades; Cade with a bullet to his head after years battling addiction. They never had a shot at happiness thanks to Trey Simmonds.

"What about Cara?" Nick asked, the urgency back in his voice. "What does she have to do with all of this? Oh God, do you think Trey Simmonds is behind her disappearance? Do you think he's hurt her, like he hurt Dea Morgan?"

"No," Jessica said. "Trey's daughter is also missing."

"Who then?"

"Someone else. Someone who's out for revenge and wants everyone in the chapter room that night to suffer as much as he has over the years."

"I told you everything, like you asked. Now you need to start giving me some answers. Do you know where Cara is? Do you know who's taken her?"

"I have an idea."

"So, tell me! I'm coming with you."

Jessica thought about the black-clad figure with the mask and the gun who had broken into her motel room. He could have killed her, right there in her bed, and no one would have known for days. But he didn't. He gave Jessica a message instead. He wanted her to find out what happened to Dea Morgan. He wanted her to know what Trey Simmonds and the Four Amigos did that September night back in 1990.

If she was on her own, Jessica might just be able to reason with him.

Showing up with one of the Four Amigos in tow? That would be like throwing a grenade into a small room. No one would come out of it alive, least of all Cara.

She said, "I don't know if I'm right but, if I am, I need to do this alone."

"What am I supposed to do? Just hang around and wait?" Zelenka was shouting now, attracting the attention of passersby on the sidewalk.

"Call the cops. Tell them Cara is missing. Tell them what you all did to Dea Morgan."

Jessica walked away and got into her truck. She didn't think Nick would make the call. She made a call of her own to Connor. He'd offered to help and, right now, she needed his help.

He answered quickly. "Jessica, hi. How're you getting—"

"Are you in the office? Can you do something for me? I'm about to hit the road otherwise I'd do it myself."

"Of course. Shoot."

"A woman by the name of Dea Morgan went missing in 1990 and her body was found by the Twentynine Palms Highway three years ago. I don't have a last-known address for her but she worked in a bar in town called the Desert Heart. She had a kid. I need you to find out what you can about the little boy—what happened to him after she disappeared; where he is now."

"You think this Dea Morgan, and her son, are connected to the disappearances of Laurie and Amanda and Mallory?"

"Yes, I do. Can you help?"

"I'm on it. I'll call you later."

Jessica got on the 10 and cursed the bumper-to-bumper traffic before finally joining the Twentynine Palms Highway at Whitewater as the late-afternoon sun began to bleed into a picturesque sunset. She'd just crossed the city limits into Twentynine Palms when the song on the radio was interrupted by an incoming call through the speaker system. Jessica answered.

"Hey," Connor said.

"You got something?"

"Sure do. The name of Dea Morgan's kid was Randal and he was seven when she disappeared."

Jessica frowned. "Randal? Are you sure? Not Buddy?"

"Definitely Randal. You're right, though. According to one old newspaper report, he was known by the nickname of Buddy back then."

"What else?"

"He spent six months in a group home before being fostered—and later adopted—by Mike and Kathy Burden. Seems like they were an older couple with no children of their own. Randal's surname was legally changed from Morgan to Burden. His adoptive parents were both doctors and the kid grew up to become a doctor himself."

"Where is Burden now?"

"He's still registered to practice medicine but I can't find any employment records for near-on the last three years."

"Home address?"

"He owns a place in the Hollywood Hills. You want me to go check it out?"

Jessica thought about it. She didn't think Cara was being held in Burden's home, was sure the woman was someplace else.

"No, hold fire for now. I'll be in touch soon."

Jessica ended the call.

Once she'd reached the Desert Heart bar, Jessica followed the truck's GPS directions, making a couple of turns which took her onto a long stretch of road where she passed an old sign for The Palms University tagged with graffiti.

She drove on past the dilapidated main university building and thought she saw a flash of dark metallic paint in the parking lot between the palm trees. A car or a truck? Jessica drove on. She didn't think she was wrong about her destination. Another turn took her to a crossroads, with weather-battered street signs pointing in three directions. Spiky shrubs dotted the sand like sleeping hedgehogs. The house was easy to spot after making the turn.

It was the only building still standing on Palmer Avenue. But only just. Jessica thought it must be condemned. The three Greek symbols above the front door were broken and corroded but you could easily tell what they'd once stood for. The house was three stories, with a big wraparound porch. Once-white siding had faded to pale gray and the windows were all boarded up. No cars were parked out front. On any other day, there would be nothing to suggest anyone had set foot inside the place in the last fifteen years.

The difference today was the front door was lying wide open.

41

BURDEN

The chapter room was dark, dank and musty.

There was no water or electricity anywhere in the building. Hadn't been for years. Even during the day, no natural light from outside touched the gloom inside because all the windows had long ago been boarded up. The only illumination was provided by a dozen candles. The effect was eerie, like the place was set up for a séance. The candles were kept out of reach of Cara Zelenka in case she tried to use the flames to hurt herself or him or to try to melt her restraints.

The chains were heavy duty in any case and extended from a metal plate bolted to the cinderblock wall to the manacles around her left wrist and ankle. There was just enough give in the chains to allow Cara the freedom to reach the plastic bucket if she needed the bathroom and to feed herself with the food he brought for her. Burden noticed she hadn't touched the sandwich or chips or fruit in the brown paper bag. She had drunk one of the plastic bottles of water though.

The mattress had been covered with a fresh, clean sheet since the last woman had lain on it. He didn't see the need to gag her.

Once she'd come around from the heavy sedative, she'd quickly realized the place she was being held was too isolated for anyone to hear her screams. The sight of the gun had also helped to reduce the panicked shrieks to a despairing whimper.

He wanted her captivity to be as humane as possible but Cara was, understandably, terrified. Her eyes were big and round. Her knees were drawn up to her chin and her back was pressed against the wall.

"What are you going to do to me?" she asked. "What do you want with me?"

Burden sat facing her on the floor and crossed his legs. Got comfortable. "I'm going to tell you a story," he said. "And I want you to listen very carefully."

◆ ◆ ◆

It was a Friday afternoon when Dr. Randal Burden's world was shattered.

Two police officers showed up on the doorstep of his Hollywood Hills home and told him they had news for him. Suggested it might be better if they all went inside and he sat down first. Burden said he was fine where he was. Just tell him and get it done with. So, they did.

The remains of a woman had been discovered close by the Twentynine Palms Highway. They had been identified as belonging to a missing person by the name of Dea Morgan. Burden's biological mother. The news came less than a year after Burden had lost both Mike and Kathy, his adoptive parents whom he loved dearly, within six months of each other.

Burden knew the answer to his next question would change everything. "How long had my mother been buried out there in the Mojave Desert?" he'd asked.

"Decades," said the younger cop.

"Probably since around the time she was reported missing," added the older one.

Burden had discovered long ago that the cops investigating his mother's disappearance had believed she'd simply run away, that she didn't want to be stuck with a kid she couldn't afford to raise properly. Now he knew his mother hadn't left him. She'd been taken from him. Before they left, the two detectives told him his mother's case was now being treated as a murder investigation. But he didn't trust them to find the answers now when they'd never bothered to look for her before. There was only one person he trusted to find out what had happened to his mother—himself.

And he knew exactly where to start.

A box full of special things was stored at the bottom of his closet. In the box was an old matchbook. He'd found it by the phone in the mobile home when he'd called 911 to report his mom missing. It had smelled like her fancy hand cream, and had reminded him of her, and so he'd kept it all these years. The name and phone number written inside had been smudged by his fingers long ago but, by then, he already knew the name and digits by heart.

The name was "Cade" and the number was local to Twentynine Palms.

Burden had long suspected the person who'd belonged to the contact details had been involved in his mother's disappearance, that she'd run off with him. But Burden had never once tried to track him down. Feared if he did find Dea Morgan via this man, that she would reject him all over again.

Now everything had changed. It had taken thirty years for Randal Burden to find out the truth. It took less than thirty minutes for him to find Cade Porterfield.

◆　◆　◆

The internet was a wonderful thing. A rich source of information just begging to be exploited.

A simple online search had quickly thrown up a match for the telephone number on an old web page for a college that had shut down several years earlier. The number had been a direct line for the fraternity house just off campus. There had been only one "Cade"—who was both a student at The Palms University and a member of the fraternity—in 1990, the year Burden's mother had vanished.

Then it was just a case of tracking down Cade Porterfield.

The man wasn't active on social media. Didn't tweet or have a Facebook profile. He wasn't married and didn't have kids. Porterfield's most important relationship was with his drug dealer. He had accrued debts and a criminal record for shoplifting as a result of his long battle with addiction. Burden found out later, when Porterfield's death finally made a NIB in the press, that his family were loaded and had paid for expensive spells in rehab for their son to no avail.

Porterfield lived alone in an apartment, owned by his parents, in Culver City. Burden had waited until nightfall, then ditched his car several streets away and walked the rest of the way. A single light glowed softly in Porterfield's apartment. The apartment complex wasn't a dive but it wasn't exactly fancy either. There were no security cameras and no secure entrance. Burden decided the direct approach would be best. He pulled on the ski mask and held the gun in front of him and knocked on Porterfield's door. Waited for the man to answer and then forced his way inside while leading with the gun.

Porterfield was shocked but didn't seem entirely surprised by Burden's intrusion. Had immediately assumed it was a robbery and told Burden to take what he wanted. Looking around the apartment, Burden didn't see a whole lot worth taking. Perhaps Porterfield's drug debts had been paid off in a similar way in the past.

As a university student, and fraternity brother, Porterfield had been handsome and fit and healthy. He was none of those things now.

Burden recognized the signs of crystal meth addiction—the gauntness and rotten teeth and the sores all over his skin. The man could easily be mistaken for twenty years older than he actually was. Even so, Porterfield appeared lucid, like he had been clean for a while.

Burden held the gun against the man's head and told him to get down on his knees. Said he didn't want money or possessions; he wanted answers about the murder of Dea Morgan. Porterfield became highly distressed, bordering on hysterical. Started babbling about how he'd loved her and how she'd haunted his nightmares for years and how even the drugs couldn't take away all of his pain and guilt.

Once he'd calmed down, he told Burden what had happened, to the best of his knowledge, inside the fraternity chapter room. How five young men had covered up Dea Morgan's murder to protect their own futures. Exactly who those other four men were.

Then Porterfield begged Burden to pull the trigger. He didn't want to live anymore. Hadn't done for a long time.

Burden pulled the trigger.

◆ ◆ ◆

Murder had never been part of the plan.

The gunshot had been loud inside the small apartment. Burden panicked. He grabbed the car keys that were sitting on the kitchen counter, pushed up the sash window, and climbed out onto a fire escape. Raced down the two stories and dropped to the ground and pressed the car key fob.

The lights of a dark-colored Dodge Dakota flashed.

Burden had intended to ditch Porterfield's truck when he reached his own car but he was worried his DNA would be all over the interior. He decided to drive it all the way home and hide it in his three-car garage until he figured out how best to get rid of it.

After a few days, another plan began to form in his mind. Maybe the Dodge would come in useful. He just had to wait until the heat was off and then change the plates.

Turned out Porterfield's neighbors didn't hear the gunshot or didn't care too much for the police. It was over a week before the body was discovered and it was obvious from the way the murder was reported in the press that the cops were treating the execution as drug-related.

The cops making assumptions yet again.

As the days and weeks passed, Burden's desire for revenge grew stronger. He'd taken no satisfaction from Cade Porterfield's death. It had been too quick. Too merciful. Burden wanted the remaining four men to suffer just like he had.

He wanted them to know what it felt like to have the most important person in the world taken from them—with no idea if they were dead or alive.

"I don't understand," Cara said. "What does your mother's murder have to do with me? Why am I here?"

Tears ran down her face and she was trembling. Burden almost felt sorry for her. He knew she did understand. She just didn't want to accept the truth.

"You're here because your brother, Nick, was one of the four men."

"No. You're wrong. You don't know Nick. He's a good man. He would never . . ."

"He did. And now he has to pay, like the others."

Cara's eyes shone with a raw, primal fear. "Are you going to kill me?"

"It depends on you, Cara. I'm going to give you a choice right now."

He was interrupted by the sound of wood splintering. The creak of hinges. Soft footsteps on the first floor above them. Sprinkles of dust fell on top of their heads. They both looked up at the ceiling.

Burden pulled a gun from his waistband. "If you scream, I will shoot you," he whispered. "Do you understand?"

Cara nodded mutely.

The private investigator.

Burden had wanted the men who murdered his mother to suffer and he relished witnessing that suffering, seeing for himself just how devastated they were by the loss of a loved one. It was how he'd discovered the Simmondses had hired Jessica Shaw to find their daughter. He'd been watching their house the night of Laurie's birthday party and had been intrigued by the mysterious blonde who'd looked so out of place. So he'd followed her to her motel in Venice and then to her place of work the next morning. Burden had then kept tabs on the PI in much the same way he'd watched Amanda and Mallory and Laurie and Cara—surveillance outside her motel room in Porterfield's truck, an overheard conversation between Jessica and the other investigator on Venice Pier while Burden pretended to indulge in a spot of fishing. Always blending into the crowd.

He had wanted Jessica Shaw to remain on the case after being fired, to eventually figure out the truth about Trey Simmonds. To let the whole world know about his dark past and what kind of man he really was. To make sure he ended up behind bars where he belonged. It was why he'd given her the matchbook. The ringleader of the gang wasn't suffering anywhere near as much as he should be since the disappearance of his daughter.

Burden had worked so hard to make sure the last known whereabouts of each woman was the same highway where his mother's body had been dumped—the motel booking in Amanda's name, Mallory being forced to use her credit card at the gas station after he'd removed the cash from her wallet, Laurie's abandoned camper van, Cara's car in the lot of a roadside cafe. A message to each of the men that someone knew what they did to Dea Morgan all those years ago.

But Trey Simmonds was still looking after number one.

That's where Jessica Shaw was supposed to come in useful. But Burden hadn't expected the private eye to figure it out so quickly, before he'd had a chance to execute the final part of the plan. He was supposed to be long gone by then, Cara's disappearance a mystery that would never be solved, just like the other three women.

Randal Burden stood up and disengaged the safety on the Beretta Px4 Storm. He was going to finish what he'd started and no one was going to stop him.

42

BURDEN

Burden crept stealthily along the hallway, with only the flickering candlelight from the chapter room to guide the way. He entered the basement. A couple of candles were lit in here too but mostly the room was in darkness. He waited for his eyes to adjust to the gloom and headed for the basement door.

He could hear footsteps on the stairwell on the other side. Slow and careful and deliberate. They were getting closer.

Burden stood off to the side, where he knew he would be concealed by the door when it was opened. His whole body thrummed with tension. His heart slammed against his chest. He held up the gun and waited.

A creak.

So faint he almost didn't hear it over the throbbing of his pulse in his ears. The bottom step. The one that always creaked. There was a pause, a moment of silence that felt like it dragged on forever, then the doorknob began to turn. The door opened slowly and someone walked tentatively into the basement. They were also holding a gun.

It wasn't Jessica Shaw.

It was a man. Like Burden, he was dressed all in dark clothing. Black pants, sweater, and boots. He was tall and well-built, with fair hair turning gray.

Trey Simmonds.

Burden froze. His already accelerated heartbeat ramped up another couple of notches. This wasn't part of the plan. Then his survival instinct kicked in. The plan would simply have to change.

He stepped out from behind the door and placed the barrel of his Beretta against the side of the man's head. "Drop the gun on the floor," Burden said. "Do it slowly. No sudden movements or I pull the trigger. Do you understand?"

"I understand." Simmonds' voice was calm and controlled, despite having a gun pressed against his skull. The calmness unnerved Burden. The other man crouched down and placed the gun on the basement floor. Burden kicked it out of reach, heard it skitter across the concrete surface, followed by the sound of steel hitting cinderblock in a dark corner.

"Put your hands in the air." Simmonds raised his hands. Burden frisked him for other weapons. Didn't find any. "Now get on your knees."

He did as he was told. Then he lifted his head and stared at Burden. There was a strange expression on his face, surprise followed by curiosity. Almost as though he were captivated. He kept on staring at Burden.

"Quit staring at me."

Simmonds lowered his eyes. "Where's my daughter?" he asked quietly.

His voice was still calm, as though he was trying to show Burden he wasn't intimidated, that he was somehow in control of the situation.

"Laurie is dead," Burden said.

Simmonds' chin dropped to his chest and his shoulders hunched. "No, not my Laurie. You're lying." It was the first real sign of emotion he had shown since setting foot in the basement.

"She's dead," Burden repeated. "And she died knowing what kind of a man you really are. What you did to my mother. Every last detail. How you tried to rape her and, when she fought back, you murdered her and dumped her body out in the desert. How you let her son grow up alone, believing he had been abandoned. Laurie cried a lot. Didn't want to believe it at first. In the end, she knew I was telling the truth. Knew deep down what you were capable of. She used her last breath to tell me how much she hated you."

There were tears on Simmonds' face now. The kind of suffering Burden had wanted to see from the man right from the start, from the day Laurie disappeared. But was he crying for his dead daughter? Or were the tears for himself, knowing his own life was about to come to an end? Burden guessed the latter.

Renee Simmonds. Zachary Dunne. Terence Wilcox. They'd all been left broken in their own way by Burden's actions. Had all suffered the same kind of pain he had endured himself. The unanswered questions, the agony of not knowing. Choosing to believe they'd been discarded by someone they loved, rather than allowing themselves to accept the worst-case scenario.

But not Trey Simmonds.

He only cared about one person—and it wasn't his daughter.

"Why Laurie?" Simmonds glared up at Burden. He sounded angry now. "She didn't do anything wrong. She was an innocent young woman with her whole life ahead of her."

"So was my mother."

"Laurie was nothing like Dea Morgan."

"What did you say? What the hell does that mean?"

Simmonds didn't answer and Burden struck him hard on the side of the head. Blood trickled from his temple down the side of his face. "Are you saying my mother didn't matter? That she wasn't as important as Trey Simmonds' daughter?"

Simmonds still said nothing.

Burden went on, "How did you know to come here?"

"The private investigator. I thought the highway thing was a coincidence at first, until she pointed out the connection to Zee and Junior. I never kept in touch with them, didn't even know their real names, so I had no idea they had anything to do with those other missing women. Not until the PI got involved. This seemed like the logical place for you to take my daughter."

"You don't give a shit about finding your daughter, not if it means exposing your own secrets. You fired the PI because she was getting too close to the truth. You were more interested in protecting yourself than you were in finding Laurie. Well, guess what? The PI didn't stop digging. She's onto you, Trey. Soon everyone is going to know what you did."

Simmonds didn't say anything. The blood from his wound dripped onto the concrete floor, like water from a faucet hitting an empty sink. "How did you find out what happened to your mother?" he said eventually. "Which one of the Four Amigos told you?"

"Cade Porterfield. Let's just say he felt a sudden desire to offload when I tracked him down."

"Porterfield is dead. I looked him up. He was shot."

"I know. I was there."

"You killed him."

"Yes."

"And now you're going to kill me too?"

"What do you think?"

"I don't think you will." He said it in that calm voice, like he knew something Burden didn't.

Burden laughed. It sounded hollow. "You really think you're going to walk out of here and carry on with your life as usual? Not this time."

"You won't shoot me. You're not capable of doing it."

Burden pressed the gun harder against Simmonds' skull and the man winced as the barrel dug into the wound. "Yeah? Tell that to Cade Porterfield."

"This is different."

"How is it different?"

"You wouldn't kill your own flesh and blood."

"What? What the hell are you talking about?"

"I'm your father, Randal."

Burden laughed again. "You're pathetic, do you know that? That's really the best you can come up with? You've been watching too many 'Star Wars' movies."

"It's the truth."

"Man, I knew you were the kind of guy who would do anything to save his own skin but this is something else."

"Your mother and I were in the same class at Brodie High School. We dated briefly and she got pregnant. Her dad was the local pastor, Randy Morgan. I didn't know about you until . . . that night."

"The night you killed her, you mean?"

Simmonds nodded.

Burden felt his focus waver. But he knew he couldn't show how rattled he was by what Simmonds was telling him—the claim that he was his father; the almost nonchalant acknowledgment of what he did to his mother. Burden had to get a grip of the situation fast.

"So, you knew she was from Brodie. Big deal. Doesn't prove a thing."

291

"It was me who bought you the stuffed cat. Remember? When you were in that kids' home? An anonymous donation at Christmastime, to be given to little Randal Morgan."

It didn't prove anything either. Even so, a cold feeling washed over Burden, a creeping sense of dread. He took a step back. He'd called the toy Mr. Cat. It'd replaced Duke the Dinosaur as his favorite because Duke reminded him too much of his mom and made him feel sad. "I don't remember any cat toy," he lied.

"If you really want proof, all you have to do is look at me."

"No."

"Look at my face, Randal. You'll see for yourself that I'm telling you the truth."

There wasn't much light to see by, only the meagre glow of the candles cutting through the gloom. Burden didn't want to look but he couldn't stop himself. He had seen Trey Simmonds plenty of times before from a distance but this was the first time he really *saw* him. Fair hair now turning gray. Ice-blue eyes. Square jawline. Even the height and build were the same. It was like a glimpse into the future, how Randal Burden might look himself in twenty years' time.

"No."

He was hit by a sudden wave of nausea. His head throbbed and he felt dizzy. He took another step back. Lowered the gun.

Trey Simmonds pounced.

He charged at Burden, low and hard, tackling him to the floor, like a defense player taking out a quarterback.

The gun fell from Burden's hand. His head cracked against concrete. The wind was knocked out of him as Simmonds landed on top of him. He tried to push him off, get some air into his lungs. Simmonds' face was damp with sweat and blood. He was breathing heavily. His eyes were wild and filled with hate.

Burden reached desperately for the gun. Felt relief flood through him as his fingers brushed cold metal. His hand closed around the grip and his finger found the trigger. He raised the gun. Simmonds grabbed hold of the barrel.

The sound of gunshot was deafening.

Then the screaming began.

43

JESSICA

Jessica pulled her Glock and Maglite from her bag. She left the keys in the ignition and the driver's side door ajar. She had no idea what she was walking into and knew she might need to get herself back out of it again in a hurry.

She crossed what would've once been the frat house's lawn but was now mostly sand and stones with the occasional tuft of tenacious sun-bleached grass.

Dusk was coming on fast now, the sky the color of a fresh bruise.

Jessica gingerly climbed the creaking porch steps, careful to avoid the missing slats. As she stepped over the threshold, she switched on the flashlight and held the gun out in front of her.

Ready and willing to shoot if necessary.

Inside the house there was a weird silence. It was too heavy, like the kind of loaded stillness that immediately follows a loud explosion. The hairs on the back of Jessica's neck stood on end and fear crawled down her back. She couldn't hear any movement but she could sense another presence within the crumbling old building.

She was sure she wasn't alone.

The living room was just off the hallway. Jessica took two careful steps to the open doorway, wincing at the squeak of her sneakers on the floorboards despite the thick layer of dust. The flashlight's beam picked out the ghostly shapes of furniture covered in dust sheets. Unopened mail was scattered across the floor. An old grandfather clock was stopped forever at ten past ten. The smell of damp and mustiness hung heavy in the air.

The living room was empty.

She moved back out into the hallway. Straight ahead was a staircase leading to the two upper floors. There was a dark smear on the wooden bannister. Jessica took a closer look. Carmine red glistened under the beam of the flashlight. Blood. There were stains on the stairs too. Recent enough that the blood hadn't dried yet.

Jessica's eyes followed the trail of blood up the stairs before it disappeared into the blackness beyond. She held her breath and listened hard. Thought she could hear the faint creak of light footsteps far above her. Breathed out and hoped it was her imagination. She cast the weak shaft of light from the Maglite around the rest of the hallway and spotted another staircase at the far end.

This one led downstairs, Jessica guessed, to the basement and secret chapter room. She threw a final look upstairs into the gloom and made a decision. If Cara Zelenka was being held in this house by Dea Morgan's son, Jessica's gut said she'd find her in the chapter room. She tiptoed over to the basement staircase, trying to avoid any more tell-tale sneaker squeaks.

The door at the bottom was wide open, betraying the faintest flicker of candlelight from inside the otherwise dark basement. Jessica's heartbeat jumped up several notches—then almost stopped completely when she felt something clamp heavily onto her shoulder.

She bit back a scream. Turned her head slowly, expecting to see a hand there. Looked into the black eyes of a fat lizard instead and almost screamed again. Its tail pounded against her back. Jessica shoved the flashlight into her pocket and grabbed the lizard and dropped it to the floor. Heard it scuttling off. Noticed there was a hole in the ceiling right above her where the little shit must have fallen through.

Jessica took some deep breaths and reached out to steady herself on the staircase newel post. Recoiled immediately when her fingers touched something warm and wet. More blood. She wiped her hands on her jeans, retrieved the flashlight from her pocket and pointed it at the open doorway along with the gun. Then she began to descend the stairs. Her legs were wobbly but her gun hand was steady.

The bottom step creaked beneath her foot and Jessica froze. Listened for the sound of approaching footsteps. Thought she heard a soft whimper from beyond the basement. She stepped inside the room and her flashlight immediately picked out a crumpled figure on the floor. It wasn't moving. Jessica's heart dropped into her stomach.

Cara.

She moved quickly toward the motionless figure. Black clothing, muscular build, fair hair. It wasn't Cara. The man was in his thirties. A bullet wound to the gut had bled out beneath him and pooled on the concrete floor. Another wound burned a tiny hole on his forehead. His pale blue eyes were open and unseeing. Jessica recognized the gun lying next to him as the one that had been pointed at her in her motel room.

Randal Burden.

Had Cara somehow managed to escape and used his own gun on him?

Jessica checked for a pulse even though she knew he was dead. Then she followed the trail of blood through a doorway and down a hallway to where the light of a dozen candles lay beyond an open door.

The secret chapter room.

She pressed her back against the cool cinderblock wall and silently counted to three. Then charged in, leading with the gun. Her eyes scanned the room for any signs of danger. She registered two couches and a long wooden table and a smaller table and some chairs.

At the far end, a woman was sitting on a mattress, hugging her knees. She was chained to the wall.

Cara Zelenka.

She peered up at Jessica fearfully through thick brunette bangs. "Please don't hurt me." Her voice was hoarse and shaky and she was trembling uncontrollably.

Jessica lowered the gun and ran over to the woman. Crouched down in front of her. "Cara? I'm here to help. My name is Jessica Shaw. I'm a private investigator. I'm not going to hurt you, okay?"

Cara paused a beat, then nodded. "Okay."

"Do you know if any other women are being held here too?"

Cara shook her head. "I don't think so. Is Randal dead?"

"Yes. Do you know what happened?"

"There was an argument out there," Cara whispered urgently, her eyes flicking between Jessica's face and the open door behind her. "A gun went off and I screamed. I couldn't help it. I was so scared. Then the other man came in here and started shouting and shaking me. Kept on asking where Laurie was. I told him I didn't know and he hit me."

Cara pushed her hair aside and Jessica could see a bruise blooming below her right eye.

"Trey Simmonds," Jessica whispered. "He's still here?"

"I think so. He went upstairs to find Laurie. I don't think she's here."

"When was this?"

"I don't know . . . maybe ten, fifteen minutes ago." Her words were fast, urgent. "I think he's going to kill me once he's done looking for her. He knows I heard what they were arguing about in the basement, that I know what he did to Randal's mom." Her eyes widened. "They mentioned your name too. Randal said you were onto Simmonds. He'll kill us both. He has a gun."

"I'm going to get us out of here," Jessica said in a low voice. She didn't know if Cara believed her. Didn't know if she believed it herself. But, as adrenaline flooded her veins, she knew her determination was stronger than her fear. "Where are the keys to your restraints?"

"I don't know. I guess Randal has them."

"Okay, I'm going to go find the keys."

Cara gripped Jessica's arm so tight her fingernails dug into the flesh. "Please don't leave me here, Jessica."

"I came here to find you and I'm not leaving without you. I'll be right back. You have my word."

Cara let go and Jessica retraced her steps back along the hallway to the basement. Led with the gun and the flashlight. The room was empty, except for the dead man on the floor. She heard a noise from upstairs. Footsteps coming down the stairs. Probably between the third and second floors. Jessica glanced down at Randal Burden. Dropped to her knees. His blood soaked through her jeans. She shoved the flashlight into her back pocket, placed the Glock on the floor. Felt in the pants pocket closest to her, while trying not to look at Burden's lifeless eyes. Came up with a set of car keys for a Dodge Dakota.

"Shit."

She tossed them aside. Strained to hear in the darkness. The footsteps sounded closer. Much closer. She leaned across Burden's body, ignoring the wetness seeping through her t-shirt, and reached for the other pocket of the pants. This time, her hand closed around two keys on a metal ring. It sounded like Simmonds was on the basement staircase now. Jessica grabbed the keys and her gun and pushed herself to her feet. Slipped in the pool of blood. Steadied herself and ran toward the hallway as the bottom step creaked loudly, followed by the crack of gunfire.

"Fuck."

Jessica raced down the hallway into the chapter room. Slammed the door behind her and tried to slide the deadbolt into place. It was rusted with age and didn't budge. She threw the keys at Cara and heard the woman start working on unlocking the manacles, while Jessica hammered at the deadbolt with the heel of her hand. Pain shot through her wrist, flecks of rust pierced the skin. The deadbolt slide began to move. She kept on hammering and it inched halfway into position before there was a series of knocks on the other side of the door.

Knock-pause-knock-knock-pause-knock-knock.

Jessica pushed one of the couches in front of the door. Threw a couple of chairs on top. Sweat ran into her eyes and pooled at the base of her spine. It wouldn't be enough of a barrier to keep Simmonds out completely but it would hopefully buy them some time.

Knock-pause-knock-knock-pause-knock-knock.

Cara had the ankle manacle off but was struggling to free the one on her wrist. Her hands were shaking too much. "He's going to kill us," she kept mumbling over and over again.

"Here, let me." Jessica took the key from her. Fumbled with the lock.

"Open the door, you fucking bitches." Loud banging started up. The playful knocking was gone. Simmonds was throwing himself against the door now, trying to force it open.

The rusted deadbolt snapped.

The wrist manacle clicked open.

Jessica helped Cara to her feet. "Now where?" the woman asked. There were no windows in the chapter room. Only one door other than the one Simmonds was trying to bust open.

"This way."

Jessica pulled Cara into a bathroom just big enough for a toilet bowl, sink and shower area. This time the lock slid into place easily but the door was made of cheap flimsy plywood. It was darker in here. Jessica pulled the flashlight from her back pocket. There was a small, pebbled window high up on the wall, just below the ceiling. The glass was completely covered by dirt but wasn't boarded up.

Cara climbed onto the cistern. "I need something to break the glass with."

Jessica handed her the flashlight. "Try this."

Cara battered the butt of the Maglite against the glass but it wouldn't yield. "It's no use," she yelled. "It's not strong enough."

A loud bang on the bathroom door made them both jump.

"Stand back." Jessica levelled her gun at the window. Cara crouched down and covered her face with her hands. Jessica fired once. Twice. The glass splintered.

Another bang. This time the door rattled in its frame.

Cara used the flashlight to knock out the remaining larger shards, then pulled herself up through the window frame. Screamed as pieces of glass pierced the palms of her hands, her sneakers slipping on the wall tiles as she tried to gain purchase. Jessica shoved at the woman's butt, forcing her through the small space.

Another bang.

Jessica scrambled up onto the cistern and Cara leaned through the broken window and grabbed her by the wrists. Broken glass clawed at her arms and ripped the front of her t-shirt as Cara desperately tried to haul her all the way through. Jessica was almost there when there was another loud bang from below. This sound was different—the harsh clatter of the metal doorknob smashing against the tiles as the door was forced open.

The bathroom lit up with a flash, accompanied by the loud report of a gun being discharged. White hot pain shot through Jessica's lower leg as she tumbled onto a hard surface outside. The desert night air was cool but her leg felt like it was on fire. She turned and fired down through the window. Heard a scream and a thud followed by silence.

The only sound was the ringing in her ears.

Jessica looked around. She was lying on crazy paving and there was a brick BBQ pit and a basketball hoop nailed to the wall. A gray Dodge Dakota was parked nearby. It took a few seconds for her to realize they were in the back yard.

"We need to get out of here," Jessica said.

"Randal's truck," Cara said.

Jessica shook her head. "The car keys are in the basement. My own truck is round the front. Let's go."

They ran around the side of the building and crossed what was left of the front lawn. The open front door gaped black and ominous like a missing front tooth. Cara was a few yards ahead of Jessica, who was limping now as pain burned through her leg where Simmonds' bullet had hit.

"The driver's side is unlocked," Jessica yelled. "Get inside."

Cara yanked the door open and threw herself into the cab and crawled across to the passenger seat. Jessica risked another look over her shoulder at the open front door.

Trey Simmonds was standing on the threshold. He was holding a gun.

His left hand was clamped over his right shoulder. He grimaced and slowly raised his right hand to aim the weapon at Jessica. She squeezed off two quick rounds from her own Glock before he could pull the trigger. Simmonds fell to the ground. Jessica followed Cara into the truck and twisted the key in the ignition and stamped down hard on the gas. The dust cloud kicked up by the Silverado was so big, Jessica couldn't see the frat house in her rearview mirror.

She didn't stop driving until they'd reached the safety of the Twentynine Palms Highway and the Desert Heart.

44

JESSICA

A couple of years back, Jessica had traveled a stretch of highway in Nevada known as "the Loneliest Road in America."

The name had come from a *Life* magazine article back in '86 on account of its complete lack of civilization, the desolate terrain largely comprising desert valleys and basins and ghost towns and hardly any services.

Jessica had only driven part of the route, not enough to pick up all the location stamps to earn a certificate from the local tourism board for "surviving" the road, but she'd seen enough to get why it'd been given the title.

Now, as she stood leaning against her truck smoking a cigarette, by the side of the road fifty miles beyond the "Next Services 100 Miles" sign outside Twentynine Palms, she thought this place might just give Nevada a run for its money.

A month had passed since Jessica and Cara had fled the frat house and burst into the Desert Heart. Both of them terrified and covered in blood and wounded, startling Jeannie and Freddy Diltz and the rest of the bar regulars.

They'd sipped brandy for the shock as they'd told the cops about a revenge plan gone tragically wrong—how Randal Burden had discovered the identities of the five men involved in the murder of his mother, how he'd shot one of them and abducted four women as part of their punishment, had then been killed by the ringleader, before Trey Simmonds had gone after Jessica and Cara.

Simmonds' bullet had grazed the flesh on Jessica's calf and the injury was already healing. She had hit Simmonds twice—on the arm in the frat house bathroom and then the hip at the front door—but neither of those shots had been fatal. She was glad. It was the first time she'd shot another person and she hoped it would be the last. Simmonds had collapsed in the doorway after the second shot. Had no chance of making it to the old college building's lot where he'd left his car. Had no way of pursuing Jessica and Cara or making his escape before the cops arrived on the scene.

Simmonds was recovering in hospital, handcuffed to the bed, with an armed police officer stationed outside his room. He'd been charged with the murder of Randal Burden and the attempted murder of Jessica and Cara. Other charges, relating to Dea Morgan, were likely to follow.

Nick Zelenka never did phone the police following Jessica's visit but he was now talking to the cops about what happened in the chapter room thirty years ago. So was Terence Wilcox. Zachary Dunne, unsurprisingly, had lawyered up.

The cops, led by Detective Valdez, were working on the basis that the bodies of Amanda Myers, Mallory Wilcox and Laurie Simmonds were buried out by the Twentynine Palms Highway someplace, just like Dea Morgan had been. It made sense to Jessica. Randal Burden had seemed hell bent on a sort of poetic justice for what had happened to his mother.

Valdez and his men had searched Burden's Hollywood Hills home, as well as a rental in his name which was located just a few streets from Cara's own apartment. They'd found fresh syringes and enough drugs to provide several lethal doses. Burden had told Cara he was going to give her a choice but she never found out what it was.

Jessica finished the cigarette and stubbed it out. About fifty yards away, a makeshift white-painted wooden cross was jammed into the desert floor. As she got closer, she could see two words were written on it in felt-tip pen. "Dea" and "Mom." A wreath of withered flowers hung in the center. No longer Dea Morgan's final resting place but a spot that had been important to her son following the discovery of her remains three years earlier. Jessica knew what it felt like to lose a mother at a young age. She knew all about the sense of injustice, the anger, the despair. Part of her felt sorry for Randal Burden. She could understand his need for revenge, the burning desire to make Trey Simmonds and the Four Amigos pay for what they'd done. But she couldn't condone how he had gone about exacting that revenge, how he had hurt innocent people along the way.

So far, the search for the three missing women had turned up no bodies.

Jessica returned to the truck. Not for the first time, she had no real idea where she was headed. She'd checked out of the motel in Venice and spent the last few weeks at Pryce's apartment, but she couldn't sleep on his couch forever so she'd loaded up the Silverado with all her stuff again this morning. She'd spoken with Connor on the phone a couple times but, so far, hadn't been back at MAC Investigations since the events at the frat house. He'd insisted she take some time to recover from both her physical wounds and the emotional trauma before returning to work. It'd given her time to think about Connor, too. She didn't know how that one was going to play out. Was Jessica in love with him? Could they have a purely professional relationship? Should she quit California and return to New York or move on to a state where no PI license was required?

Jessica didn't know the answer to those questions.

But, as mile after mile of empty desert flashed by her window, Jessica did know one thing. It didn't matter how many gas stations or motels or bars or people you passed along the way, the loneliest road was usually the one you traveled by yourself.

EPILOGUE

The breeze ruffled her short blonde hair as she walked along the beach in Rosarito searching for someplace quiet away from the crowds.

She'd move on again to another beach, another town, before Labor Day and the influx of American tourists.

The white sand was warm beneath her bare feet and the ocean was the same color as her eyes behind the big sunglasses. The Baja sun had turned her usually pale skin a deep golden tan.

A little Mexican boy of around seven or eight ran over to her, a Polaroid camera in his hand. "*Dos dólares por una bonita fotografía?*" he asked hopefully.

The tie-dye maxi dress was new and she knew she did, indeed, look pretty today but she shook her head. "*No fotografía.*"

He looked disappointed and she reached into her wallet and pulled out two dollar bills. The little boy shrugged, grabbed the cash and ran off again with his camera to find someone else to haggle with.

A half mile along the beach, she found a suitably secluded spot and sat down. Pulled a copy of the *Los Angeles Times* out of her big straw bag and flicked through the pages until she found the article she wanted to read.

The latest update on the Trey Simmonds case.

He had now been charged with two counts of murder—Dea Morgan and Randal Burden—as well as two attempted murder charges. A half-dozen women had also come forward to allege they had been sexually assaulted by the once respected businessman and pillar of the community. Despite all of the allegations against him, his wife, Renee, was standing by him.

The body of their daughter had still not been found.

Laurie Simmonds set the newspaper aside and thought about Randal Burden and the time she'd spent with him in that basement room. The way he'd cried when he told her what her father and his college friends did to his mother. How they'd disposed of her body and then carried on with their lives having destroyed his own as a child. Laurie hadn't wanted to believe him but had known, just from the expression on his face, that he was telling the truth.

He told her he wanted to make those men suffer the same way he had, for them to know what it felt like to lose someone they loved.

Laurie had thrown up in the bucket he'd set next to her for her bathroom needs and she had cried and asked if she was going to die.

The answer to that question was entirely up to Laurie, he'd said.

Burden was going to give her a choice. Start afresh with a new identity and enough cash to set herself up someplace else on the condition she never contacted her family again. Or die right now in a filthy basement room and wind up in a shallow grave out in the Mojave Desert like Dea Morgan had.

If she took the first option, and then broke the condition, he would find her and kill her. Same if she attempted to contact the police.

Randal Burden had two syringes. Which one he used would be her decision.

Laurie had woken up groggy and disorientated in an old car she didn't recognize on a quiet road outside Escondido. In the glove compartment was a passport with her photo and someone else's name and a driver's license and papers for the car. She'd also found a fat brown envelope stuffed full of cash.

Now that Randal Burden was dead, she could return to her old life without fear of repercussions. But what would she be returning to? A father who was a rapist and murderer? A mother who was willing to stand by him and who had never allowed Laurie to live her own life?

No.

She didn't know what choice the other two missing women, Amanda Meyers and Mallory Wilcox, had made. They hadn't been found either. But there was no going back for Laurie Simmonds.

She took the sketch book from her bag and turned to a fresh page. Relished the prospect of a completely blank canvas.

ACKNOWLEDGMENTS

First of all, my biggest thanks go to my readers. I've been blown away by the incredible response to the Jessica Shaw series so far and it really helped when writing this book. I very much hope you enjoyed reading *Dark Highway*.

Thank you to my brilliant agent, Phil Patterson, for all your support and encouragement—and to the rest of the team at Marjacq for the fantastic work you do. It's very much appreciated.

A huge thanks to my editor, Jack Butler, and everyone at Thomas & Mercer. I'm so lucky to have such a great publisher. You took a chance on me and my books and, for that, I'll always be grateful. A special mention for developmental editor Charlotte Herscher—your input, once again, has been invaluable.

A big shout-out to the bloggers who have helped to spread the word about my books, especially Sharon Bairden, Mary Picken, Noelle Holten, and Gordon McGhie. And not forgetting *Daily Record* books columnist Nicola Smith. Thank you!

To Lorraine and Darren Reis, Danny Stewart, Lawrie Anne Brown and Louise Robertson, whose friendship and support means so much. Thanks, also, to my crime-writing buddies—you know who you are!

To Mum, Scott, Alison, Ben, Sam, and Cody—I couldn't do this without you. You mean the world to me. And to my dad, who's always in my thoughts, and who would be loving this crime-writing adventure as much as I am.

ABOUT THE AUTHOR

Lisa Gray is an Amazon #1, *Washington Post*, and *Wall Street Journal* bestselling author. She previously worked as the chief Scottish soccer writer at the Press Association and the books editor at the *Daily Record Saturday Magazine*. She is also the author of *Thin Air* and *Bad Memory*, and now writes full-time. Learn more at www.lisagraywriter.com and connect with Lisa on social media @lisagraywriter.